The Desert Eagle's slide locked back, empty

As his fuzzy brain told his hand to reach for his Beretta, it also told him he would never get to it in time. The price for knocking the wind out of the gunman was a near-concussion, and his enemy had already recovered from the loss of breath.

The Executioner had no intentions of giving up. The grim determination to go out fighting never left him. But he was a realist, as well, and he knew his odds of survival were slim.

The gunman suddenly turned and, weapon still in hand, raced out of the broken back door.

The Executioner staggered to the doorway and looked out. The backyard was empty. Whoever it was who had come to kill Buxton was gone.

And Bolan knew no more about him than he had before.

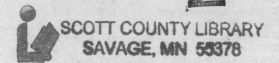

MACK BOLAN ®
The Executioner

DON PENDLETON'S
THE EXECUTIONER®
VENDETTA FORCE

A GOLD EAGLE BOOK FROM
WORLDWIDE®

TORONTO • NEW YORK • LONDON
AMSTERDAM • PARIS • SYDNEY • HAMBURG
STOCKHOLM • ATHENS • TOKYO • MILAN
MADRID • WARSAW • BUDAPEST • AUCKLAND

First edition December 2002
ISBN 0-373-64289-X

Special thanks and acknowledgment to
Jerry VanCook for his contribution to this work.

VENDETTA FORCE

Printed in U.S.A.

A hero cannot be a hero unless in a heroic world.
—Nathaniel Hawthorne

What is a hero? Somebody who does what needs to be done when it needs to be done. That's all— nothing more, nothing less.
—Mack Bolan

To Jim Cirillo and Sheldon Ritholz
of the NYPD Emergency Squad.

Prologue

The man wore a long-sleeved navy blue T-shirt with no markings and new blue jeans. Unwashed, unfaded. Because dark blue didn't reflect light during night ops, and it didn't raise eyebrows the way all black did.

Clayton Rudd turned the Chevy Impala onto Bell Street and pulled over to the curb in front of a sprawling ranch-style house in the upper-middle-class neighborhood. Rolling to a stop halfway between two streetlights, he killed the engine and reached into his pocket for the Szaball. The Szaball was a simple device made to increase grip strength. It was nothing more than a pliant orb of thin rubber filed with rice, slightly smaller than a tennis ball. But it worked—both as a grip strengthener and a tension reliever, and it was so basic that it made him want to slap his forehead and say "Why didn't I think of that?" It had probably made the inventor rich.

Rudd squeezed the ball in his right hand ten times as he stared down the semilit street. Wednesday night. Almost midnight. No traffic. Transferring the ball to his left hand, he glanced at his watch as he squeezed out another ten reps. Unless something unusual had happened, everyone in the two houses would be sound asleep.

Rudd looked at the house on the other side of the street four lots down the block. A gray-brick, split-level dwelling, it had no burglar alarm. He had checked, and the fact had surprised him, considering the past profession of the man who lived there with his wife. But sometimes when people retired, they got careless. Especially cops. They seemed to think the real danger was over, and the most violent thing that might happen was to get a fish hook caught in one of their fingers. Mackenzie? MacIntyre? What was the guy's name? It had slipped his mind. Not that it mattered. MacWhoever would be asleep in the house with his wife. Their only child, a son, was away finishing his last year at Colorado State. That was good. The kid could have been a problem. Not only did college kids come and go at erratic hours, according to what Rudd had learned the boy was six feet five inches tall and played defensive tackle for CSU. He didn't want to go up against anyone like that.

The old man could have been a problem, too. At least a few years ago. Harvey MacWhat'shisname—funny, he could remember the first name but not the last—had been a highly decorated police officer. He had also been a firearms and close-quarters combat instructor. But now he was retired, getting paunchy, and was saturated with arthritis.

Rudd looked at the house directly across the street from the retired cop's. Jefferson Bowers. Real-estate magnate. Socialite wife. Both of the Bowers drank too much, fought with each other frequently, and the local cops had been forced to come out four times during the past year. Thank God he had access to police reports. It made things so much easier.

Rudd squeezed the ball ten more reps with each hand, letting it roll around into different areas of his palm to hit the forearm muscles from different angles. His fingers tried to stiffen as he dropped the ball on the seat beside him, but he rubbed his hands together until they relaxed once more. Grip was important to Rudd. He exercised his hands and forearms even more than the rest of his body, which was put through a stringent daily regimen.

Rudd glanced into the rearview mirror and saw no signs of life up and down the block. He pulled a black leather athletic bag over the seat. Sliding a pair of surgeon's rubber gloves onto his hands, he opened the door and got out. A moment later he was walking quickly across the street and cutting between two houses. He vaulted a chain-link fence and stopped long enough to pull a .22-caliber Ruger target pistol—carefully fitted with a sound suppresser—from his belt beneath his shirt. There had been no dogs between him and his objectives when he'd checked for the final time the night before. Being ready for the unexpected was what kept him alive, and he believed in covering all bases.

The man in dark blue vaulted two more fences before landing in the ex-cop's backyard. MacAskill. That was the name. He knew it had been something Scottish. Funny how little bits of information came and went in one's mind.

Rudd did a final 360-degree check of the backyard before jamming the Ruger back into his jeans. He stepped onto the back porch, moved silently to the door and shook his head. The door consisted of a wooden frame in which were set fifteen small glass windows—another security slipup—unworthy of an ex-cop like MacAskill. Rudd could even see the inside brass lock through the glass. Setting down the bag, he pulled out several strips of previously cut duct tape and applied them to the window nearest the lock. He had seen burglars and spies on television do the same thing, then use a pistol or hammer to break the glass. On film, it always worked perfectly. But in real life, Rudd had found that some of the glass always escaped the tape and fell to the floor inside, creating noise. So he simply pushed against the window until the glass cracked almost silently, then removed the tape and set it on the porch next to the bag.

Reaching through the opening, Rudd unlocked the door and slowly opened it. An irritating screech sounded—the hinges needed oil—but not loud enough to be heard in the far end of the house. At least he hoped not. He stepped into the kitchen, pulled the bag in after him, drew the Ruger and crouched behind a breakfast table for a full five minutes before continuing.

Rudd crossed the kitchen tile, the rubber soles of his dark blue cross trainers making no sound. The hallways was carpeted and presented no problem. He set down the bag again just outside the master bedroom and waited, listening.

Two sets of snoring came through the open door—one loud and hoarse, the other softer and feminine. Keeping to the shadows, he entered the room and crept to the foot of the bed.

A faint glimmer from the streetlight outside flickered into the room, and soon Rudd's eyes had adjusted. On the nightstand next to MacAskill was a Smith & Wesson Model 66 four-inch barreled revolver. Standard-issue of most departments twenty years before, and some of the old boys such as MacAskill had clung to their wheel guns all the way to retirement. Rudd's eyes moved from the weapon back to the man. At one time MacAskill looked to have been powerful, but now the muscles in his shoulders had atrophied and hidden beneath a layer of fat. The woman next to him looked small, dainty even. In her early fifties, she was still attractive. Too bad. Rudd didn't like killing women.

The man in dark blue started to draw the Ruger again, then hesitated. The sound-suppressed rounds wouldn't carry beyond the walls of the room, and the small caliber would keep the blood to a minimum. But there would be some blood, and Rudd hated blood. These days, he couldn't afford to take chances with anybody's blood.

Leaving the Ruger in his belt, Rudd crawled up between the two sleeping figures on the bed. Both stirred in their sleep but neither awakened. Slowly he reached out with both hands simultaneously, his well-developed fingers closing around the two throats. MacAskill's neck was flabby, but beneath the top layer was the remnants of a once-muscular neck. His wife's throat was slim, and he heard the pop as her larynx crushed almost immediately.

MacAskill came awake and his eyes bulged. For several seconds, Rudd could see on his surprised face that he didn't know where he was or what was happening. He began to kick his legs spasmodically, and his hand reached for the revolver on the table.

Releasing the dead woman's throat, Rudd reached across and brushed the weapon to the floor. MacAskill tried to pry his hand away, but his strength was gone. A few moments later, the legs quit kicking and he closed his eyes. Rudd checked both pulses. Nothing.

Going back to his bag in the hallway, Clayton Rudd pulled out a Ruger 10/22 rifle. He checked the 10-shot magazine, then pulled back the bolt and chambered a round before flipping on the safety. After rolling the dead man to the side, he sat on the edge of the bed and lifted the phone. He would be posing as Harvey MacAskill, so he didn't dial 911—a retired cop wouldn't do that for the kind of call he was about to make. Instead, Rudd dialed the local nonemergency number.

When the female dispatcher answered he said, "Neighbors across the street are at it again. Drunk, yelling, screaming, throwing things. Keeping my wife and me awake, anyway." He gave the woman the address of the house across the street.

"We'll send a cruiser right out, sir," the dispatcher said. "Would you mind giving me your name?"

Rudd laughed into the phone. "You got it right there on caller ID," he said. "But I'll give it to you anyway. MacAskill."

"Oh, yes, Lieutenant MacAskill, I remember you. It's the Bowers across the street again?"

"Yeah," Rudd said. "My favorite neighbors until they invite Jack Daniel's over every evening."

The woman giggled. "You retired off the job right before I came on, I think. But from what I've heard about you, you could just go over and take care of them yourself."

Rudd laughed again, trying to make it sound like an old man glad to be remembered. "Hey, sweetheart," he said. "I served my time. Now I get to sit on my ass like every other citizen and scream that I'm a taxpayer and tell you I pay your salary."

This brought on an even grander set of giggles. "We still hear that, I assure you. Good talking to you, Lieutenant. I'll get the car right over."

"Thanks, honey." Rudd hung up. He moved up to kneel on the

bed between the dead couple and opened the window facing the house across the street.

It wasn't an emergency and response time was slow. Rudd noted that it took more than twenty minutes by his watch for the black-and-white squad car to arrive. Not good, even for a routine call.

The patrol car parked along the curb. A male officer in his late twenties got out from behind the wheel. A short stocky female exited the passenger's seat. They both adjusted the equipment hanging from their Sam Browne belts as they walked wearily toward the front door. Another pair of drunks to try to reason with. Just another routine call.

But it wasn't going to be routine this time.

As the male officer rang the doorbell, Rudd put two quick .22 Hornet rounds into the back of his head. He staggered and leaned into the brick wall next to the door.

The female officer wasn't sure what had happened. As the man began to slide down the brick to the ground, Rudd heard her say, "John?" She knelt quickly over the body.

Rudd heard what he thought was the beginning of a scream in her throat as he pulled the trigger again and caught the woman just below the clip holding her blond hair above her neck.

1

During the past three months, 147 law-enforcement officers had been assassinated. Shot down in the streets by snipers, ambushed on phony disturbance calls and murdered in a variety of other ways. And the big man who opened the door to the police station had decided to do something about it.

The booking room looked very much like police station booking rooms the world over. The paint-chipped walls had started out industrial green but turned brown from years of dirt and tobacco smoke. The wooden chairs circling the room were splintered. A few even lay broken and discarded, piled in one corner. The front desk was equally timeworn, scarred by fists, elbows, nightsticks and cigarette burns. Grunts, moans and curses filled the air, coming in a variety of languages. In addition to the voices, the shuffle of feet and the clink of handcuffs and leg irons could be heard over the whirl of the ancient ceiling fan twenty feet above the floor.

But it wasn't the decor or the racket that caught the big man's attention as he stepped into the booking room. It was the smell. It was a mixed odor of sweat, body odor, stale beer, urine, feces and vomit.

It was a smell of human pain. Of agony. Of death.

He walked to the end of the line in front of the booking desk and took a place behind cops and prisoners waiting their turn. He was tall, broad in the shoulders, and the loose khaki-colored sport coat tapered in to a slim waist at the top of his dark brown slacks. In his plain white shirt and simple striped tie he looked no different than any of the detectives or plainclothes officers in the room. But a closer inspection would have made the trained eye wonder.

Mack Bolan had a certain presence about him that wasn't apparent in anyone else in the room. It was hard to define exactly, but it had something to do with experience, ability and self-confidence.

Bolan waited as a loudly cursing prostitute was signed in by the desk sergeant and then dragged through a door to be fingerprinted and photographed. Two more officers stepped up to the desk with a drunk.

The man known as the Executioner glanced around the room. He wasn't a cop, but he had been in many police stations around the world, and he knew how they operated. It wasn't quite eight in the morning; the prisoners being booked were the result of the past night's arrests. The usual types were represented—drug addicts, pimps, prostitutes and probably a burglar or two. Many were ahead of him in line with their arresting officers. Others cops had decided to sit out the wait with their prisoners in the chairs against the walls.

The loud thud of an ink stamp came down on the desktop, and Bolan turned back that way. The desk sergeant, an unlit cigar stub shooting from the corner of his mouth, lifted a sheaf of papers and jammed them into the hand of one of the cops next to the drunk. "Next!" he yelled as the men disappeared though the door.

The line moved forward, and an obviously drug-high prisoner tried to keep his balance with the assistance of two men dressed in sport coats. Directly behind them was a lone detective who stood next to a well-dressed man. The detective had discarded his coat, and a shoulder holster bearing a Glock 21 hung over his shirt. The well-dressed man had carefully trimmed hair and an equally coiffured mustache. The handcuffs securing his wrists behind his back seemed incongruous with what looked like a thousand-dollar suit and five-hundred-dollar shoes. The man remained silent, but his nose was stuck in the air in an attitude that bespoke the fact that he believed he didn't belong there. He stood stiffly, his eyes on the ceiling, as if sending his mind somewhere else would allow his body to accompany it.

Two more sets of prisoners and cops were between Bolan and the desk. Behind the well-dressed man, three uniforms did their best to keep an angry couple from getting at each other. It looked like a domestic disturbance in which both husband and wife had been arrested. Behind them, and directly in front of Bolan, a burly worker wearing a dark green shirt and matching pants was trying to talk his uniformed captor into letting him go. The man in blue ignored his pleas.

Bolan noticed the well-dressed man turn sideways to face the officer who stood next to him. The two began to speak in low voices. They didn't seem to be arguing, but the prisoner's shoulders moved animatedly. He looked as if he were used to using his hands when he talked and feared he wouldn't get his point across without them. His actions were in sharp contrast to the arrogance he had shown earlier.

A few choice curses sounded over the general clamor about the room. Bolan looked to the desk to see that the stoned prisoner had fallen to the floor. "Dammit, Brody," the sergeant screamed across the desk. "Can't you and Johnson even hold that son of a bitch up long enough for me to fill out this form?" The two cops lifted the man back to his feet and the sergeant started writing again. The rubber stamp came down once more. But as it did, a different sudden movement caught the big man's eye.

In a flash, the formerly docile man in the expensive suit stepped into the cop next to him. Both hands closed over the butt of the Glock in the exposed shoulder holster. A microsecond later, the pistol had cleared leather.

In the corner of his eye, Bolan saw a female officer's hand drop to her Sam Browne belt. "Gun!" she shrieked.

All around the room, hands slapped leather and ballistic nylon as cops tried to pry their weapons from their hips. More screams and shouts sounded above the usual noise in the room. Other cops screamed "Freeze!" and "Drop the gun!"

Bolan moved forward quickly. Brushing the prisoner in the dark green work clothes to the side, he moved past him and his arresting officer. By the time he reached the prisoner who had grabbed the Glock, the weapon was aimed at the uniform next to him. The big man saw the tendons in the gunman's wrists flex as he started to pull the trigger.

Then a fist slammed down on the forearm of the well-dressed man. A shocking crack sounded as if wood had been broken. The man screamed as the Glock fell from his hand and clattered to the dirty tile.

Bolan drew back his fist again as the man in the suit grabbed his injured wrist with his other hand. The fist shot forward again, this time in a right cross to the would-be shooter's jaw. Another cracking sound filled the room.

The prisoner in the expensive suit was unconscious before he hit the ground.

The room fell silent. All eyes turned to the big man as both police officers and criminals stared in awe. None of them—cop or con—had ever seen this man before he'd entered the building a few moments earlier. Those who had seen him then had noted that, yes, there was something a little different about him.

But now that difference had just been demonstrated.

Bolan stepped over the unconscious form on the floor, picked up the fallen Glock and handed it to the officer with the empty shoulder holster. Although he looked somewhat like a cop, and was about to pass himself off as one, the truth was that he was not and never had been a police officer.

The big man walked up to the desk and looked across it at the sergeant. Reaching into the khaki sport coat, he produced a badge case and flipped it open to reveal a shield that read Houston Police Department.

"Detective Mike Belasko," the big man told the sergeant. "Just been transferred in. Can you point me toward Captain Medford's office?"

With shock still covering his face, the sergeant pointed to a door on the other side of the room.

MACK BOLAN HAD BEEN known by many other names over the years, but regardless of what he looked like or was called, it was the same warrior's soul that inhabited the body that now walked through the door bearing the words Captain Thomas Medford, Major Offenders Unit, Investigations Command.

Going undercover for either short- or long-term operations was nothing new to Bolan. Usually when he employed role camouflage he masqueraded as a criminal. Good guys pretended to be bad guys in order to catch bad guys. But this time it would be different.

This time, the Executioner was a good guy about to portray another kind of good guy in order to catch the bad guys.

Tom Medford's eyes had been glued to the top of a stack of paperwork on his desk since he'd answered Bolan's knock with a "Come in!" The soldier watched the man squint at the paper, then lift it. Medford moved the page back and forth, closer then farther, in front of the reading glasses perched on his nose and secured by a braided leather lanyard around his neck. Each new distance brought a frown and a squint.

Bolan remained silent as the man tried to focus his eyes. The shiny skin of Medford's scalp did its best to hide, unsuccessfully, beneath a comb-over. The graying hair, matted with too much hair spray, grew from the right side of his head and then crawled to the other side.

Finally Medford tore the glasses from his face, slammed the paper back down on the desk and looked up at Bolan. "Can you read that last sentence?" he asked.

The soldier took the paper off the desktop and smiled. "'It is this officer's opinion,'" he read, "'that both Mr. and Mrs. Baker should be prosecuted: Mr. Baker being charged with second-degree burglary, and knowingly concealing stolen property, and Mrs. Baker on the latter charge only.'" He looked up. "It's signed—"

"I know who signed the damn thing," Medford snapped. "Ronnie Vogt. That kid's handwriting looks like he's older than me. You combine that with the way my eyes are getting, and I've got a major problem on my hands... Belasko, isn't it?"

Bolan nodded. "Mike Belasko."

Medford leaned forward again, took the report back from Bolan and dropped it on his desk. He stayed over the desk long enough for a quick handshake, then said, "Sorry about the rude welcome just now. I'm getting older, and I'm afraid I'm not taking to it very well. Reading glasses, arthritis, hair falling out. Seems to all happen at once."

Bolan simply nodded again.

Medford snatched the glasses off the desk and flipped the lanyard over the back of his head. It looked like a well-practiced movement, and the little half-spectacles settled on the bridge of his nose. He dug through the stack on his desk until he found a manila folder, then opened it. "Luckily, this is all typed," he said. He squinted anyway as he began leafing through the pages.

Bolan waited silently. He knew what the man was studying. It was Detective Mike Belasko's Houston PD personnel file.

Hal Brognola, Bolan's contact at the U.S. Department of Justice and director of the Sensitive Operations Group out of Stony Man Farm, had arranged for computer wizard Aaron "The Bear" Kurtzman to hack into the Houston files and insert the phony file. For all practical purposes, Bolan was on the payroll, had full medical and dental coverage and was even on the retirement plan. Among other things, he had been twice decorated, and was one of the department's firearms and close-quarters combat instructors.

Medford closed the file. "Impressive career," he said. "And that little minidrama they told me just occurred in the booking room makes more sense now that I see you're one of the unarmed instructors." He paused and looked up over the glasses. "But tell me, why didn't you just shoot the son of a bitch?"

Bolan shrugged. "Too many innocent people around. And your desk sergeant was directly behind the guy. Right in the line of fire."

Medford nodded. "Quick thinking. I like that. And we don't

have to go through as much bullshit with Internal Affairs, either. Although it wouldn't have hurt my feelings if you'd killed the guy. You know who that was?"

Bolan shook his head.

"Dr. Benjamin Knafee. A heart surgeon. Now, you'd think anybody would be satisfied with the phenomenal amount of money they make. But not him. He's been fronting cocaine and heroin money for the last twenty years. The narcs finally nailed him. But he'll either get off with one of those legal 'dream teams'—damn, I hate that cliché—or end up with a suspended sentence. He may lose his license to practice medicine, but what does he care? He's as rich as an oil sheikh." The aging captain sighed, then said, "But such is life." Returning to the subject of his new detective, he went on, "The memo I got from the chief says he's transferred you because he wants you on the cop killings." He tapped the file. "You had a major role in a serial killing investigation a few years ago. Which one was it again?"

"The Christ Church Killer," the soldier said. It had been a major case a few years earlier—the victims all being women members of the church, which was still on the original site where it had been founded in 1839. The killer had turned out to be the choir director. Kurtzman had inserted a major role in the case history for Bolan, which he would erase along with the rest of the phony personnel file as soon as it was no longer needed.

Medford frowned behind the reading glasses. "I worked the Christ Church case," he said. "Funny, I don't remember you."

Bolan smiled. "There were a lot of us on it, Cap," he said. "I got more credit than I really deserved. I remember you, though. You were the one who joined the choir undercover. You were the first to suspect the director." Bolan had done his homework on the case, and the rest of his fake file, to support his cover.

Medford fairly beamed. "Yeah, what a freak that guy was. Turned out he wasn't even a choir director—all his credentials from all those Bible colleges and seminaries were forged. You remember when we found that out?"

"I remember when Patterson did," Bolan said. "Your hunch led to the background investigation, and that led to me zeroing in on him. It was easy after that. Like I said, I got more credit than I deserved." He waited, hoping he was well enough established now that they could get on with the important subject and quit wasting time.

The man behind the desk squinted at Bolan. "I'm beginning to remember you now," he said, nodding his head. "Damn. Just getting old, I guess."

The soldier suppressed a smile.

Medford picked up the phone on his desk and punched a button. "Vogt out there?" he said into the instrument. "Then find him and send him in here." He hung up and looked at Bolan. "Ronnie Vogt—the kid whose handwriting is sure to make me go blind in another month of so—is your new partner." He took off the reading glasses and pulled a bandanna from his desk. As he polished the lenses, he added, "Vogt's a good kid, really, if he could just use a pen." He paused a moment, and his face grew puzzled. "One thing bugs me about you, Belasko. It's personal, but I'm going to ask you anyway. If you don't want to answer, just tell me to go to hell."

He liked Medford. The man had enough confidence to give his subordinates their dignity without worrying about losing their respect. "Shoot," Bolan said.

"The file has you transferring in from Information Services. You were there—" he glanced down at the closed folder as if he could see through the cover "—two years was it?"

"A little over."

"Why? I mean...with your background...and you just don't look like the kind of guy who'd like the Administrative Division."

"I didn't," he said. "But I needed a break." Both Bolan and Brognola had known that even in a department as large as Houston, a high-profile investigator would come in contact with the Major Offenders Unit if assigned to any of the investigative branches. But by hiding him away in Administration for two years they had given memories time to fade. "My wife died, Cap. Cancer. I needed something routine for a while."

Medford glanced down at the desk again, obviously sorry he'd asked the question. Finally looking up, he said, "Okay, then. We've got something of an informal joint task force up and running. You and Vogt are both assigned to it."

Bolan nodded. Over the past few months, a total of 147 police officers had been murdered across the United States from Washington to Florida, Alaska to Hawaii. The first three, however, had been in the Houston area. The next two had been in Eastern Louisiana, and an unusual number had been somewhere in the South and Southwest. No lone man could be behind all of the killings. It had to be a terrorist group of some kind, either foreign or domestic. But the fact that the killings had started in Houston meant there was at least some connection there. And with no better leads, the soldier had decided that Houston was as good as any place to start.

The task force Medford had mentioned was local only, made up of Houston area police officers and various sheriff's deputies. So far, there hadn't been enough evidence to link the murders across state lines and give the FBI jurisdiction. But the Feds were all waiting in the wings, chomping at the bit to get in on the action. The problem was that while everyone suspected the assassinations were connected, they couldn't put together enough direct evidence to warrant a federal investigation, which was driving the G-men and liberal politicians crazy. There were even rumors in the Senate that a bill proposing a new federal police agency that would combine all U.S. law enforcement and give them jurisdiction over state, county and local police was in the development stage because of the killings.

Bolan was not against federal law enforcement. In fact, although he operated as an independent agent he worked hand in hand with Brognola and the Justice Department. But the idea of one national police that could, at will, take over cases from locally appointed and elected officials didn't sit well with Bolan. The potential for abuse by any organization that strong was simply too high. Such an agency reminded him a little too much of Hitler's Gestapo. It also sounded a too much like the old KGB.

A knock came at the door. Through the translucent glass Bolan saw the shadow of a broad-shouldered man of medium height. Medford yelled "Come in!" in the same voice he'd used when Bolan arrived. The door opened.

Ronnie Vogt entered the room. Medford had twice referred to the detective as a kid. Perhaps the captain *was* getting old. Vogt was certainly not old, but he had to be in his midthirties. And the premature lines on his face—the lines of a man who has seen more than his share of human suffering—made him look even older.

"You wanted to see me, Cap?" Vogt said.

Medford nodded. "Your new partner," he said, indicating Bolan with a wave of his hand. "Mike Belasko." He tapped the file on his desk. "Impressive file. You ever met before?"

Vogt shook his head as he walked over and extended his hand. "Big department," he said, quoting the same words Bolan had used to Medford earlier. It was the maxim cops of all big departments fell back on when they didn't recognize a fellow officer but felt that they should. "No, we've never met. But I've seen Mike in action." He paused and shook his head again, this time in amazement "I was out in the booking room earlier. Tell me, you got a red cape on under that jacket?"

Bolan shrugged. "Right place, right time and lucky," he said.

Again, Medford's hand fell on the file. "And the right training and experience, I'd say."

Glancing to Vogt he added. "Belasko has been one of our firearms and close-quarters combat instructors for years. And if I remember what I read, you're former Army. Green Beret, wasn't it?"

At least that part of the Executioner's file was accurate. "Long time ago, Captain," Bolan said modestly.

Vogt started to take the chair next to Bolan but Medford said, "Don't sit down. I'm through. Go catch me a cop killer. I'd rather retire on a deputy chief's salary than a captain's."

Vogt nodded, then glanced at his watch. "We've got a task force meeting in forty-five minutes, Mike. That's probably the best way to get your brought up to speed. You ready?"

Bolan nodded.

They were almost out the door when Medford called, "Vogt!"

When they turned, the captain was holding up the report Bolan had been forced to read for him earlier. "Learn to write like a human instead of a chimpanzee, okay?"

"You got it, Cap," Vogt said. He was laughing to himself as the Executioner followed him out into the hall.

"WITHOUT FURTHER ADO, my fellow senators," said the president pro tem of the Senate, "I give the floor to the Honorable Owen Killian, senator from the great state of New York."

A polite applause sounded throughout the half-filled Senate chambers as Killian rose from his seat and walked to the podium. Although the microphone had worked just fine for the president pro tem, he still tapped it twice before clearing his throat. He paused dramatically, looking out over the floor, trying to make personal eye contact with each member of the Senate before beginning. It was a technique he had first employed as a member of New York's champion high school debate team, and he had never seen any reason to discard it during the thirty-five years that had come and gone since. It had helped him get elected first as a New York City councilor, then slid him into the mayor's office. He had used the eye-contact technique to earn two terms as governor, and after one term in the House of Representatives he'd switched to the Senate and never left Washington. Something about his eyes, he had learned, had an almost hypnotic effect on both constituents and fellow politicians. Perhaps it was the fact that he could look a person squarely in the eye, lie like a whore telling a john exactly what she knew he wanted to hear and make it sound like the most sincere truth the person had ever heard.

"Fellow senators," Killian finally said in the rich baritone he had cultivated over the years. "You all know why I asked to address you today, for I have spoken to you individually about this matter that has been most heavy on my heart in recent days. During the past three months, 147 law-enforcement officers have been ambushed, shot by snipers, bombed or otherwise killed across this great land of ours. Men and women who, for ridiculously low pay and the requirement of higher background checks than either you or I have ever had to undergo, still chose to don the mantle of blue to protect and serve the rest of us. One hundred forty-seven, my fellow senators. What does that mean? It is only a number, and since we knew none of these officers personally, it is a mere statistic. A number, and a small number at that for those of us who deal in millions and even billions when deciding budgets. But this number, though small by comparison, is far greater than any number that represents dollars. For this number does not represent money. It represents human lives."

Killian paused to wipe away the lone tear that had begun to drip down his face. When he continued, he let his voice quaver slightly. "Human beings. Gunned down, blown to shreds, or otherwise *murdered* in the prime of their lives. Dying, so that we might live." He quit speaking entirely, forcing a small choke from his throat and holding up a hand to indicate he needed a moment to pull himself together. That last part had not been in the speech written by his aide. It had just come to him as he spoke. Should he carry that thread forward when he began again? Easter was only a few weeks away. Should he compare these officers to Christ's sacrifice or would that be carrying it too far? Probably. At least for the moment. Save it for later. Stick to the script and the overall plan.

As soon as he thought the pause had been sufficient, Killian leaned back toward the microphone. "I ask your forgiveness for the delay," he said in a voice that was steady but sounded world-weary. "I will try to go on." Again he searched the faces. Before he had begun, he had drawn deadpan expressions from the vast majority of the men and women seated before him. Now he saw more interest on the faces of many. On a few he saw concern, even sorrow. There were those, of course, who were still without expression—all of them of the opposing party, and all men or women who he knew were never likely to side with him simply because he was *him*. On one man's face now, however, he saw outright contempt. Senator Richard Lane. Lane was a former member of the Libertarian party who had finally come over to the two-party system in an attempt to defeat it from the inside. Everyone—including the voters who had elected him in his home state of Idaho—knew it. He was still called the "Libertarian" in Washington.

Killian didn't let the scorn on Lane's face bother him. It was to be expected. Okay, the Libertarian wasn't affected by his eyes or any of his other acting abilities. But it didn't matter. Lane might be able to see through him. He might know Killian had ulterior motives. But he didn't know what they were. And even if he did, he could never prove them. Lane was a Washington outcast, and no one would listen to him.

"One-hundred forty-seven men and women," Killian repeated. "One hundred twenty-one male officers. Twenty-six female. There are 204 little children who will grown up without a father or mother. These are children who will grow up and spend the rest of their lives knowing their parent was murdered!" He hadn't planned to let his voice rise in anger as it was doing now. But it sounded good. He'd keep it up and watch the faces. "Are we going to let them grow up with the additional knowledge that we, the government of the United States of America, the most powerful nation in the history of humankind, did not find these murderers and distribute justice? Or at least do everything in our power to find those responsible for these abominable acts?"

Killian's voice was shaking again but this time, rather than in sorrow, it was with a righteous anger. Making sure his trembling hand could clearly be seen above the podium, he reached for the water glass next to the microphone. As he drank, he purposely let a little of the water drip carelessly onto his shirt. When he had set the glass down again, he spoke as if he had struggled to gain control of his emotions once more. "Fellow senators," he said, "we face a challenge here that state and local law-enforcement officers are simply not equipped to handle. There are communications problems, jealousies between departments and other problems that are far too serious to overcome quickly, if they can be overcome at all. And each day that passes without apprehending the party or parties responsible for these nefarious murders means more men or women in blue will die." He paused, making a final quick glance at the faces. He had, waiting, the first of several ace cards that he planned to play over the next few weeks. But he wanted to make sure they were ready for it.

They were. At least enough of them were.

"Ladies and gentlemen, fellow senators of this great land, I propose that a Senate committee be formed to investigate these murders. And that this committee oversee a task force handpicked from the FBI, BATF and other federal law-enforcement agencies, and that they be granted jurisdiction in this matter over all state and local law enforcement."

There was a moment of silence, then a few hands began to clap. But there were a few unhappy murmurs along the floor, as well. Neither the approval nor disapproval was particularly fervent, but Killian hadn't expected it to be. Most of these men and women seated before him were career politicians like himself, and they didn't build a career in politics by stepping into the wind until they knew which way it was going to blow. Until they did, most of the senators didn't want to appear so committed to either side that they'd have trouble reversing themselves later if it became expedient.

But at least one man in the room didn't care. He had as much as said he didn't care if he got elected again, he was going to do what he believed was right regardless of what it cost him. It was an almost unheard-of concept in Washington, and had alienated most of the other politicians while simply confusing the rest. The man was Richard Lane, and Killian was not surprised when, completely out of order, the senator from Idaho stood.

"I'd like to ask a question," Lane said.

Killian rolled his eyes dramatically and a few soft laughs were heard around the room. Commenting on Lane's lack of protocol, Killian had once told a newsreporter, "He's like the bad kid in school who gets into big trouble all the time. When he does something small, the teacher's so tired of dealing with him it just goes ignored." Such was the case with Lane. So Killian skipped the "floor recognizes the senator" part and just said, "Go ahead, Richard."

"I know how busy you are, Senator," Lane said sarcastically, "but have you ever had time to read a little document called the U.S. Constitution? I know we just pretend it doesn't exist most of the time these days, so I was wondering if we're going to ignore it again on this issue, too."

Killian sighed, loud enough to be sure the mike picked it up. "My staff has researched this," he said in his weary voice. "Our opinion is that there is no violation of—"

"The letter of the law?" Lane interrupted. "Is that what you were about to say, Senator? Because I have no doubt you have found a loophole somewhere. You amaze me. You can find holes so small a minnow couldn't swim through them, but by the time you're through stretching them they won't keep out a whale."

"Senator, I—"

"Don't *Senator* me, Killian," Lane said, his voice rising. "We all heard your dramatic little song-and-dance just now, and you'd have been much better off with a career on Broadway. I, for one, know what you're really up to. This task force as you call it is nothing more than a first step toward a federal police agency. You want your own private army when you run for President. That's what you really want!" By now he was shouting angrily.

For a split second, Killian was taken aback. He hadn't said a word to anyone yet about his ambitions. How did Lane know?

The answer was, Lane *didn't* know. He was guessing, fishing. But he was doing a damn fine job of it. Killian forced himself to relax again. It didn't matter. This was Richard Lane. No one would listen to him.

The president pro tem, seated to the side of the podium, picked up a small phone and spoke into it. A few seconds later, two uniformed men walked into the room.

"Senator Lane, you are out of order," the pro tem said, standing and leaning into the microphone. "And it's not the first time, I might add."

"It won't be the last, either!" Lane yelled. "It's not me who's out of order! It's this whole place! Everybody spends ninety percent of their time here patting themselves and each other on the back, calling each other 'honorable this' and 'honorable that,' talk-

ing about 'great states and great lands' and saying one thing while
they mean another."

"Senator, I'm going to have to ask you to leave."

"That won't be the first time either!" Lane screamed at the top
of his lungs. He began throwing papers and files into his briefcase
as the two security men came to a stop behind his chair. When he'd
finished he slammed the lid shut, then leaned into the microphone
in front of him one last time. "I know what you're after, Killian.
And I'm going to make sure everybody knows what you're trying
to pull. You're going to try to use these murders to create a federal
police agency and then take the credit when your cronies in the
news media make it look like you stopped the killings personally.
Then you'll run for President on that platform. Hey, America! See
what I did for you? No more murder, no more rape, all because
Senator Owen Killian got us our own Orwellian police force!
Why, we shouldn't even call you Mr. President! You'll be the first
dictator this country has ever had!"

By now the security men had taken hold of Lane's arms. The
senator shrugged them off. "Is it *you* or *me* who needs help walking?" he practically spit into their faces.

With his briefcase under his arm like a football, Richard Lane
strode out of the Senate.

Killian watched him leave. He sat, but not before scanning the
faces to whom he had spoken. He'd made some progress. Not
enough, though. Too many still weren't convinced. The senator
from New York smiled inwardly. Soon, he would have all the support he needed. If not from ideology, then at least from fear of the
voters turning against them.

Because if the people of the United States of American thought
a lot of cops had died in the past few weeks, wait until they saw
what was in store for them a few days from now.

THE TASK FORCE was an informal gathering of area law-enforcement officers assigned to the police assassinations around Houston. A suite at the Houston West Drury Inn, at the intersection of
the Katy Freeway and Addicks Road, had been rented. Most of the

furniture in the living room had been moved out and a conference table and chairs moved in. Charts and maps covered the walls in place of the paintings and mirrors that had been there before, and would return when the investigation was over and the police went back to their respective departments.

Representatives of the Houston PD and investigators from several of the surrounding cities and counties were present. The men—and two women—all looked like battle-hardened street vets who has seen more than their share of human malevolence. They stood in groups around a conference table drinking coffee when Bolan and Vogt walked through the door. Vogt introduced Bolan to officers from Morgan's Point, Pasadena, La Porte and several other of the smaller incorporated cities that made up greater Houston. Besides deputies from Harris County, which surrounded Houston, deputy sheriffs from the surrounding counties of Brazoria, Galveston, Liberty and Fort Bend had also sent men to become part of the team. The last person to whom Vogt introduced Bolan was Deputy Archie Burnett of Harris County. A big man with a raspy voice, Burnett was in charge of the meeting, which was about to begin. He shook Bolan's hand and said, "Glad to have you on board, Belasko."

Bolan nodded.

Burnett grinned from ear to ear. "We can use all the help we can get. Not enough men on this case anyway, and we've got two guys out with this flu going around."

Then, turning away from the soldier to address the rest of the room, he raised his voice and bellowed, "Okay, they ain't paying us these fantastic salaries to drink bad coffee. Let's get to work."

There were a few snide remarks made about fantastic salaries as the men dropped into seats around the table.

Burnett moved to the head of the table but remained standing. From a stack of folders to one side of the table, he took the top one and slid it down to Bolan. He opened it up to see the case history. Copies of all reports, witness lists and contact numbers and everything else they had so far concerning the cop killings.

"Everybody meet Belasko?" Burnett asked.

Around the tables, heads nodded.

"Good," Burnett said. "For his sake, let's go over this thing from the beginning. Won't hurt anybody else a bit to review things from the start, either." Burnett had taken off his sport coat and, besides a .40-caliber Browning Hi-Power with stag grip panels, a collapsible ASP baton rode on his basket-woven belt in a matching leather carrier. Drawing the ASP, he flipped it to full extension, then turned to a map of Harris County on the wall directly behind him. "We'll start with the most recent officer assassination and work back. It took place here, less than a week ago." He used the ASP as a pointer to indicate one of the pushpins in the map. "Houston Heights, just off highway 610, near Kelley. Lone officer—Joe Kenard, some of you knew him—answered a call reporting a disturbance in a supermarket parking lot. When he arrived, he found the parking lot peaceful. As he got out of his cruiser, he was approached by what we must suppose he took to be a store clerk wearing an apron. Six witnesses in the lot saw them talking. Four of these saw the clerk reach into his slacks, produce a small revolver, then empty it into Kenard. Some of the witnesses said five rounds were fired, some said six. All were head shots, all exited except one—.38 caliber—and the medical examiner reported that the head was too messed up to determine the exact number of rounds. But regardless—five or six—none of the witnesses remember the killer pulling the trigger after the last round. In other words, no empty clicks after the roars." Burnett stopped for air, then his eyes fell on Bolan near the other end of the table. The soldier didn't know whether what the Harris County man said next was a way of welcoming him to the group or testing him. "What can you tell me about the killer from all that, Belasko?"

The Executioner leaned forward slightly. "The fact that he didn't fire on an empty chamber meant he knew his gun. Whether it was five rounds or six doesn't matter. He knew how many he had, and the stress of the moment didn't get to him and make him lose count. He's familiar with weapons."

Burnett nodded approvingly. "What else?"

Bolan looked the man in the eye. "He either knew, or suspected, that Kenard was wearing a vest. That's why he went for the head."

Burnett smiled again. "Very good. Pretty much what we've guessed ourselves. Which means he does his homework. He knows weapons, pressure doesn't get to him and he's studied cops."

"Any witness descriptions?" Bolan asked.

There were a few polite chuckles around the room, and they let him know what the answer was about to be.

Burnett nodded, his smile hardening. "Sure are, four of them. The guy was either short, medium height or extremely tall. He had either blond or brown or black hair, and was either a black man or a white man. Except for one witness who said he was either Mexican or Japanese. Figure that one out for me if you can because I couldn't."

Bolan nodded. Such discrepancies between witnesses were not unusual after traumatic events. "How'd he leave the scene?"

Burnett had lifted his coffee cup to his lips, and one of the other cops—Don Macy of Morgan's Point PD, Bolan remembered—spoke for him. "One of the witnesses, a Radio Shack salesman who worked across the street and had gone to the store for some smokes, had no idea. He froze when he saw the shooting, and he still hadn't thawed out the next day when we went for a follow-up interview."

"I still think that's bullshit," came a voice from the other side of the table.

Bolan looked over to see a stocky detective with curly blond hair and a matching mustache and goatee. Another of the Houston PD men. What had his name been? Alexander. Robert Alexander.

Burnett forced a smile. "Bob interviewed the kid and thinks he knows more than he gave out."

Alexander turned to eye Bolan. "He saw something. Or knows something," the stocky man said with no uncertainty in his voice. "He talked to the first cop on the scene. He was blubbering and didn't make sense, but the uniform told me he knew something." Alexander paused, then added, "By the time I got there, though, he'd turned mute. He'd also been joined by this skinny little blond girlfriend. My guess is she scared him into forgetting anything he saw."

"Besides Alexander, three other men tried getting him to talk," Burnett said. "Then we ran Karen at him." The big deputy nodded toward one of the two women on the task force. Bolan had met her earlier: Karen Cohlmia was a sultry brunette with dark skin and mysterious Mediterranean eyes. Her every pore breathed sexuality. "Figured this geek might open up for her."

"*I'll* open up for you Karen," Alexander said.

The female detective gave him the finger but laughed good-naturedly along with the other cops. When things settled down, she looked at Bolan. "I didn't have any more luck with him than Alexander's ever going to have with me," she said. The response brought on more rowdy comments from the men.

"All those interviews took place the day of the shooting and the day after," Alexander said, bringing everyone back to the subject at hand. "The little geek was so scared he took vacation days and left town. We've kept an eye on his house. He just got back last night."

"Anybody try him since he got back?" Bolan asked. "See if he'd changed his mind?"

Alexander nodded. "Karen and I both talked to him this morning. Same story. Brain freeze."

"Bottom line," Burnett said, "he's sticking to his story." He cleared his throat. "Anyway, another of the witnesses swore the killer drove away in a car. But she didn't get a license, didn't know the make or model and none of us put much stock in her. She was eighty-years-old, and was mixed up on a lot of other things, too."

"Yeah," said a voice from somewhere down the table, "like what her name was and whether she should vote for Truman again. I interviewed her."

"The other two witnesses said the shooter ran straight into the kid, knocked him down, then ran behind the supermarket and that's the last they saw of him. There's an alley runs behind the store, where they make deliveries and dump the trash, and on the other side is a residential neighborhood."

"If that's true, then the guy should have gotten a good look at him," Bolan stated.

"My guess, too," Alexander said.

Bolan leaned in slightly. "Did he say anything like that to the uniform before you got there?"

"Nah, like I said, he was just blubbering incoherently. Then the girlfriend showed up and he went mute on us."

"Anybody in the houses along the alley see anything?" the soldier asked.

Macy shrugged. "Some of them said they heard the shots. Some of those thought they were firecrackers. Others, I think, just *said* they heard something because they thought they should have." He paused. "One old man though, last house at the far end of the alley, away from where the shooting took place, said he heard somebody running past his window."

He paused, frowned, then looked at Vogt. "Wait a minute. Ronnie, aren't you're the one who talked to him?"

Next to Bolan, Vogt nodded. "Yeah. He might have heard somebody running but he wears a hearing aid. Barely gets around. Funny old man, though. Real crackpot."

"In any case," Macy said, looking back to Bolan, "the trail ends there. At least for now."

Burnett took the floor again, moving on to the second murder, which had been a week before just outside of La Porte. A deputy sheriff had been found in his car, parked on the side of the road. His throat had been cut, and he'd been stabbed several times with a large knife. There were no signs of a struggle, however. The third had been a few weeks before that in Galveston, where a city officer had been bludgeoned to death on the beach and not found until the next morning by surfers. At that time there had not seemed to be any connection between the three deaths.

"Then the two happened just across the border in Louisiana," Burnett said. He had finished his coffee and taken a seat. "We started checking around, and suddenly cops were going down every day or so somewhere. Lots of different techniques. And not enough evidence to prove to a judge that they were connected." He paused and looked Bolan in the eye. "But we *know* they are. And so does every other cop in the country."

There were murmurs of agreement around the table. Bolan understood. Like soldiers, cops developed their instincts with experience. Maybe it was some sixth sense, and maybe it was just the fact that their unconscious minds picked up evidence the conscious didn't register. But they learned to trust hunches.

Don Macy spoke again. "None of us here particularly want the FBI taking over this thing, but we could use their resources and intelligence distribution."

"Aren't they helping anyway?" Bolan asked. "In an unofficial capacity?"

"Sure," Macy said. "But not completely." He paused, opened his jacket and pulled out a pack of cigarettes. It seemed the cue for everyone to suddenly ignore the No Smoking sign on the front door of the suite, and suddenly the room looked like London on a foggy day. "You look like you've been around a while, Belasko," Macy went on. "So you know what it's like working with the Feds. They always hold back stuff. More worried about taking the credit than catching the bad guy. They aren't going to get real interested until they're in on the deal. Some of them still don't even think the crimes are connected."

Burnett picked up the ball once more. "Okay, let's have the rundown on what's gone on since the last meeting." He looked at the man seated to his right.

In counterclockwise order, the investigators around the table told what leads they had followed. Many had reinterviewed witnesses. Others had canvassed the neighborhoods where the murders had taken place looking for new witnesses or other leads. Vogt had revisited the scenes, looking for any sort of physical evidence that might have been overlooked the first time around. None had been found during the initial crime-scene investigations, and the Houston detective hadn't turned up anything new. It had been a long shot at best, but long shots sometimes came through. And one thing had become increasingly clear to Bolan as the men gave their reports: long shots were all they had. For all practical purposes, there were no good leads. Whoever was killing the cops not only knew how to kill, they knew how to cover their trails.

Archie Burnett made a few comments and then a few suggestions on what should be done next. But it also became clear to Bolan that the big deputy was more of a coordinator than the boss of the task force. All in all, the group was little better off than if they'd been working independently.

Finally, as they were about to break up, Burnett turned to Bolan once more. "We've been on this thing for weeks, Mike," he said. "You lose your objectivity after a while, and we could use some fresh ideas. You got any?"

The soldier shook his head. "Not at the moment. What I'd like to do is go talk to some of the people who were in the supermarket parking lot. Maybe the old man who thought he heard running. You never know when somebody will think of something later, and they don't always call it in."

"More power to you," Burnett said. "You've got the names and addresses of all the witnesses there in the file."

"Right."

"Okay, then, " Burnett said. "Anything else?"

No one spoke.

"Then gentlemen, let's hit the bricks," Burnett said. "I don't want even one more of our brothers to hit the pavement. We nail whoever is behind all this."

2

There wasn't a day that went by when Jack Crenna wasn't in pain. Arthritis in his knees, hips and shoulders from over forty years as a pipeline welder, climbing in and out of ditches and working in hundred-degree-plus heat under the hot Texas sun. Both knees had been replaced, and he walked with two canes on good days and didn't walk at all on bad. On those days, he got out of bed only to go to the bathroom and answer the door when the local Meals-on-Wheels van brought his lunch. Most of the time he ate it. Sometimes he ate a bowl of cereal for supper, too. But other times, his stomach wouldn't even take that.

Yes, Crenna thought as he shuffled down the hall from the bedroom to the living room, his body hurt. But not as bad as his heart. He looked quickly at the calendar on the wall then turned away just as quickly. The two-year anniversary of Elsie's death was coming up, and he didn't want to know the date. The problem was, he did know. His body might be failing but, at eighty-four, his mind was as sharp as it had ever been. A damn shame, too, he thought as he carefully lowered himself into his TV chair and reached for the remote control. It would a lot easier if he'd bought a ticket to Alzheimerville like the few friends he had left. Friends he never saw, of course, because they couldn't find their way to his house even if it occurred to them to try, and while he he'd know how to get there, his body wouldn't take him. A chuckle rumbled his chest, and even that small movement sent pain shooting through his shoulders. It seemed that all he had left was his sense of humor, so he guessed he'd better thank God for that. On the other hand, he thought the government ought to place a moratorium on medical research. People were living too long, and he was one of them. They either lost their body or they lost their mind or they lost both but they still kept on breathing. It was no kind of life. Except maybe for a laugh or two here and there.

Crenna searched the remote control for the power button, switched on the set and saw Regis and that new girl who'd taken Kathie Lee's place. He didn't like her as well as Kathie Lee. Wasn't as pretty. Wasn't as funny. Didn't remind him of Elsie the way Kathie Lee did, and didn't make him laugh the way Elsie used to do. Of course not even Kathie Lee had done that. He was about to hit the channel button when he heard the doorbell ring.

He looked at his watch. Too early for Meals. He frowned, then called out, "Jes' a minute there. Takes me a mite longer to get up than it used to." Holding both arms of the chair, he struggled to his feet and grabbed the canes he'd leaned against the lamp table. He wondered who it might be. Mailman? Too early. Neighbor checking to see if he'd died in his sleep? Sometimes they did. Home invasion? Only if they were so desperate for drugs they thought a ten-year-old television was worth the effort. Sure were a lot of invasions on the news these days, though, and he considered going into the bedroom for the old Colt 1911 he'd walked off with fifty years ago after the war. But it would take him a good ten minutes to get back in there. Maybe another five to get down on the floor under the bed. That's if it turned out to be one of those days where he *could* get down on the floor.

Crenna laughed out loud as he thought of an old television commercial. "I've fallen! And I can't get up!" he said to himself.

So the hell with it. Let the home invaders kill him and take the TV. He'd just go off to see Elsie.

Shuffling toward the door, he called out, "Who is it?"

"Houston police, Mr. Crenna," a voice said through the door. "Detective Vogt. You remember me?"

"I remember you, son," the old man called out as he continued his wobbly adventure across the carpet to the door. "And if you remember me, you'll remember that it's gonna take me a minute to get to you."

"We'll wait."

"*We* then, is it?" Crenna asked. "You brought reinforcements? That's good, son, 'cause what's really taking me so long is I'm flushing my marijuana cigarettes down the toilet."

He heard laughter come through the door.

"You'll never take me alive, coppers!" Crenna shouted and he heard more laughter. Good, he thought as he neared the door. Long as somebody was laughing, maybe the next breath he took was worth the effort.

Finally he reached the door, held both canes with his left hand and painfully twisted the doorknob with his right. Fire shot through his shoulder as he slowly swung the main door open and peered through the storm-door window. One of the boys who'd talked to him before stood on the porch holding up one of those wallets with a badge on it. And he'd brought along a new face. Bigger guy. Seemed like every policeman in town had talked to him during the past few weeks. But he didn't mind. Company was company.

"Sorry," Crenna said. "Dunkin' Donuts is down the street, boys."

The cop he remembered laughed. The other one—tough looking fellow—just smiled. "Come on in," Crenna said. "Get the storm door yourself if you don't mind. It's unlocked. I'll start on back toward the chair and I ought to be there in time for supper." He heard more chuckles as he made a slow trek back toward the living room. The storm door opened behind him, and footsteps entered the house.

"You want some coffee?" Crenna said over his shoulder as he neared the chair. "I can put some on."

"No, thanks, Mr. Crenna," the voice of the man he remembered said.

The old man reached the chair and began his turn, pivoting on the canes. "No coffee?" he said in mock surprise. "You can't be real cops." He started the lowering process, his knees creaking, grinding, cracking and sending needles of pain to his brain. "Maybe I better see that badge again." He finally reached the chair cushion and breathed a sigh of relief. "It's hell getting old," he said. "I don't recommend it to either of you two boys. Now, what can I do for you?"

BOLAN FOLLOWED Ronnie Vogt into the house and stopped, waiting as the old man made his way precariously across the room. The soldier's first instinct was to lend the man a hand. But he suspected such action might get a cane swung at his head as an insult to Crenna's dignity. The old man's body might be gone but he had plenty of spunk left, and Bolan liked him immediately. As they waited, Bolan took a look around the room. Worn-out green carpet. Fake wood paneling on the walls. Well-worn couch and love seat with a floral print—picked out, no doubt, by the woman whose photographs were on the walls and bookshelves, and was obviously deceased. Other little things told Bolan there was no woman in the home. The carpet needed vacuuming. There were scattered magazines, an old autographed baseball and a few other stray items on the lamp table.

"Now, what can I do for you?" Crenna said after making a couple of jokes.

"We just came back to see if you remembered anything more," Vogt said.

"Well, take a load off your feet. Wouldn't want them getting flat." He pointed toward the couch with one of his canes. "Just kidding, you know. Don't take me seriously with stuff like that and the coffee and doughnuts jokes."

"We don't take offense," Vogt said. "But has anything else occurred to you since we last talked last?"

"Boys, I'll tell you again, like I've told every police officer who has come by. It was a bad day, and I was in bed most of it. Bedroom's back there by the alleyway. I was just lyin' there, wishin' I could go to sleep when I heard what I thought was some kids shootin' off firecrackers. Pop-pop-pop-pop-pop. Sounded a long way off. Then some feet came runnin' by the window, and that's that." He paused and took a deep breath. "Can't even say who those feet belonged to because I was lyin' down facin' the other way. But somebody went runnin' past the window, plain as day."

Vogt hesitated a moment before saying, "Mr. Crenna, I notice you wear a hearing aid. How does it work for you?"

For the first time since they'd arrived, Crenna appeared to lose his sense of humor. "Are you having to yell right now?" he asked, a little on the testy side.

"No, sir, I'm not."

"Then I'd say it works pretty well, wouldn't you?"

Bolan scratched his nose to cover the smile that threatened to come over his face. The old man still had his vanities.

Vogt cleared his throat. Bolan knew he'd been over all this before, and it was obvious that he suspected they were wasting their time. "Mr. Crenna, did anything else at all unusual happen around that time?"

Crenna shook his head. "Not unless you want to count the fact that the Meals-on-Wheels brought me fried okra with my lunch. Told 'em many a time not to do that, and they usually don't mess up." His good humor had returned now that they'd left the subject of his hearing, and he shot them a grin that was thirty years younger than his face and a hundred years younger than his body. Bolan glanced to the side. His eyes fell on the map table where the baseball and other objects lay, haphazardly waiting to be knocked off by a stray cane or arm. He realized one of the items didn't fit the rest of the picture.

Half-hidden behind the lamp was a Szaball gripping ball. Bolan had seen them and used them himself. He glanced at Crenna's hands and saw that the knuckles of both were swollen with either gout or arthritis. The old man's hands didn't look like they could grip anything. Maybe he used the ball in an attempt to ease the pain. But they looked far beyond the point where the gripping ball would have helped.

"Mr. Crenna," Bolan said, "do you suffer from arthritis?"

"Well, yes," Crenna responded, grinning again. "I think suffer would be the right word. At least I don't enjoy it."

Bolan laughed softly. He couldn't help liking Crenna and the way the old man laughed his way through the trials and tribulations life threw his way. " I couldn't help noticing your grip exerciser on the lamp stand there," he said. "Does it help the pain in your hands?"

"No, no," Crenna said, shaking his head. "I assumed it might, but it just irritates them more. Seems to inflame them. I just thought I'd try it though when I saw it lying in the yard that day."

"*That* day?" Bolan asked. "You aren't talking about the day you heard someone run past your window, are you?"

"No, the day after that. I was feelin' a mite better, and I went outside. Like to get out any time I can because I can't so much of the time. It was there in the yard, so I thought I'd give it a try. Bent down and picked it up. Thought I'd have to call a crane to straighten out again, but I got it done." He laughed at himself again.

"You don't remember seeing it the day before? The day before the running at the window?" Bolan asked.

"Don't even remember it the morning of the running."

The soldier frowned. "I thought you said you were in bed that day."

"I said most of that day. I was up in the morning and went out for a spell. Then the barometer started droppin' and I felt like somebody was beatin' me with a hammer while somebody else stuck me with a branding iron. So I went back to bed." He glanced at the table next to him. "That thing wasn't there in the morning. Can't say about the afternoon."

Bolan looked back at the ball. It was a long shot, but he had a gut feeling about it. If whoever had shot Officer Kenard had run down the alley, he could easily have cut across Crenna's front yard when he reached the corner. The grip developer might have been in a pocket and fallen out. Was that ridiculous? It seemed so on the surface. Why would a man getting ready to shoot a police officer take an exerciser along? It seemed like a strange time to worry about muscle development. So why did the Executioner have such a gut feeling about it?

Because grip exercisers were also stress reducers, Bolan suddenly realized. Like the "worry stones" some businessmen rubbed when they were anxious, or the strings of beads counted and manipulated by some people in Middle Eastern countries.

It was still a long shot, but it couldn't hurt to keep it in mind as Bolan went about working on his own personal profile of the killer. "Mr. Crenna," he said. "Do you mind if we take the ball along with us?"

Crenna chuckled. "Not doing me any good," he said. "Besides, don't want to go to jail for concealing stolen property."

"I'm sure it's not stolen," Vogt piped in. He was giving Bolan a curious look that said he had begun to wonder a little about his new partner. "My guess would be someone just lost it."

"Take it anyway," Crenna said. "Like I told you, it's too hard for me."

Bolan stood, walked to the lamp table and picked up the ball. Too rough for fingerprints. Besides, Crenna's attempt to use it—regardless of how feeble and unsuccessful—would have smeared any prints. He dropped the exerciser into the side pocket of his sport coat.

"Anything else you can think of?" Vogt asked, looking at Bolan.

Bolan shook his head.

"Then I guess we'll get out of here and let you get back to your business," Vogt said as he stood.

"Oh, please do," Crenna said. "I was just about to execute an unfriendly takeover of Microsoft when you interrupted me. Then again, I might just see what's on television instead."

Bolan and Vogt both shook hands with the man.

"You take care of yourself, Mr. Crenna," Bolan told him.

"You do the same, son," Crenna said. "You don't mind letting yourself out, do you?"

"Not at all."

"Good," Crenna said, tapping the phone on the stand next to him. "I'm expecting a call from that blond girl...what's her name...yeah, Pamela Anderson. Sure would hate to miss it while I'm trying to get back across the room." He beamed at them and again thirty years left his face.

The old adage of smiles being infectious had to have been true, at least in this case. Because Bolan and Vogt were both smiling as they left the house.

CLAYTON RUDD KNEW he was taking a chance driving his own vehicle, but it wasn't a very big one. Besides, he was on a tight schedule. He had to get back and do something very important that night.

Rudd squeezed a rubber ball as he slowed his car just before the Twelfth Street exit in Moore, Oklahoma. Taking the off-ramp, he cut down, then up again until he came to a stop sign on the east side of Interstate 35. A left turn took him back across the highway, and he followed the directions he had memorized to an industrial area a few blocks north of Twelfth. Half-hidden among the body shops he saw the sign: Stor-Yor-Stuff. An eight-foot chain-link fence circled the grounds but the main gate was open, and he turned into the drive.

Rudd shifted the ball to his right hand, wondering for the thousandth time where he'd misplaced the Szaball. Had to have lost it somewhere, but he had no idea where. He'd pick up a new one first chance he got, but until then he'd have to make do with this rubber thing he'd picked up at the drug store. But he didn't like it. It didn't soothe his nerves the way the Szaball did when the rice inside grinded back and forth.

Steering with his left hand now, Rudd slowly cruised along the lines of rental sheds. Number 77 appeared, and he pulled in front of it. He smiled. Lucky 7. In fact, twice lucky. Not that he was going to need much luck. This one was going to be quick and easy. The only obstacle was time. He had left only one loose end so far, and he planned to tidy it up this night.

The driveways around the sheds were deserted, and Rudd liked that. Not that anyone would pay much attention to him even if they weren't. People came and went from these things all the time, stashing furniture and other items they didn't currently use, or picking up boats to go to the lake or anything else they needed. That was what these things were for, after all.

Leaving the engine running, Rudd dropped the rubber ball on the seat next to him, exited the vehicle and walked to the ribbed overhead door. A padlock secured the bolt, but the key in his pocket snapped it easily open. He rolled back the door and glanced inside.

The big man in Washington had been true to his word. The Harley-Davidson stood against the wall just as he'd been told it would. On the concrete floor next to it was a battery-powered lantern. There was plenty of room inside the shed for his car, as well.

Returning to his vehicle, he drove inside, then got out, flipped on the lantern and closed the door behind him.

Rudd wasted no time opening the trunk of his car and pulling out a soft-sided suitcase. He set it on the ground and began undressing. No one had paid him any attention on the drive to Oklahoma, and there was no reason they should. But he had learned long ago to plan for any contingency he could, and he had dressed completely contrary to his normal attire. He removed the three-button pullover polo shirt and looked down at it in the lantern light. Little gold golf clubs and flags were knitted into the fabric, screaming to the world that whoever wore it had to love the game dearly. Rudd didn't. He had played once and found it the most boring pastime imaginable. Rather than put the shirt into the suitcase, he simply folded it and set it in the trunk.

The tasseled loafers—a style he abhorred as feminine and nearing out-and-out gay—came off his feet and went next to the shirt. Next went the stone-colored jeans. Standing now in his underwear, he bent to the suitcase and unzipped it. He pulled out a navy blue T-shirt—plain, no logos or emblems or wording that would stick in the mind. It was a tight fit over his well-developed shoulders and arms, and he tucked the tail into a pair of grungy denim jeans. The cuffs of the jeans, in turn, went into the tops of his black leather tanker boots. Rudd wasn't a biker, but he liked the boots. The straps, which wrapped around the ankle and calf and took place of shoestrings, were quick and easy.

Pulling the sleeveless denim jacket—purposely oil-stained to match the jeans—out of the suitcase, Rudd laid it on the fender next to the open trunk. At the bottom of the suitcase was the shoulder rig. Made of ballistic nylon, it was different than most such rigs, carrying the weapon on the strong side of the body rather than the usual cross-draw configuration. But the weapon he carried in it was different, too, and the system worked perfectly with it. Rudd shrugged into it, fastening the retaining straps to his belt before donning the greasy jacket.

He lifted the lantern, then checked himself in the reflection from the car window. When he twisted certain ways, tiny portions of the shoulder straps could be seen. But they were black and wouldn't be noticed on top of the dark blue T-shirt. No problem.

The navy blue baseball cap came last. Rudd laughed to himself as he put it on backward the way the street gangs and wannabes wore them. Without further ado, he rolled back the garage door and wheeled the Harley outside. He left it on the kickstand while he closed and locked the door, then he hit the starter and rode away.

A few minutes later he was back on I-35. Traffic was thin that time of day. But the Oklahoma City area was always thin, even during rush hour, when compared to Dallas or Houston or someplace like L.A. He kept five miles under the speed limit, leaving Moore and entering Oklahoma City, then taking the SW Twenty-ninth Street exit. Again following his memorized directions, he drifted along with traffic to Shields, then followed Shields as it became Martin Luther King on the other side of the downtown area. Passing a sign announcing Bricktown and the new Riverwalk—every town had to have a Riverwalk these days and they were little more than concrete troughs—he stopped at several lights.

Rudd felt himself gearing up with enthusiasm as he neared the Murrow Federal Building Bomb Memorial. There, years earlier, had stood a building that housed many local federal field offices including the FBI, DEA and BATF. Then along had come Timothy McVeigh and now there was a memorial instead. It was also a place where politicians and special-interest groups held rallies for support, and this day the Mothers Against Drunk Drivers were sponsoring some event. There would be cops aplenty. But none of them would be expecting trouble like they would had it been a Ku Klux Klan march or New Black Panther rally.

Rudd rode on, turning past the memorial, barely giving it a glance. There were men, women and children milling about outside, ready to go in and hear the speeches. There were also cops. But they weren't the ones he was looking for. Like a lion following a herd of gazelles, he wanted the one separated from the pack. The one on the fringe. The one who had no reinforcements and no suspicions.

He found the cop he was looking for two blocks from the memorial site. He saw him as he waited for a light to change.

The uniformed man was young. Mid to late twenties. And he was acting young, prancing and preening as he flirted with two young women on the sidewalk. A police motorcycle was parked at the curb, and the cop was decked out in full regalia with storm trooper boots, tight riding pants, and his helmet jammed between his chest and his left arm. He had carefully sculpted, thick black hair and a matching mustache.

Rudd waited for the light to change, hoping the girls would walk. He didn't want to kill them—they were too good-looking. Red became green, yet he waited until the car behind him leaned on the horn before riding through the intersection. As he coaxed the Harley slowly past the trio on the sidewalk, one of the girls began writing on a piece of paper, undoubtedly giving the cop her phone number. She used the young police officer's back as a stabilizer, and all three of them laughed when he wiggled his back and smiled.

Rudd felt mildly sorry for the girl. She was involved in a mating dance that would never be completed.

Driving a block on, Rudd pulled a quick U-turn and started back as the cop waved goodbye to the girls. The officer returned to his motorcycle and hopped into the saddle from the back like a cowboy in an old B-western. A wide grin of anticipation curled his lips as he watched the girls walk away.

Rudd accelerated slightly as he drew back toward the police officer. The man was on the opposite side of the street now, and he'd have to cross over to get close to him. But there was no traffic right now.

Besides, a man about to commit murder should be willing to break a few traffic laws.

Rudd reached under his jacket, unfastened the restraining snap on his belt and swung the Ingram MAC-10 out to the end of the strap. The tiny machine pistol was almost a relic now, not in use as it once had been. But he had always liked the weapon, and it had always done what it was supposed to do.

Something made the motorcycle cop look up when Rudd was still twenty feet away. He saw the MAC-10 extended from the arm of the man on the Harley, and the smile faded from his face. There was a moment in which he tried to decide if what he was seeing was real before his hand began dropping to the gun on his hip.

And it was during that moment that Rudd emptied the entire 30-round magazine of 9 mm bullets into him. With the Ingram's incredibly high rate of fire, it took under three seconds. The first few rounds struck the officer in the chest, knocking him back but being stopped by the vest beneath his uniform. Rudd had loaded every third round as a tracer, and even in the sunlight they could be seen. He walked his point of aim upward as the police officer jiggled and jerked, and the last ten-to-fifteen rounds all but decapitated the man.

Rudd rode past without looking back, letting the machine pistol fall back under his arm and covering it with his jacket. He turned past the memorial and drove slowly, watching the faces of those outside the building, particularly the other cops. Everyone, police officer and citizen alike, had turned toward the sound of the gunfire. They stared that way, wondering what had happened much as people all over Oklahoma City had wondered, Rudd suspected, the day they'd heard the loud boom that led to the memorial.

He was already past when the cops along the street began making their way cautiously toward the noise, their hands on their holstered weapons.

Rudd kept below the speed limit, skirting the downtown area, then cutting back to Shields and heading south. He stayed off the interstate. Fifteen minutes after he'd pulled the trigger, Rudd was back inside the storage shed.

He changed clothes quickly, not out of fear but because he was in a hurry. Tossing the motorcycle gear into the trunk, he slipped back into what he thought of as his Joe Golfer disguise, backed the car out onto the driveway and locked up the Harley. It would probably be left there for several weeks or months before anything was done with it.

Whistling softly, Rudd drove back down Twelfth Street, then took the access ramp back onto I-35. He turned on the radio and learned he was famous. He checked his watch. He was cutting it close but if he stayed right at the speed limit, he could probably get home, get what he needed to do done and still catch a couple of hours sleep before he had to be at work the next day.

BY THE TIME Bolan and Vogt left old Jack Crenna's house their shift was almost over. Vogt took the wheel and started back in the general direction of the station. "You said you wanted to talk to the Radio Shack guy, too," he reminded Bolan. "You see any reason to do that tonight, or you want to wait until tomorrow?"

Bolan had no intention of waiting. But neither did he intend to take Vogt along with him. If the man was holding back information, traditional police interrogation had already proved useless—even with more than a healthy dose of sex thrown in in the form of Karen Cohlmia.

No, it was time for more of an Executioner approach to intelligence gathering. And for that, he needed to be alone.

"We can do it tomorrow," Bolan said.

Vogt reached to the dashboard and turned on the radio. A jolt of ultrahard Christian head-banger music rocked forth, and Bolan leaned forward and turned down the volume.

"What's wrong, Mike?" Vogt said. "You don't love Jesus?"

"I love Jesus," Bolan came back. "Enough to not want His, or my, eardrums blown out."

Vogt laughed and drove on. "Want me to take you back to the station or drop you at home and sign out for you?" he asked. "Come to think of it, I don't even know where you live."

The truth was, Bolan didn't know, either. He had arrived in Houston early that morning on a plane flown by Jack Grimaldi, the top pilot for Stony Man Farm. Running late, he had barely made it to the station to check in for his first shift. His luggage was still at the airport, as was Grimaldi, waiting to fly him anywhere he needed at a moment's notice. "Just take me back to the station with you," he said. "Got my car there anyway."

"Good enough," Vogt said, and continued to fight the Houston traffic.

A half hour later they were pulling into the parking lot. After signing out Bolan said, "See you in the morning." Getting in the Nissan he'd rented at the airport, he headed back toward George Bush Intercontinental Airport and, once on the grounds, took the access road to the private plane terminal.

Grimaldi was seated at the table in the cabin of the Learjet reading a copy of *War and Peace*. He looked up when Bolan came on board.

"A little light reading?" the soldier asked as he moved to the lockers behind Grimaldi.

The pilot chuckled. "Hadn't read this in years," he said. "Not bad." The pilot had taken off his faded brown leather bomber jacket, and Bolan could see the grips of Grimaldi's ever-present .357 Magnum Smith & Wesson sticking out of his belt.

The Executioner had packed several bags for the mission, and they sat on the floor in front of the lockers. Lifting them, he said, "Thanks for the help with my luggage, Jack."

Grimaldi pretended not to hear him, but the corners of his mouth flickered.

Thirty minutes later, Bolan was checking into the Houston Inn Drury West, and making sure he got a room far away from the suite where the task force met. After all, they thought he had been on the PD for years. That meant he'd lived there in Houston, which in turn meant a house or apartment rather than a hotel. But the soldier wanted to be close by, and the Drury was big enough to get lost in. Even if he was seen in any of the restaurants or clubs within the complex, he could always say he'd needed to stop by the task force suite to pick up something. Several secretaries had been assigned there, and there was at least one working the phones around the clock.

After sticking his key card in the door, the Executioner carried his luggage inside and dropped it on the closer of the two beds. Moving to the sliding glass door that looked out over the pool, he drew the curtains closed, then returned to the bed. The khaki sport coat came off and was dropped next to the suitcases on the bedspread. Next came the Glock 21 he had carried in his cop guise. His shoes and slacks followed.

Bolan unzipped the larger of the two suitcases and pulled out one of his blacksuits. Made of skintight stretch material to avoid snagging, he slid it onto his body. The blacksuits held numerous pockets that had already been filled with gear. Reaching back into the suitcase, Bolan found his ballistic nylon shoulder rig and slid it over his shoulders. Under the left arm he carried a 9 mm Beretta 93-R submachine pistol capable of either semiauto fire or 3-round bursts. The Beretta also had a front grip that stayed tucked up under the barrel until needed. It had been threaded for a sound suppressor, and the holster was custom-made to fit the longer, bulkier overall package. The suppressor made it much heavier and more awkward to carry, especially concealed, but it was an inconvenience Bolan never questioned.

The almost silent 9 mm slugs had saved his life, and the life of other innocents, too many times over the years to even think about leaving it at home.

The second gun had become his trademark—a .44 Magnum Desert Eagle.

The Desert Eagle went into a Concealex holster on his right hip. The hard plastic covering had been formfitted to the gun and required no retaining straps or snaps. The Eagle would fly out of the holster like lightning, with no obstructions. In addition to the two pistols, he carried extra magazines for the Beretta on the shoulder rig opposite the machine pistol, and for the Desert Eagle on his belt. The big Magnum mags rode next to a custom-made bowie knife. The sleek curves of the wicked-looking ten-inch blade could chop their way through jungle, separate a man's arm from his body or silence a sentry with one skull-crushing cranial cut.

Bolan pulled the black leather boots out of the suitcase but dropped them into a smaller bag. He sat on the edge of the bed and opened the file Burnett had given him that morning.

Carl Buxton was the Radio Shack clerk who had gone to the supermarket for cigarettes the day Officer Joe Kenard had been ambushed by the phony store clerk. According to the file, Buxton lived close to the area where both the Radio Shack and grocery store were located. There was even a map indicating where it was, and a route traced out leading from the station house to the scene.

Bolan found the Drury Inn on the map and traced his own visual route to Buxton address. Memorizing it, he tossed the file on the bed and stood again.

Wearing his blacksuit openly, with guns and knives hanging all over him, wasn't very prudent. It was a long time until Halloween, and if he didn't want to elicit the attention of hotel security and probably screams from the other guests, he'd need to cover up. He realized that getting from the room to the car might well be the most dangerous aspect of what he intended to do that night. The black outfit usually served him for battle. This night, it would play a more psychological role. But in any case, he needed it hidden until he got to Buxton's house.

Bolan stepped into the pants he had worn earlier, sliding them up over the legs of the blacksuit. They were a little snug but not noticeable. The khaki jacket went over his weapons, and a glance in the mirror assured him that he now simply looked like a man wearing a black turtleneck under a sport coat. A little late in the season for a turtleneck maybe, but nobody was going to notice that and decide it meant he was armed for war.

The soldier slid into the loafers he'd worn earlier that day, then picked up the small bag that carried his boots. On the outside he again looked like Houston Police Department Detective Mike Belasko.

But beneath the outer layer of clothes lay the Executioner.

BUXTON LIVED in a one-story house that looked to be about twelve hundred square feet in a low-middle-income residential area near the supermarket. Bolan parked down the block, noting that the light was on in the bedroom as he slid out of his jacket and pants. He replaced the loafers with his combat boots. In the small bag was a black ski mask he had brought along. It would serve two purposes. First, it should intimidate Buxton. And it would cover the Executioner's face. He and Vogt planned to meet with the man the next day, and it wouldn't do to have him start screaming the second he saw that Bolan was the same man who had broken into his house the previous night.

Before Bolan could get out of the car, the light in the bedroom went out and what looked like a lamp appeared behind the curtained living-room window. The soldier closed the car door quietly, then jogged down the street to the house. It wasn't that late yet, but none of the neighbors seemed to be out. Just in case someone was watching, he carried the ski mask crumpled up in his hand. He'd have to hope the black-on-black of his weapons, holsters and the blacksuit itself, combined with the shadows and dim streetlights, kept his weapons invisible to any curious eyes.

Reaching the house, Bolan went directly to the window. Inside, he could hear soft classical music playing. The sound was clear and crisp, as it should have been for anyone with an employee discount. The curtains, however, were drawn tight and he could see nothing but the glow of the lamp. He was about to move away to look for another way in when he heard a giggle. He pressed his ear against the glass. A woman's voice was speaking, but he couldn't make out the words.

Moving quietly around the side of the house, the soldier saw a window leading into the bathroom. It was high, and the wood around it looked rotten. It was likely to crumble under his weight if he pulled himself up. Circling farther, he opened a gate in the rusty chain-link fence to the back, then closed it again behind him. The house had no back porch. One window led to the kitchen, another to the second bedroom. The kitchen window was locked, as was the door.

The soldier readjusted his shoulder harness, then reached into one of his pockets and produced a flashlight. Aiming the beam at the door, he studied both it and the lock. The wood was as old and rotten as what he'd seen around the window on the side of the house. That meant it would not only creak and squeak if he tried to enter quietly, it meant loud creaks and squeaks. Even picking the lock could prove noisy and give Buxton time to go for a weapon.

No, Bolan realized as he flipped off the flashlight and stuck it in a pocket. There was only one way to enter this house under the circumstances. Loud and fast. He'd have to hope the giggling female voice he'd heard in the front room was keeping Buxton's mind on other things and he didn't have a gun out already.

Bolan slid the ski mask over his face. He stepped back, raised a boot and kicked.

The old door didn't just swing inside, it flew completely off the hinges and into the kitchen, striking the refrigerator on the opposite wall and breaking into three pieces. But by then Bolan was inside the house, the big Desert Eagle leading the way in his right hand.

As he pivoted toward the hallway that had to lead to the living room, he heard s shriek come from that area of the house. Then a terrified female voice said, "What was that!"

Bolan raced down the hall toward the light. Less than five seconds after entering the house, he was standing in the living room with the big .44 Magnum gun aimed at the two skinniest people he'd ever seen.

And both were naked.

"Oh shit!" Buxton said. "Look...I didn't tell the cops anything...I didn't...I swear...."

"Shut up," Bolan said. "Put your clothes on. Both of you."

The girl on the couch with Buxton had to be the skinny blond girlfriend Anderson and the other task force members had mentioned. The one they suspected had convinced Buxton to forget everything he'd seen. "You...you aren't going to rape me, are you?" she sputtered from trembling lips.

Through the eye holes of the ski mask, Bolan looked at the frail bones sticking out all over the body as if she were anorexic. Just beneath the waxen skin, blue and green veins and arteries crawled across her arms and legs like angry spiders. "No," he said. "But I'm going to kill you if you don't hurry up and get dressed. Both of you."

Both Buxton and his girlfriend kicked into high gear at the threat, setting a new record for speed dressing. They got mixed up on underwear and hurriedly slid into that of the other person, then pulled on blue jeans and T-shirts. Bolan saw no reason to tell them about their mistake. "Sit back on the couch," Bolan ordered when they were finished.

They obeyed, all but turning to stone.

The soldier's original plan had been to break in and scare Buxton into telling him what he knew. But a new card had been dealt him now, and he decided to play it. It was obvious from Buxton's initial response that the clerk thought Bolan was the shooter come back to get rid of a witness. That could be used to great advantage.

"You told the cops what I look like," he accused the frightened man.

"No!" Buxton fairly screamed. "No! I didn't! I didn't!"

"What *do* I look like?" Bolan demanded.

"What?" The question obviously confused the man even further.

"You heard me," Bolan said. "Tell me right now what I looked like to you!"

"Wel..." Buxton said, obviously stalling for time in order to decide what he should say. "You were...tall."

"Did I look as tall as I do tonight?" the soldier asked. "Tell me the truth!"

Buxton was convinced Bolan was crazy now. He said, "Well, you look even taller tonight."

"Did I look broader the other day or today?" Bolan knew he had to work fast and keep the man off balance if he was going to get the truth. The questions he was asking were unusual, to say the least.

"Well..." Buxton said.

The girl next to him whispered something too low for the soldier to hear. Buxton immediately said, "You looked broad both times. Real handsome, in fact."

Bolan stepped in and pressed the barrel of the Desert Eagle against the man's forehead. For a moment, it looked as if Buxton were about to faint. He closed his eyes.

It was time to change tactics. "I'm not fishing for compliments," Bolan said in a far less agitated voice. "And I know these questions sound odd. But I need to know. And I need to know the truth. You tell me, and I'll let you live."

The skinny blonde next to Buxton was trying to put it all together and have it make sense, and she was a half-beat ahead of her boyfriend mentally. She had guessed first that the man in black holding the gun on them needed his ego refueled. But now she made another guess.

"Are you...with the government?" she asked quietly.

Once again, Bolan saw a new angle and took it. "Yes," he said, turning his ski-masked face her way. "And your boyfriend has stumbled onto a government operation he can't possibly understand. But if he tells me all he knows, he'll live. If he doesn't, I regret I'll have to kill you both." He paused to let it sink in. "Understood?"

Heads nodded atop the skinny necks of both Buxton and his girlfriend. Buxton was still dumbstruck. But goose bumps broke out on the blonde's ashen skin, and she nearly shook with excitement. "Tell him what he wants to know, Carl. You'll be helping your country!"

"Tell me what I looked like that day," Bolan prompted again. His voice was low now, soothing, even gentle. His entire approach had changed from the one he'd expected to take when he kicked in the door. But a warrior had to be flexible. Had to be able to change battle plans in the middle of the fight if an opportunity presented itself.

"You were a little shorter," Buxton said. "And not quite as heavy."

"Hair," Bolan asked. "What color was my hair?

Buxton began to tremble again. "I...don't remember," he said. "*Really.* I was too scared...don't kill me...."

"How about my face? Any features stand out?"

"No...please don't kill us.... I'm telling you the truth...I don't remember...."

A frown of concentration had come over the blonde's face as she listened. "Is this like...maybe a clone you guys made has gone bad or something?"

The last stupid question came from watching too many movies, and Bolan ignored it. "Think," he said in the quiet, encouraging voice. "Try to remember."

"I have tried, " Buxton choked out. "But I just can't remember. You've got to believe me. I'm telling the truth. Don't kill us, please. I couldn't tell the cops what you look like even if I'd wanted to. I was too shocked. And when you knocked me down and then told me you'd kill me if I talked...I just went blank."

Bolan wasn't surprised. But he had hoped for more. He had learned little of value, and he was tired of Buxton's whining and the skinny blonde's stupidity. In a rare display of anger he jerked suddenly away from the two people on the couch.

That rare display saved his life.

As the Executioner moved, the familiar buzz of a bullet raced past his ear and the equally familiar explosion of a handgun going off sounded from the hallway.

3

Clayton Rudd pulled into a gas station across the street from the supermarket where he'd killed the cop. What was his name again? Joe Kenard, if he remembered right. He rarely paid much attention to the cops he killed. He picked them at random, as did most of the other guys doing this. He'd heard there was one of them who was using the situation to rid himself of some pesky acquaintances at the same time he carried out orders, but he'd never tried. Maybe he should. On the other hand, he preferred easy to revenge. And when this was over, he'd have no hard feelings toward anyone. He'd be on top of the world and wouldn't care.

A few people came and went in the supermarket parking lot, doing some last-minute, late-night grocery shopping. Rudd doubted that the cop shooting was still on any of their minds. People had a short memory for things like that. He had worn no disguise that day, and he wore none this night but he suspected he could go right in and buy out the produce section without anybody looking at him twice. People not only had a short memory, they were just plain stupid. And even those who weren't were usually cowards.

Like Carl Buxton.

Rudd glanced at his wrist as he waited for his tank to fill. He'd made good time driving back to Houston from Oklahoma City. It was a long trip by car, but he wasn't particularly tired. Maybe it was the adrenaline, or maybe the knowledge that this hit would be such an easy kill and would take care of one of his worries. The clerk was just a side detail, but one that had to be taken care of to insure it didn't come back and bite him in the ass at some later date. Rudd was ninety-nine-percent certain that Buxton was too scared to tell the cops what he looked like. But he had gotten a good look at Rudd's face when he'd knocked him down and fallen on top of him, and Rudd didn't like that one percent that was left over.

The automatic pump clicked off and Rudd took the nozzle out of the tank. He glanced across the street, catty-cornered from the supermarket, to the strip mall across from it. He could see the Radio Shack sign two storefronts down.

Hanging the pump back up, Rudd got back into his car and drove to the side of the station, parking just outside the men's room. He should have shot Buxton after crashing into him. But he hadn't been thinking—the surprise collision had broken his concentration, and he'd been in a hurry to get out of there. Bad mistake. And it wasn't the only mistake he'd made. On the way back from Houston it had finally dawned on him where he'd lost the Szaball. He had pulled it out of his pocket as he ran down the alley, using it to relieve the stress. Somewhere—probably in the alley—he had lost it. At least he hadn't had it when he got home. It wasn't anywhere in the car, and he couldn't remember what he'd done with it when he'd gotten into the automobile.

It wasn't that bad, Rudd told himself. The rubber coating on the surface was porous; no prints could have been lifted from it. And there were thousands of the Szaballs in circulation these days. No way to trace him through that. Still, losing the ball bothered him almost as much as Buxton seeing his face, and it was a feeling he couldn't shake.

Rudd got out of the car again, opened the trunk and hauled his suitcase into the men's room. He locked the door behind him, then checked himself in the mirror. Needed a shave. He'd have to remember to make sure he got that done before going into work in the morning. Quickly he opened the suitcase and changed into the same navy blue T-shirt and blue jeans he'd worn in Oklahoma City. He debated on the sleeveless denim jacket, then decided to leave it off. It was warmer there in Houston. And besides, he wasn't going to be packing the Ingram MAC-10. Reaching down, he dug through the bag and found the Beretta 92-SB. That would be enough for Buxton. One round through the head. He tucked the 9 mm Beretta into the waistband of his jeans and pulled the blue T-shirt over it.

Rudd drove quickly to Buxton's house, parking two yards away. Through the front window he could see a dull glow but no other light was visible. He'd circle the house to find the best way in. Getting out of the car, he patted the Beretta into place in his belt and cut across the lawns.

The driveway was gravel and he walked carefully over the rocks, careful not to make any noise. He had learned to walk softly in the Army, and he was proud of that, and the other abilities he'd picked up. The memory of those days brought a smile to his face, but the smile faded as he remembered how it had all turned out. The problems he'd had there at the end had not only ended his Army career, it had screwed up his plans for the rest of his life.

Rudd reached the corner of the house and ducked into the shadows before drawing the Beretta. Well, life threw him a few curves. He had to learn to hit them. He'd missed the first, but he still had two strikes left. And the last pitch thrown his way—the one that had launched him on this quest to kill cops—would change his life around all over again. Things were only going to get better from there on in.

Creeping around the corner, Rudd stopped in his tracks when he saw the back door. It wasn't just wide open, it was gone. What kind of fool was this Buxton? What kind of man got so scared that he left town for over a week but then came back and stayed in a house with no back door?

Rudd felt himself frowning hard. He didn't like surprises like this. It was like running into Buxton in the first place—it rattled him. He reached into his pocket but the ball wasn't there. Okay, he told himself. Next stop after this was to get a new ball.

Still uneasy, Rudd opened and closed his fingers, stretching them out first before curling them into a rock-hard fist. He repeated the process ten times with his left hand as he crept toward the back door. When he reached the cavernous opening, he dropped to one knee before peering around the entrance. In the dark kitchen he could see the pieces of the door. The house was old, and he had noticed the work of termites as he made his way to the back. Had the door just rotted away and fallen apart?

Yeah. Then it had thrown itself into the kitchen. Right.

A real feeling of uneasiness came over Rudd now, and he decided to go in, get his business done and leave quickly. Just because his body didn't feel tired didn't mean his brain wasn't. He'd had a long drive up, a lot of stress during the OKC hit—even if it didn't feel like it—and then a long drive back. He was probably just tired, jumpy and seeing ghosts where there weren't any. There was some logical explanation for the door being the way it was, but he didn't need to know what it was. He just needed to get in, kill Buxton, get out and head home.

The fingers of Rudd's empty hand shot out and in, open then closed, open then closed, as he rose from the ground and walked quietly into the house. He could see the faint light coming from the front—the same light he'd seen through the window. He walked quickly but quietly through the kitchen, then down the hall. When he reached the halfway point he could see most of the living room. And what he saw caused him to suddenly press his back against the wall.

Rudd's fingers straightened and curled with new intensity. Son of a bitch! he thought. What timing! He'd come to kill Buxton at the same time some big bastard in a black jumpsuit and ski mask decided to pull a home invasion! He concentrated on his breathing, trying to steady his nerves as a new flood of adrenaline shot through his veins. Would this big guy kill Buxton for him? He couldn't count on that, and he was too tired to wait around to see. It would be easier just to shoot both of them.

Rudd leaned out of the shadows just enough to listen to their conversation. The home invader was talking to Buxton and some blonde even skinnier than Buxton was. They were cringing on the couch as the man spoke in a low voice, probably imitating some TV or movie star whose voice he thought sounded low and threatening.

With the sights lined up on the man's ski mask right where the temple would be, Rudd took another deep breath, let out half of it and began the slow trigger squeeze. He felt the slack go out of the trigger. Then, a microsecond before the trigger broke, the man in black suddenly jerked back. The movement surprised Rudd, and he jerked the trigger.

The Beretta leaped in his hand, sending a 9 mm hollowpoint round exploding from the barrel to zip past the head of the man in black.

THE EXECUTIONER DROPPED to the ground, squeezing the Desert Eagle's trigger as he fell and sending a 240-grain semijacketed .44 Magnum hollowpoint round back in the direction from which the shot had come. He didn't expect it to hit. He could only hope it would buy him time. He was in the middle of the only room in the house that had any light, there was no immediate cover available and he couldn't see his assailant in the shadows of the hall.

Two more rounds sailed over his head as Bolan landed on his belly. He fired two more of his own down the hall, the recoil going from the gun to his hand then up his wrist and out his arm. The big Eagle moved in his iron grip. The Magnum rounds sounded like dynamite exploding within the confines of Buxton's tiny living room, and the acrid odor of burned gunpowder filled Bolan's sinuses.

As soon as he'd pulled the trigger the second time, Bolan rolled to his right, away from the two people on the couch. The invisible gunman pulled the trigger again at that exact moment, and another bullet hit the floor where his chest had been a second earlier. The copper-jacketed lead ripped through the moldy carpet at an angle, creating a furrow three inches long, the smell of singed shag mixed with the cordite.

Bolan knew he had only seconds left. He was the epitome of a fish in a barrel. On this side of the room the only furniture was the stereo and speakers that sat on makeshift bookshelves of two-by-eight boards and concrete blocks. There was a window but, unless the hidden gunman couldn't hit the proverbial broad side of a barn, he'd take rounds as he rose. More while crashing through the glass.

But that wasn't the only problem. Even if he got out of the house safely, it would mean leaving Buxton and his girlfriend alone with the gunman. And killing Buxton had to be the reason the man had come in the first place. The Executioner didn't know the identity of the man in the hallway, but he had to be the same man who had killed Kenard, then run straight into Buxton as he made his escape. He had come back to kill the man who might identify him. He hadn't expected to run into anyone else at the house.

The Executioner was a surprise, an unexpected obstacle to overcome.

Bolan rolled back left, firing again, barely evading a double-tap that ricocheted off one of the concrete blocks of the bookshelves. It had been only a few seconds since the first shot had been fired, and during that time Buxton and his girlfriend had lived up to the freezing. But now they thawed, and with the thaw came yelling and screaming.

The Executioner rolled to a halt in the center of the room. Beneath his chest, he could still feel the heat of the round that had ripped into the carpet. He fired again, blindly, hoping he might hit the gunman who was somewhere in the shadowy hallway, but if not at least keep him off balance. And as he fired, he made a decision.

The room offered no cover. And there was no escape. There was only one chance. Slim, but existent. He would charge the man in the hallway, taking the fight straight to the enemy. All he would have in his favor was the element of surprise.

Bolan pulled the trigger again as he scrambled to his feet and dashed toward the hall. Another round left the hand cannon just as he ducked into the darkness. A bullet from the unseen gunman buzzed past his ear like an angry hornet, then he heard a snort of surprise as he ducked into the shadows. The next thing he knew, he was making contact with another human being.

Bolan's shoulder hit the gunman in the belly and he heard a loud "Oooomph!" as air rushed out of the man's lungs. But a microsecond later, the Executioner's felt as if someone had struck him in the side of the head with a ball peen hammer. He fought to remain conscious, jerking the Desert Eagle back toward him at the same time and feeling it scrape across flesh as he did. His foggy mind told him the barrel had rubbed across a chin.

A voice from far away, which he knew had to be his own thoughts, told him his temple had made contact with something hard. He didn't know what, and it didn't matter—the damage was done. He staggered, trying to raise the Desert Eagle but his arm refused to listen to his brain. As if it were happening slow motion, Bolan watched the shadowy form of the other man stumble back into the kitchen. In the dim light he thought he could make out the familiar shape of a Beretta in the other man's hand. He strained to see a face, but it was hidden in the semidarkness. He couldn't even register a hair color or style, and then he had no time to try because the gunman raised the Beretta to fire.

Calling on all of his willpower, Bolan got the Desert Eagle up knee-high and jerked the trigger. Another ear-shattering roar came from the Eagle as the bullet left the barrel at close to 1400 feet per second. But the Executioner's arms were still weak, and they failed at the last second, the Eagle wobbling to the side of its target. The round missed the gunman, and the Executioner saw a large hole appear in the cabinet below the kitchen sink.

The Desert Eagle's slide locked back, empty.

As his fuzzy brain told his hand to reach for his own Beretta, it also told him he would never get to it in time. He was half conscious and his movements were slow, sluggish. The price for knocking the wind out of the gunman was a near concussion, and his enemy had already recovered from the loss of breath. Bolan hadn't yet reclaimed his senses from the blow to the temple, and he wasn't going to for a while.

The bottom line was that the gunman would see him standing there in the hallway with an empty weapon. The man would take his time, getting a perfect sight on the head or heart and killing the Executioner at his leisure while the haze in Bolan's head forced him to fumble for his other gun at half speed.

The Executioner had no intentions of giving up. Even as these thoughts passed through his injured brain, his hand crawled toward the 93-R. His fingers felt light as he tugged at the weapon in the shoulder rig. The grim determination to go out fighting never left him. But he was a realist as well, and he knew his odds of survival were slim. If it was all to end there, so be it. He had lived most of his life knowing it would someday come to this, and that it would be over in very much this way. The Executioner's jaw set tight. His only regret would be if the killer then walked into the living room and added Buxton and his girlfriend to his list of sins.

But the gunman suddenly turned, weapon still in hand, and raced out the broken back door.

The soldier's brain was still rocking as he concentrated, putting one foot ahead of the other and making his way across the kitchen like a stroke victim learning to walk again. By now he had the Beretta in his left hand, the selector switch on burst mode. The empty Desert Eagle, still in his right hand, felt as if it weighed a hundred pounds. As he neared the door, it occurred to him that the same dark hallway that had almost gotten him killed had also saved his life. The dim lighting had prevented the man in the kitchen from seeing that the Desert Eagle had locked back, empty.

Bolan staggered to the doorway and looked out. The backyard was empty. Whoever had come to kill Buxton, and had been killing police officers, was gone.

And Bolan knew no more about him than he had before.

SENATOR OWEN KILLIAN rose to a sitting position on the bed, punched a finger at the buzzing alarm and rolled over. "Don't get up, darling," he said to his sleeping wife. "I have to be in early. You go on and sleep."

Miriam Killian never opened her eyes to acknowledge whether she'd heard him.

Rising from the bed, Killian slid his feet into his well-worn leather slippers and walked to the closet. A moment later he had wrapped a green terry-cloth robe around his pajamas and was padding into the kitchen. The coffeemaker had come on thirty minutes earlier as he'd set it to do, and he reached over the machine into the cupboard.

A key being inserted into a lock sounded from the living room as Killian took a seat at the breakfast table. He heard the front door open. Then Judith appeared in the kitchen carrying the morning *Post* in one hand, a purse the size of Cincinnati in the other. The portly matron handed him the newspaper, and said, "Good morning, Senator."

"Morning, Judith," Killian said as he spread the paper out across the table. "Sleep well?"

"Always do," Judith said as she did every morning. "You had your shower yet?"

Killian ignored the minor irritation the words caused him. She knew he hadn't, just as she knew he hadn't showered *every* morning when she asked him the same question. Judith liked to clean the bathrooms first, and it drove her crazy to scrub the sink just to have it dirtied with shaving cream and toothpaste five minutes later.

Well, Killian thought as he glanced at the headlines, he didn't care. Periodically Judith needed to be reminded who worked for whom, and this was as good a way as any. "No," he said, "I haven't taken my shower yet. But you go right ahead and clean the bathroom if you'd like. I'll be a few minutes here with the paper." He ignored the rush of disgusted air that escaped the cleaning woman's mouth. She disappeared from the kitchen, resolved to her damnation of cleaning the bathroom, only to have it soiled again later.

Killian pulled his reading glasses from the front pocket of his robe and studied the headlines. The two police officers who had been killed a few days ago were still on the front page. But the headlines all concerned the Oklahoma City motorcycle cop who'd been machine-gunned by another motorcyclist the day before. It had taken place almost on top of the bomb memorial site, of all places. That, in itself, was news and the headlines read Death Revisits Sooner State. The reporter—Bill Michaels of the *Washington Post*—offered several possible explanations. The motorcycle assassination technique was a favorite of the drug cartels in South American, he noted. It could've been a cartel hit. The killer appeared to be dressed like an outlaw biker, so that was another possibility.

The senator chuckled as he raised the coffee cup to his lips and took a sip. Next to the story was a photograph taken by the *Daily Oklahoman,* which gone national. It showed a frowning man with broad shoulders and a small mustache staring at an overturned police motorcycle. The caption read Top Cop Claims Assassinations Related. Returning to the story itself, Killian learned that the man in the picture was Stanley Langford, the director of the Oklahoma State Bureau of Investigation. "There have been too many officers killed in the past three months to call it coincidence," Langford had been quoted as saying. "I know it, and every police officer in the country knows it." The quote brought a wide smile to Killian's face. It was statements like these that would keep his own steam going in his drive for a Senate committee and a federal task force. He took another sip of coffee.

Killian finished what had been printed on the front page and was about to turn to where the story had been continued when he heard the familiar buzz. He turned in his chair to the alcove set in the kitchen wall, pulled the phone from the charger, then twisted back to the table again. "Good morning," he said into the receiver. "Senator Killian speaking."

"Senator, glad I caught you, good morning!" came the voice on the other end. "Bill Michaels, here."

In the background Killian could hear the busy buzz of the newsroom. "Hello, Bill," he said. "Good work this morning."

"You've seen the story, then?" the reporter asked.

"Just about to turn to Page 10-A for the rest."

"You've read most of it, then," Michaels said. "The rest is just a recap of the other killings." He cleared his throat. "Heard you had quite a little display in the Senate chambers after your address yesterday."

Killian sighed. "Well, you know Libertarian Lane," he said.

"I'm doing a follow-up on it," Michaels said. "Mind if I quote you on that?"

Killian thought about it for a moment, then said, "Why not? And you can add that the man is making a complete fool of himself these days, and has set any progress his party might be making back a decade."

"His party?" Michaels said. "But he's no longer a Libertarian. "He ran on the—"

"I know which ticket he ran on," Killian said, "but we all know that was simply to get his foot in the door. He's one leopard who hasn't changed any spots."

"That's great...I'm writing as fast as I can...okay, got it. Anything else?"

"That sums up my feelings."

Michaels cleared his throat again. "Then let's talk about your feeling on getting the Feds into this cop-killer case—assuming that there is a case, and the murders all go back to the same source."

Killian glanced down at the paper again. "Assuming?" he said. "Bill, don't you read your own writing anymore? What was it the 'Top Oklahoma Cop' said?"

"Okay, Senator. You got me. So tell me, just what are your intentions on this?"

"I want these assassinations stopped, and I want to see the most effective law enforcement we can have in this country. This man— OSBI Director Langford—summed it up as well as I could. Everybody knows there's a connection. The problem, Bill, is that it's too much for the locals, and to get the FBI in we have to show definite federal jurisdiction. And we can't. At least not so far." He took another sip of coffee. "Well, forget about all that for a moment. Forget the fact that the methods of assassination haven't all been the same and that there's no obvious link. Everyone knows that when we finally get to the bottom of these killings we'll find they all go back to the same source. Lane talked about loopholes in the law yesterday. If you ask me, *this* is the loophole—everyone knows it but no one can prove it. In my opinion, the fact that no two murders are the same is evidence of the connection in itself. Whoever is behind all this is going out of their way to make sure they don't look related." He paused to clear his throat. "Bill, can you tell me that you don't believe these killings are all connected?"

Michaels laughed good-naturedly. "No, I can't. I believe they are. But this story isn't about what I think. The people want to know what *you* think, and you still haven't answered my question."

Now Killian laughed. "Typical politician, huh? Spoke for fifteen minutes and didn't say a thing." He heard someone else in the newsroom shouting Michaels's name.

"Just a second, Senator," Michaels said. Killian heard him shout back at whoever had yelled for him, then come back on the line and say, "Sorry for the interruption, Senator. Something breaking on the West Coast but yes, you circled me quite well and it was very typical of a politician. So let me help you a little. How about what Senator Lane said? Are you really pushing toward a national police force that would combine all the federal agencies and have nationwide jurisdiction over states and municipalities?"

Don't forget the county sheriffs, Killian thought. But instead of voicing those words, he sighed wearily and said, "I want to see whatever is necessary happen so that our cops and citizens don't get murdered," he said, then paused, thinking. Was the time right to take another step? Anything he said right now was going to find print. So be it. "I hadn't really thought about a national police, Bill. But now that you mention it, I see no reason to rule out the idea."

Michaels paused a moment, then said, "Lane seems to think that would violate the Constitution."

"Lane thinks everything violates the Constitution. The man's an anarchist. He doesn't trust any kind of government and he's antiauthority." Should he say sociopath? No, that would be going too far at this point.

"So, in your opinion, a federal police agency would be legal?"

"I don't know," Killian said, not falling into the trap. "If any of my staff have time, I'll see if they can check into it because it's worth checking into." He had already told Michaels he hadn't thought about a federal police force until now. He didn't want to contradict himself by admitting he had his people working day and night to find a loophole in the Constitution. "Bill, I'll say this— the Constitution of the United States of America is the most remarkable document in the history of the world." He thought a second, then remembered he would be quoted. "Except for the Bible, of course. But it was written well over two centuries ago, and times were much different then. The Constitution is still very much alive in spirit. But times have changed, and we, the government, must change with them."

"Is this like your stance on the Second Amendment?" Michaels asked.

"Very similar," Killian agreed. "When the Second Amendment was written, guaranteeing the right to bear arms, those arms were muskets, butcher knives and tomahawks. The founding fathers could never have imagined weapons of mass destruction like high-capacity 9 mms and assault rifles. They were shooting lead musket balls in those days, Bill. Could they have ever predicted cop-killer bullets?" Killian chuckled, making sure it was too quiet to be heard over the phone. He had been one of the driving forces to outlaw the armor-piercing ammunition they had dubbed cop-killer bullets. It had made no difference that not one law-enforcement officer had ever been shot by one.

Conversation between the two men stopped momentarily. All Killian could hear was the sound of a pen scratching paper as Michaels took notes over the tumult of the newsroom behind him. Then, suddenly, the racket seemed to increase tenfold.

"Senator," Michaels said, "can you hold on just another second?"

"Happy to," Killian said. "I'm anxious to learn what all the fuss is about myself." He suspected he knew.

Michaels was gone for half a minute or so. When he came back on, he was out of breath. "Another one, Senator. L.A. cop this time. Found dead in his apartment after missing his shift yesterday. And you aren't going to believe how this one was killed."

Poisoned, Killian thought. "Tell me," he said.

"Well, the medical examiner hasn't released his report yet, but one of the investigators said it had all the signs of a poisoning."

"It seems our enemies are becoming increasingly more creative to keep from providing us with a link between their crimes," Killian said.

"Does start to look that way, doesn't it? Listen, Senator, can't thank you enough."

"No need for thanks," Killian replied. "Just spell my name right."

Michaels laughed. "You got it, Senator. Be in touch."

There was a click in Killian's ear as the reporter hung up.

Killian pushed the off button and returned to the paper. Poisoned. A strange way indeed for a cop to be murdered. Even a veteran journalist like Michaels seemed shocked.

The senator wondered how Michaels would feel about the Illinois state trooper who was scheduled to be beaten to death with a baseball bat later in the day. And that was nothing compared to what was coming up soon after that. What he had planned next would strike deeper into the hearts of the citizens of the United States than the World Trade Center attacks or Oklahoma City bombing. It would be more than they had ever dreamed possible. Of course there would then be obvious connections. The FBI would enter the case. But by then, Killian was confident that he could use his rhetoric skills to convince America that it was even too big for the FBI. What they would accept, and even beg for, would be an agency with unlimited powers to investigate such terrorist operations.

And if the couple of thousand police officers he estimated would die had to be sacrificed, so be it.

Killian poured himself another cup of coffee and headed for the shower.

BOLAN'S HEAD STILL throbbed when the wake-up call came. He lifted the receiver next to the bed and pressed it to his ear, only to get the beeping sound of an electronic call. Rising from under the sheets, he walked into the bathroom and flipped on the light.

The sudden brightness brought new pain to Bolan's face and the side of his head. Squinting into the mirror, he saw the swelling just above and to the side of his left ear. Not as bad as when he'd returned to his room at the Drury Inn. But, in the short few hours since, the skin around his temple had discolored, turning a dark blotchy black and blue with strains of yellow mixed in.

Bolan moved to the shower and twisted the knobs. With the spray as hot as he could stand it, he stepped in. The hot water had a soothing effect on his still-foggy brain, bringing him around. He had wondered if he'd suffered a concussion and had stayed up with ice on his head until he was convinced he didn't. This morning, he knew if there had been any concussion it had been mild.

The soldier unwrapped a miniature bar of soap and tossed the paper into the trash can next to the toilet. As he began to soap down his body, he went over the events of the previous evening. As best he could remember, his blind dash down the darkened hall had taken him squarely into the hidden gunman. He recalled the sound of air rushing from the man's lungs a split second before he'd knocked himself on...what had his head hit? The other man's skull? Maybe the chin. Whatever it was it had been hard and fairly pointed. He supposed it could have even been the bony area of the shoulder. The collision had been like a Volkswagen crashing head-on with an eighteen-wheel big rig. He was lucky he'd stayed in the hall where the gunman couldn't see either his diminished fighting capacity or the slide locking back after he'd fired his last round from the Desert Eagle.

Bolan twisted the cap off a miniature bottle of hotel shampoo. He remembered going back inside and telling Buxton and his girlfriend they should go back to wherever they'd been hiding the past few days. But he remembered it as if it had all been underwater. Not that it mattered. The salesman and his girlfriend had been packing their clothes even while he told them.

By the time he'd finished his shower, Bolan's brain was working full speed again. He dried off, then wrapped the towel around his waist as he shaved. The purplish black and blue mark on his face would be questioned by Vogt and the other cops. The soldier glanced to the shower. Slipping on the soap and hitting the side of the tub sounded as good as any other story.

As soon as he'd brushed his teeth, Bolan walked back to the phone and took a seat on the bed. A few minutes later, he had Hal Brognola on the line. After the Justice Department man had listened to the events of the night before, he said, "You heard about the cop in Oklahoma City?"

"Not until now," Bolan said. "What happened?"

Brognola told him.

The soldier stared at the carpet beneath his bare feet. "What time did all this go down in OKC?" he asked.

"Late morning," Brognola told him. "Before noon anyway." Knowing why he'd asked, the head Fed man said, "It could have been the same guy. He had plenty of time if he flew in and out of OKC. He could have even driven it."

Bolan reached up and rubbed his temple with his free hand. "Could be," he said. "But even if it was the same man, we know there's more than one guy involved in all this. We aren't talking about the world's greatest serial killer here, Hal. Nobody assassinates a 147 cops in three months. It's a group. And there had to be at least two of them involved in Oklahoma City."

"Explain?"

"I don't mean on the actual hit," Bolan said. "I mean in the planning. If the OKC shooter drove into town, I suppose he could have ridden the motorcycle or brought it with him on a trailer. But does that seem likely?"

"No," Brognola agreed.

"Which means unless he stashed the bike there beforehand, someone else had it waiting for him. And there's the weapon. What did you say it was?"

"A 9 mm submachine. We don't know what kind yet. Only a couple of people even saw the shooting go down, and neither of them knew guns." Brognola went silent for a moment, then said, "Is the type of gun important right now? If it is I can—"

"No, not yet. Maybe later. What I'm getting at is if he drove to OKC, he could have brought the subgun with him. But if he flew, it was waiting for him with the bike. You don't just drop a sub-machine gun in your carry-on and wink at the guards at airport security."

"No argument," Brognola said. "I..." His voice faded out, and Bolan heard a feminine voice in the background. He couldn't make out what was being said, but a moment later Brognola came back on. "That was my secretary. Cop killed in Los Angeles. Poisoned. Your guy couldn't have—"

"Depends on what kind of poison was used and how fast-acting it was. But no, I doubt it was the same guy."

"We'd be stretching things again," Brognola said.

"Yeah, but that doesn't mean the poisoning and this guy aren't still connected. Even though we're talking multiple killers here, we know there's a head to this snake somewhere, too. One individual behind it all. Or at least one terrorist group."

"What are you thinking, big guy?" Brognola asked. "Foreign or homegrown?"

"Don't know. Home, would be my guess. The foreigners lean toward ridding us of politicians rather than cops."

Brognola laughed over the phone. "Nobody's *all* bad, I guess."

"Take this number down." He gave Brognola the phone number to his room. "I'll have the cell with me, too. Wish I could talk more but I've got a new job. Hate to be late my second day."

"How's that going?"

"No problems. They've teamed me up with a guy named Vogt. He's sharp."

"He have any idea that you aren't what you appear to be?"

"No. Not yet. But like I said, he's sharp."

"What do you have planned if he figures things out?"

"I don't know. We'll cross that bridge when we come to it." Bolan knew why Brognola had asked. The Stony Man Farm director was all but certain that when they'd traced the cop killers, they'd find another cop involved somewhere. Someone within the group of murderers knew too much about cops and how they worked not to be, or have been, in law enforcement. That being the case, Bolan could trust no one in blue—not even Vogt. "I'm going down to the task force meeting in a few minutes. Then I may have Jack take me out to L.A. I'd like to know a little more about this poisoning thing."

"It may not even be related," Brognola said. "Cops get killed for other reasons, too."

"I know. Call it a hunch." He paused, trying to think of a way to ditch Vogt for the rest of the day. "Hal, have Kurtzman double-check the employment file he hacked into the PD for me. Make sure I've got plenty of sick leave built up. This bump on the head may turn out to be my ticket to L.A., without arousing suspicions about who I really am."

"You got it, big guy," Brognola said.

Bolan hung up and called Vogt's home number. "I'm running late," he said. "I'll meet you at the suite."

"See you there," Vogt said.

Thirty minutes later Bolan was again in the task force suite drinking coffee. Several of the men he'd met the day before asked about the bruise on the side of his head, and he gave them the slipped-in-the-shower story. Karen Cohlmia, the good-looking female detective he'd met the day before, looked him in the eyes and grinned. "Slipped in the shower my ass," she said. "My guess is she crossed her legs."

The soldier just smiled.

Vogt was the last to arrive. As soon as he was there, Burnett started the meeting. It was far shorter than the one the day before when they'd been trying to bring Bolan up to speed. Nothing new of any significance had been learned. The two men who had been out with the flu were back, and Bolan met Chuck Larson of the Tomball police and A. K. Spencer from Chambers County. Larson was a fit, fiftyish former Special Forces man with a balding flattop haircut. Spencer had a round boyish face beneath a dense growth of unruly straw-colored hair, and had cut himself shaving that morning. He tapped the Band-Aid on his chin and pointed to Bolan's bruised head. "You know, if you and I could come up with a good story we might get a medical retirement out of these things. Or at least some sick leave."

The soldier smiled politely. "If it doesn't quit hurting pretty soon, I may take some of that sick leave and go to the doctor."

Spencer nodded. "Never hurts to be careful with head injuries," he said.

Bolan followed Vogt out to the car and got into the passenger's seat, holding his head. He had decided he did need to go to L.A., so he might as well make it look good.

Vogt slid in behind the wheel. He started the engine, then turned to stare at the soldier's bruise. "How'd you say that happened again?" he asked.

"Nothing too exciting. Slipped getting out of the shower."

"And hit your head on...what?" Vogt's face looked skeptical.

"One of the knob handles, Vogt," Bolan said, faking mild irritation and rubbing his head again. "Why? You want to put me on a polygraph?"

Vogt backed out of the parking space and drive out to the highway. "No, no," he said. "I haven't known you very long, but I saw you in action yesterday in the booking room. Slipping in the shower just...well, it just doesn't seem like something that would happen to you. Take it as a compliment."

"I will," Bolan said. "But believe me, I can make the same dumb mistakes as anyone else."

They had planned on reinterviewing Buxton that morning, and Bolan wasn't surprised when Vogt headed to the Radio Shack store. He also wasn't surprised that the skinny man hadn't shown up for work that morning.

"He was scared to death after that shooting," the sales manager said. "Thought the guy was going to come back and kill him. I tried to tell him that only happens on TV, but he wouldn't listen and took vacation days. I thought he was going to be back today. Guess I was wrong."

"We'll try him at home," Vogt said.

Again, Bolan wasn't surprised to find no one at Buxton's house. And he was glad Vogt didn't decide to go check the back. "Probably still scared and hasn't come back yet," he said. "We'll keep tabs on the place and try again."

Bolan nodded. "You have anything else planned today?"

"Just a few odds and ends. Nothing very likely to crack the case. Why, your head hurting?"

Bolan nodded. "I think it might be a good idea to have the doctor look at it," he said.

"Want me to take you?"

"No, I can drive. Just get me back to my car."

Vogt did just that. Bolan said goodbye in the parking lot.

"SO," JACK GRIMALDI said as the Learjet began its descent over LAX, "how are you going to approach the L.A. cops? As a Fed or a Houston cop?" He turned to glance at Bolan in the seat next to him.

Bolan had debated that very issue himself during the flight. He wanted to learn more about the poisoning death of the Los Angeles officer, and the fastest way to do that would simply be to go to the investigators working the case. He could "badge his way" in, and as a professional courtesy—as well as a fellow cop who highly suspected that the poisoning was another in the epidemic of police murders—they'd cooperate with him. At least to some extent. Would he get a warmer reception flashing his Houston credentials or those of the U.S. Department of Justice provided by Brognola? Good question.

The federal government still wasn't involved in the investigation of the police assassinations. Therefore the official stance had to be that the killings weren't related. If he showed up as a Fed, the L.A. cops would know he was there on his own and without the Justice Department's sanction. Add that to the basic distrust many state and local officers had of the Feds, and the soldier could predict problems—half-lies that jealous and competing agencies often fed each other.

"I'm going Houston," he told the pilot.

The wheels hit the runway and Grimaldi slowed the engines. "Good call," he said. "Not that you asked for my advice."

"It's an open invitation," Bolan said. "You've been around too long not to have picked up something."

They came to the end of the runway, and Grimaldi guided the plane toward the hangars. "You calling me old?" He grinned.

Bolan kept a deadpan expression. "No. But have you looked in the mirror lately?"

Grimaldi did so, and his grin widened. "Brad Pitt, eat your heart out."

Taking only a briefcase, the soldier dropped from the plane and strode toward the private craft terminal. As soon as he'd decided to continue playing the part of Detective Belasko rather than use his Justice ID, he had called Brognola back. Aaron Kurtzman had hacked his way back into both the Houston computers and the older Teletype communications system and advised Los Angeles's homicide division that the HPD was sending Bolan to meet with them. The communiqué had said only that they suspected they might have a homicide of their own that tied into the dead cop. But any officer who hadn't been hiding under a rock for the past three months knew what it really meant.

Three men awaited Bolan's arrival in the terminal, and none of them had to be told who he was. "You must be Belasko," a middle-aged potbellied man in a cheap green blazer and rust-colored slacks said, extending his hand. He wore aviator sunglasses and the evidence of several meals on his tie. "I'm Tim Saxon. Homicide." His warm smile stretched his face. "This is my partner, Alex Windsor."

Bolan shook hands with Windsor, who was tall, emaciated and had suffered from severe acne at least twenty years previously when he'd been a teenager. In his black suit and tie he looked more like a sad undertaker than a cop. He nodded when he shook hands but didn't speak.

Saxon hooked a thumb toward the third man who had stood slightly to the side of the other two. The smile stayed on his face, but all of its warmth faded away. "Meet Dwight Jessup. Los Angeles Internal Affairs Division." As Bolan shook the hand of a gray-faced man who seemed devoid of emotion, Saxon added. "He's in this because the deceased was a cop." Saxon paused, then added, "Among other reasons."

Bolan frowned slightly, wondering exactly what that meant.

"Watch yourself around him," Saxon went on. "I know you're Houston PD, but I've got no doubt Jessup knows all the head-hunters in your department."

Out of the corner of his eye, Bolan could see that the smile was still frozen in place. The statement had been said as a joke, but it hadn't been meant that way. As within all departments, the members of the IAD squad, whose job it was to go after fellow cops, weren't going to win any popularity contests.

"Let's hit the car," Saxon suggested. "We can fill you in on the situation as we drive to the medical examiner's office. But first, who hit you in the head with a sledgehammer?"

"Nobody. Slipped on a bar of soap getting out of the shower and hit the knob."

"Damn," Saxon said. "Lucky. That could have killed you, right there on the temple."

Bolan nodded and followed the men silently to a dark green Ford sedan in a No Parking zone in front of the front door. Through the windshield on the dashboard he could see the cardboard sign that read Los Angeles Police.

The soldier got into the back next to Jessup. Windsor took the wheel and Saxon flopped in front on the passenger's side, turning to place an arm on the back of the seat so he could face Bolan. "Have a good flight?" he asked as Windsor started the engine and pulled away from the terminal.

Bolan nodded. "Not bad at all."

"I saw the bird you dropped down in. Fancy. You guys got many of those?"

The soldier faked a laugh. "Learjets? No, just the one. I got lucky today. The chief didn't have any out of town luncheons to speak at."

Saxon laughed boisterously. "I know how that goes. We get the scraps the brass can't eat around here, too." The other two cops remained silent. Windsor, because humor didn't seem to be part of his personality profile, and Jessup because he was obviously with two men who didn't like him, didn't want him with them and he knew it.

"Can you run down what happened?" Bolan said.

Saxon sighed as they pulled out onto the highway. "Okay, cop's name was Thurman, Jonathan Edward. Went by Jonny. He moonlighted by tickling the ivories at some of the piano bars."

Bolan sat quietly, waiting for him to go on.

"Anyway, I didn't know him, and neither did Windsor. Probably why we drew the case." He paused, pulled a cheroot out of the shirt pocket beneath his sport coat and stuck it in his mouth. A cigarette lighter was right beneath the No Smoking sign, and he used it to light the long thin cigar. "Now, Jessup here, he knew him. Or at least knew who he was." Taking a long drag off the cheroot, he said, "I figure if I smoke in the car like this, it'll take Jessup's mind off all the bribes I take." Again, he smiled. But again, there was malice behind it. "Dwight, you want to tell the rest of the story on Thurman or you want me to?"

Jessup spoke for the first time, and his voice was as monotone and nondescript as the rest of him. "You go ahead and finish your story, Saxon," he said. "Then I'll tell him the truth."

"Ahhhh! Rack one up for the opposing team!" Saxon said, then turned back to Bolan. "Thurman was divorced. Lived alone in a fairly seedy place near MacArthur Park. Word is it was all he could afford. Divorced wife, two kids, high alimony and child support payments."

"And other expensive habits," Jessup said.

"Dwight, I thought you wanted to wait?" Saxon said as Windsor took them off the highway and into downtown L.A. He went on. "When I got to the scene, two patrolmen were already there. It hadn't started out as an official call. He'd just missed his shift the day before, and the second day one of his buddies figured they better check on him. Might be sick or something. After roll call, they went by and found him." He drew on the cheroot again, and the end glowed orange and hot. "Looked like a poisoning."

"Of a sort," Jessup said. "Drug overdoses are certainly a form of poisoning."

For a moment, the car went silent, and the only noise was the hum of the engine and the street sounds of downtown Los Angeles. Saxon's smile faded to a grimace of hatred, and it looked as if it were taking every ounce of self-control he had to keep from drawing his gun and emptying it into the Internal Affairs man. When he'd composed himself again, he said, "That's about it on my end, Belasko. We're waiting on the toxicology report." He stubbed out what remained of his cigar in the ashtray and then said, "So why don't you do your gig now, Jessup." The man's name came out sounding almost like a profanity.

Jessup continued to stare straight ahead, not looking at Bolan as he spoke in his monotone. "IAD has been watching Thurman for several months," he began. "The man's ex-wife is the sister of one of the Redondo Beach Rebels—strongest outlaw biker gang in the area next to the Hell's Angels. The Rebels have a heavy slice of the methamphetamine trade in Southern California."

"My uncle was a bootlegger during Prohibition," Saxon growled. "That make me dirty, too?"

Jessup ignored him. "Detective Saxon also neglected to tell to tell you that four months ago Officer Thurman applied for, and drew, a plainclothes assignment with Narcotics. During the interview before his transfer was approved, one of the standard questions asks if the applicant has any family members or friends involved in the use or distribution of any dangerous drugs. Thurman's answer was no."

Saxon wasn't about to let that one pass, either. "An ex-wife makes an ex-brother-in-law and that's not my definition of family. Sounds like the man just told the truth to me, Jessup, and if you thought that situation was still so bad, why didn't IAD's background investigation turn it up?"

Jessup's face colored slightly—the first sign of emotion Bolan had seen since meeting the man. "We missed it somehow, initially. But the bottom line is that we know it now. And since Thurman was assigned to Narcotics, two different investigations into the Redondo Beach Rebels have gone up in smoke. Both of which Thurman knew about."

They had reached the medical examiner's office building, and Windsor pulled into the parking lot.

"Let me get this straight," Bolan said. "Saxon, you think Thurman was poisoned by parties unknown?"

The beer-bellied detective replied, "Affirmative."

The soldier turned back toward Jessup. "And you think he was involved with the Rebels meth trade and used, too. ODed?"

"That would be my guess at this point," Jessup agreed. "But I will concede to what Saxon said earlier. We have to wait on the toxicology report to find out."

Bolan reached up and rubbed his jaw. "I guess there's no doubt in your mind why I'm here," he said to none of the men in particular.

"All the way from Houston?" Saxon said. "Only one reason I can think of. You think this is another one of the hits by whoever it is who's taken it on themselves to rid the world of police. After all, Houston is where it all started." He dug the cheroot stub out of the ashtray and lit it again, taking one last drag before they entered the building. "And I agree with you. The fact that none of the cops have been poisoned before fits the pattern of no pattern. It's how the perpetrators are keeping the Feds out."

Jessup's thin lips moved only slightly, forming a smirk almost as expressionless as the rest of him. "And I believe when we're through, Detective Belasko, that you're going to find that you've wasted your time and the money of the citizens of Houston, Texas. Thurman was a dirty cop. He tipped off the crank dealers, and he used himself. He simply gave himself a bad dose and died."

Windsor parked the car several rows back from the main entrance and the conversation continued as the men opened the doors, got out and began walking toward the building. "You forgot we've got an eyewitness of a scruffy looking dude leaving Thurman's apartment the day before he was found."

As he walked, Jessup lifted his arm and flicked an imaginary piece of lint off his sleeve. "People who deliver illegal drugs are often 'scruffy' looking, Detective Saxon," he said. "Or so I'm told."

"Yeah, well, I'm glad somebody told you. 'Cause I doubt you picked it up from any *street experience*."

They were met at the door by another man who was obviously a police officer. He pushed on the fire bar, opened the door and stepped back to let them enter. He had to have been awaiting their arrival, and was one step from being out of breath with excitement as he dispensed with greetings and got right to the point. "A lot's happened since you left for the airport, Tim," he told Saxon in an excited voice.

The men stopped in the entryway between the glass doors they had just entered and another set that led into the building proper. "Toxicology back?" Saxon asked.

"Yep, and you were right." The new cop cast a gloating look at Jessup, then looked back to Saxon. "Worst self-ingested thing they found in his blood was alcohol. And last time I heard, even the Rat Squad let us drink beer." He gave the Internal Affairs man another glance.

"So what was the cause of death?" Bolan asked.

"Mike Belasko, the Houston guy," Saxon interjected.

As they shook hands, the cop who had opened the door said, "Ted VanKrevlin, Narcotics. Jonny and I were friends. The cause of death was poisoning, all right."

"What substance?" Jessup demanded. He seemed not to believe it.

"Nicotine sulfate," VanKrevlin answered.

The soldier nodded to himself. Nicotine sulfate was one of the easier homemade poisons and could be cooked up in any kitchen. Many insect poisons contained as much as forty percent of the substance, and that percentage could double if allowed to evaporate into thin syrup form. It would not only work if ingested, it absorbed through the skin and simply spilling it on a person could kill within minutes.

Around the ring of police faces, Bolan saw a conflict of emotions. They were relieved that their fellow officer hadn't been on the take or a drug abuser. But they still mourned his passing. Whenever a cop died, anywhere in the world, the rest of the police "family" felt the loss.

"But that's not all," VanKrevlin went on. "Davis took a photo lineup by the apartment of the lady across the hall from Thurman's—the one who saw the lowlife looking character leaving the day Jonny died. She picked out his brother-in-law, no sweat."

"What's his name?" Jessup asked.

"Sam Underwood," VanKrevlin replied.

"The Wolfman?" asked Saxon.

VanKrevlin seemed surprised. "That's him. Know him?"

Saxon nodded. "We looked at him on a murder of one of the Angels a few years back. Wasn't him." He looked VanKrevlin in the eye. "We have enough for a search warrant, you think?"

VanKrevlin shook his head and spit on the ground. "Already tried. That cranky old bastard Judge Lamberton wouldn't sign."

"Then let's at least pick him up for questioning at his house," Saxon said as they got in into the car. "The law says that we've got a right to search the immediate area for our own safety, right?"

Bolan suppressed a smile. What constituted as the immediate area was a matter of judgment, and had to be the call of the officer on the scene. Testifying later that the search had been conducted for the safety of the officers present—meaning they were worried about weapons or hidden parties who might ambush them from cover—was a widely used pretext for actually searching for drugs, stolen property and other evidence of a crime. It came in handy in situations like this, and while Bolan was never in favor of violating the constitutional rights of law-abiding citizens, neither was he in favor of criminals like Underwood hiding their evil deeds behind the law.

Jessup started to speak. "If you think I'll stand by while you—"

Saxon cut him off. "Shut the fuck up, Jessup," he said. "A fellow cop got murdered. So why don't you try being a cop yourself for once instead of a grade school tattletale."

Jessup's jaw clamped tight.

A moment later the five men were crowded into the sedan and speeding toward Redondo Beach.

4

Sam "Wolfman" Underwood, the poisoned cop's former brother-in-law, had gotten his nickname from his long hair, beard and the thick matting of hair that covered his arms, legs, chest and back. During the drive to Redondo Beach, Bolan learned this, as well as the fact that Underwood had served terms in both Folsom and San Quentin for armed robbery and manslaughter. VanKrevlin also told him Underwood had recently completed a year in Los Angeles County for possession of methamphetamine.

Neither prison nor the county jail, however, had rehabilitated Underwood. He'd gone right back to his old ways the moment he'd been released.

VanKrevlin, as part of the narcotics division, had a current address on the Redondo Beach Rebel. It was an old two-story house several blocks inland from the beach, and Windsor drove past it without stopping so they could see what they were jumping into before they left the ground. Or, as VanKrevlin said, "Any time you mess with the Rebels you want to be careful. I don't like the sons of bitches. But you have to keep a healthy respect for them or you get killed."

Bolan had dealt with outlaw bikers many times in the past and found them to be little different than most criminals. Some were tough. Others just played at being tough. But the Rebels were very much like the Hell's Angels in that they didn't do much playing, and most of them would just as soon kill a cop as look at him. The Executioner had also found, however, that they were much braver when the odds were around ten to one in their favor.

A dozen or so Harley-Davidsons were parked outside the house and, in contrast to the house itself, gleamed with care and cleanliness. The house needed paint, and some of the windows had been broken out and replaced with scraps of plywood or cardboard. The lawn looked as if it hadn't been mowed for months, but most of the long strands of grass had been pushed down to ground level by the tires of the motorcycles.

There was no sign of activity.

Driving two blocks down, Windsor cut a U-turn and then pulled to the curb. He threw the transmission into Park but left the engine running. Then, turning to his partner, he said the first words Bolan had heard him speak since they'd met. "What do you want to do, Tim?" he asked Saxon in a high-pitched squeaky voice.

The potbellied detective was staring down the street at the motorcycles. "Got to figure at least a dozen of them inside. Maybe more, maybe less, but that's how many bikes are out front."

"We should call for backup," Jessup stated flatly.

Saxon looked at him with contempt. "We don't need any fucking backup, Jessup," he growled. "We're picking the man up for questioning, not arresting him. And we don't even know if he's there."

"That's right," VanKrevlin said. "This is where he's staying but he's not on the lease. It's more of a crash house for the whole club. They come and go."

"If they have a meth lab in there, we could get blown to hell," Jessup argued.

VanKrevlin and Saxon looked at each other as if they'd both just seen a spaceship land in the yard next to them. Then they looked at Bolan. "Can you believe this guy?" Saxon said. "Where does the Rat Squad find them?"

Bolan knew what they meant. Any cop worth his salt would know that there would be no crank lab in such a high-profile hangout for bikers. The Rebels might be degenerates, they might be ruthless, and they might be pure evil. But they weren't stupid.

"Why don't I go up, knock on the door and have a look?" the Executioner said. "They won't recognize my face."

"Good idea but you're out of your jurisdiction," Saxon said. "Besides that, you look more like a cop than any of us."

Bolan couldn't suppress a smile at the irony of the comment, but the others thought he had taken it as a compliment. The truth was that he was slightly amused. He might have both U.S. Department of Justice and Houston PD credentials in his pocket but, of the five men crowded into the car, he was the only one who wasn't a cop.

Saxon turned to Windsor. "Did you take the coveralls and the toolbox we used on that stakeout out of the trunk?"

Saxon's near-silent partner just shook his head.

"Okay, then, I'm elected," Saxon said, sliding out of his sport coat and unknotting his necktie. "They probably know VanKrevlin's face on sight, and Jessup—" he glanced over his shoulder with the mirthless smile again "—well, what can I say about you, Jess? I don't think undercover work's really your cup of tea, is it?" He reached for the door handle.

"Wait," Jessup said, pulling his briefcase from the floor to his lap.

"What?" Saxon asked impatiently.

Jessup opened the lid and pulled out what looked like a slightly oversized ballpoint pen. "At least wear this," he said. "We can listen to you when you talk to them."

Bolan looked inside the briefcase and saw that it contained an electronic receiving unit. The fake ballpoint was evidently the transmitter.

Saxon snatched the transmitter out of Jessup's hand and shook his head. "Leave it you guys to always have your eavesdropping toys handy," he said with open sarcasm and no smile this time. "Hey, you sure this will work on criminals? It isn't just set for cops, is it?" Before Jessup could respond he got out of the car and opened the trunk.

A moment later Saxon appeared next to the vehicle. He carried a toolbox and wore a pair of olive green coveralls that read ACME Plumbing Service on the back. The transmitter-pen was in the right front breast pocket of the coveralls.

VanKrevlin was amused. "ACME Plumbing," he said. "I like it. Right out of a Bugs Bunny or Road Runner cartoon."

"Up yours, Van," Saxon said. "We'll test the transmitter when I get close to the house. Then I'll turn around." He glanced to the front window and Windsor. "Hit your lights twice if you hear me, Windy."

Windsor nodded.

Saxon took off down the street, swinging the toolbox so easily that Bolan knew it had to be empty. There was really no need for a verbal test of the bug. Every step the man took on the concrete sounded over the receiver in Jessup's lap. The Executioner didn't realize there was a delay, however, until he saw a small Scotty dog run into the front yard of a house as Saxon passed. The dog barked once, and they heard it outside the car roughly a half second before the sound came over the airwaves.

"Testing, one two three, testing," Saxon said a few moments later as he crossed the street to the block where Underwood's crash pad was located.

As soon as Windsor saw his partner stop and look back, he flashed the headlights on and off, then on and off again.

"Okay, I saw them," Saxon said before turning back and continuing toward the house. "Even in our bright Southern California sunshine, where the song claims it never rains, I saw the light."

Bolan waited impatiently as the man walked on. He didn't like it, and knew he should have been the one to pull this impromptu undercover reconnaissance duty. He was eminently more qualified if sudden violence broke out. But how was he supposed to explain that to these Los Angeles cops without blowing his cover? The answer was, he couldn't. So he waited.

The Executioner had come to L.A. to see if this poisoning was linked to the other police assassinations. So far, he didn't know. Sure, cops were being killed all over the country and many of the murders had to trace back to the same source. But that didn't mean all of them did. Cops were killed all the time for other reasons, and that wasn't going to stop just because someone, or someones, had decided to speed up the process. The fact was that the rise in cop killings made the front page of the papers every day, and that kind of publicity even spawned copycats.

"Let's pull up a little closer, what do you say?" Bolan said as Saxon neared the house. "We can't see the front porch from here."

"Good idea," VanKrevlin said. "Windsor, go up to the stop sign. They aren't going to notice us there."

Windsor, as usual, did as he was told without comment.

Bolan knew there was another side of the coin to this situation, however. The longer he was there, the more it looked like the Redondo Beach Rebels—Underwood in particular—was behind the murder of Officer Thurman. And the fact that Underwood was Thurman's ex-brother-in-law stacked the odds in favor of more personal reasons for the murder. A sudden thought crossed his mind.

Could it be the Rebels behind all this? Like the Hell's Angels, the Redondo Beach Rebels had grown far beyond the motorcycle-riding thugs they had begun as, and were heavily involved in drugs, prostitution and other forms of organized crime. They had power and connections across the nation, and in many foreign countries as well. They had the ability to pull off this string of assassinations. But did they have a reason?

Not that Bolan could come up with. Still, he needed to stay there long enough to find out for sure.

Windsor came to a halt at the stop sign at the end of the block just as Saxon started up the steps to the front porch, toolbox in hand. Bolan watched him rap on the door with his palm. Thirty seconds later, when he had gotten no response, he repeated the movement. He had to do it once more before a woman wearing nothing but a white bra and black thong panties opened the door. She was rubbing sleep from her eyes.

VanKrevlin could see her, too. "That's Thurman's ex," he said. "Cathy. Probably up several days on meth and crashing now."

"Good afternoon, ma'am," Saxon's voice came over the receiver. "You called the plumber?"

"I didn't call no damn plumber," the woman said and started to close the door.

"But ma'am, wait...please..." Saxon said, reaching out to keep the door from closing. "Maybe I got the wrong address. Could you help me just a minute?" He reached into a pocket of his coveralls.

From somewhere in the house, a male voice was caught by the pen-shaped transmitter. "Who the fuck is it?"

"Just some dumb-fuck lost plumber," Cathy Thurman shouted back in a voice that would have made a fishwife proud. "Shut up and go back to sleep."

Saxon produced a small pad of paper and held it out in front of him. "Okay, I've got here that a Mr. Sam Underwood of this address called in with a stopped-up toilet. He doesn't live here?"

"He lives here...he's my brother," Cathy said. "But we ain't got no damn stopped-up toilet."

The sound of padding feet came over the airwaves, and then the door swung back wider to reveal a shirtless man wearing ragged blue jeans. He had long hair and a beard but unless he'd shaved his chest he wasn't anyone who could have earned the name Wolfman.

"What the fuck do you want, man?" he demanded.

"Just trying to find out where my mistake is," Saxon said cheerily. "Sam Underwood called in from this address and needed help with a toilet." He started to return the pad of paper to his coveralls. But when he did, the spiral edge caught on his lapel and the pad was ripped from his hand. His natural reaction was to grab for it, and when he did he released the toolbox in his other hand. The metal box hit the concrete porch with a clang loud enough to be heard all the way down the block. A half-second later, the same clang sounded again over the airwaves through the receiver. The clasps on the toolbox sprang open, and the box bounced once, then settled on its side with the lid open.

Nothing fell out.

"What you doing carrying around an empty toolbox, asshole?" asked the big man with no shirt. "You ain't no plumber!" His hand disappeared behind his back.

"Move in!" Bolan said, reaching for the door handle.

But they were too late.

The Executioner kept his eyes on the house even as he opened the door. But he, and the other cops in the sedan, were helpless to interfere as the butcher knife appeared in the shirtless biker's hand and then shot forward.

Saxon's own hands moved to his belly in an attempt to defend himself, but they were too slow.

The men in the surveillance car heard the sickening, wet, swish of a blade entering soft tissue as the knife perforated Saxon's chest.

BOLAN DREW the Glock 21 as he vaulted from the car and sprinted toward the house. When the man with the butcher knife saw him coming, he pushed Saxon backward off the porch, grabbed Cathy Underwood and threw her back into the house behind him, then slammed the door. The Executioner heard the click of a dead bolt sliding into place as he hurdled the steps.

No simple dead-bolt lock was going to stop him. Lowering a shoulder, Bolan hit the door, following it in as it swung open. In the corner of his eye, he saw the man holding the bloody butcher knife just to his left. The bloody blade was held over his head in a reverse grip. As it descended, the Executioner pivoted off the center line and brought up the Glock, jamming it into the man's throat. He pulled the trigger, and a .45-caliber hollowpoint round blew into the man's neck at contact range. An explosion of red showered the room, momentarily blinding Bolan. When it had cleared, the biker was still miraculously on his feet. Half of his neck was gone, and what remained had been blackened by the powder that exited with the .45-caliber round. He stared down at the crouching Executioner with eyes of surprise, then fell to the side.

But Bolan's problems weren't yet over. As the man who had stabbed Saxon fell, he revealed another man right behind him.

Shorter, he had been hidden by his fellow Rebel and the bullet that had passed through the shirtless man's throat had gone over his head. Instead of a butcher knife, this biker gripped a sawed-off double-barreled shotgun.

Bolan dived to the floor as the Rebel pulled both triggers at the same time. The side-by-side shot a double dose of 12-gauge buck-shot over his head like twin hurricanes.

The Executioner landed on his belly, brought the Glock back up and triggered a lone round into the shotgunner's chest. The cut-down weapon fell to the ground, and the biker toppled over it. In the man's back, the hollowpoint's exit wound gaped open and was the size of a fist.

VanKrevlin, a SIG-Sauer in his hand, shot into the room. Bolan shouted, "Get down!" just as a rifle barrel appeared around a cor-ner. VanKrevlin hit the ground as the Executioner fired just to the side and above the rifle, hoping to drill through the wall and hit his mark. But the rifle jerked back out of sight.

If he had hit the man, it wasn't bad. For a moment, the house went silent. "Where are Jessup and Windsor?" Bolan whispered to VanKrevlin.

After hitting the floor, VanKrevlin had rolled behind a thread-bare couch. "They took the back," he whispered.

Quickly the Executioner surveyed the house's floor plan. The front door opened into the living room, just to the left of the stair-case leading to the second floor. The doorway where the rifle had appeared led to a hall, which in turn would lead to at least one downstairs bedroom, maybe two. Just past the staircase was a swinging door. Behind it, Bolan guessed would be the kitchen, and there was probably another door from that room leading into the same hall, farther down.

What was upstairs? The Executioner didn't know. More bed-rooms and baths. And people. He could hear scampering footsteps overhead. How many? Impossible to tell. He turned his attention back to the hallway. Now that the thunder of the Glock and shot-gun had faded, he could hear excited voices whispering from the back of the first floor.

"Get the Uzis, you bastards!" a hoarse voice whisper-yelled.

Uzis. Plural. Their implications weren't lost on the Executioner.

Bolan rolled to semiconcealment behind a large reclining chair. It offered only a partial hiding place—just enough to get him out of immediate sight if someone burst from the hallway. But unless a round struck one of the metal struts inside and glanced off, even a feeble .25 ACP was likely to drill straight through it. All he could hope for was that it would cause a moment's pause on the part of anyone entering the living room.

A moment was more than the Executioner would need.

Bolan heard gunfire break out at the rear of the house. Pistol fire rather than another shotgun or rifle or one of the Uzis the voice had mentioned. Did the fire come from the guns of Jessup and Windsor? Or had one of the Rebels shot them both with a handgun? Again, impossible to know at that point. And there was nothing he could do to help the two cops if they'd been hit. Going after the enemy now, by rushing down the hall, would be suicide. Besides, if he left the living room, he afforded an opportunity for whoever it was he heard upstairs to descend and attack from the rear.

Bolan took a deep breath, keeping the Glock trained on the opening to the hallway. The only logical course of action at the moment was to wait. To wait patiently. To wait until the enemy grew weary of waiting themselves and lost their own patience.

To his side, Bolan could hear VanKrevlin's deep breathing. Patience in such situations was difficult, the Executioner knew. The natural human instinct was to dispose of the threat. To do anything to put an end to the strain the brain was experiencing from the life-threatening encounter. But sometimes natural human instincts—even those related to survival—could get a person killed. And it was natural human instinct—not his own but that of the Rebels—that Bolan was counting on. The pressure they were under should be enough to create enough impatience to be their downfall.

VanKrevlin glanced over at Bolan and whispered from behind the couch. "I, uh, I know this is L.A., and it should be my call," he said. "But you got any good ideas on what we should do next?"

He laughed nervously. "It appears you're no stranger to this sort of thing."

Bolan nodded. "Nothing," he whispered.

"Pardon me?"

"We do nothing. For now."

VanKrevlin's voice was strained. "Okay. We do...nothing. Tell me, you *have* been in situations like this before, right?"

"Once or twice," he said.

"So we do nothing," VanKrevlin repeated.

"Exactly," Bolan whispered. "We wait them out. Make them come to us. We'll have the tactical advantage."

VanKrevlin cleared his throat. "You...uh...you heard that part about Uzis a minute ago, didn't you?"

"I did."

"And you still want to do nothing?"

"I do."

"You don't have any better ideas than that?" VanKrevlin said.

"No. But if you do I'm willing to listen to them while we wait."

"How about we get out the door and run for the car. We can call for the whole damn SWAT team."

Bolan shook his head. "I don't like the idea of getting shot in the back. Any other ideas?"

"No," VanKrevlin said. "That was it. I was hoping you'd come up with something. Sorry, but I don't like this waiting strategy."

"Neither will they," Bolan said. "In fact, they'll like it even less than us. And in a minute, one of them is going to show himself."

The soldier wasn't always right, and this proved to be one of those times. It didn't take a full minute. Ten seconds after he'd spoken, he saw a shadow moving down the hall. The runner was inexperienced, because he didn't take that shadow into consideration. Bolan watched him easily, saw him stop three feet from the opening to the living room, drop to his knees and knee-walk forward, a long gun of some kind gripped in both hands.

Bolan glanced briefly to the corner of the doorway and saw the bullet hole he'd put there earlier. It had gone all the way through, and a thin beam of light shone through the hole. The wall looked to be made of standard half-inch plasterboard. It wasn't a support wall, and being of inside construction it wouldn't even contain any fiberglass insulation to slow a bullet. Just an inch of wallboard and air between him and the man creeping down the hall.

The Desert Eagle might have done the job better, but the Glock would do. Aiming just behind the corner, Bolan waited until the shadow was behind his sights, then pulled the trigger.

The Glock jumped slightly with the recoil and a shower of white plasterboard dust puffed out into the room. A shriek sounded in the hall, and Bolan saw the shadow fall from his knees to a sitting position. The Rebel's feet slid out in front of him, and into view in the opening. The shadow still gripped the long gun in one hand but grabbed its shoulder with the other. The biker seemed unaware that his lower limbs were exposed.

The Executioner pumped out two more rounds, one into each of the man's feet. A banshee wail went up in the hallway as he swung the Glock back to the wall. Indexing on the shadow and the exposed feet, Bolan lowered his aim slightly to where the gunman's chest would be and fired again. Another roar. Another cloud of white dust.

But this time, there was no scream. Just the gurgling sound of a lung shot. The shadow jerked convulsively, and a mist of blood shot from the man's mouth, looking like a cloud in the silhouette on the wall. The man in the hallway finally fell forward, facedown in the doorway. The long gun he had carried turned out to be a .44 Magnum Ruger carbine.

The house fell silent again. Another minute went by. Then two. After five minutes, VanKrevlin whispered, "Does waiting ever get on your nerves?"

"No," Bolan said.

"Really?"

"Really."

"How do you do it?"

"Practice. Now, be quiet."

"Okay."

The voices began in the back again. Low murmurs. Loud enough to hear but too low to distinguish the words. Above his head, the floor of the second-story creaked again with footsteps, the old wood protesting so loudly that Bolan could have pinpointed the exact position of the feet making them. He considered firing upward, through the ceiling. But the floor was solid wood instead of plasterboard, and the Glock didn't have the penetrating power of his Desert Eagle. Besides, he couldn't be sure that the feet he heard above him didn't belong to an innocent.

More gunfire erupted at the back of the house, there was a pause, then pistol fire was returned. It sounded like only one gun shooting from outside the house in, and again Bolan wondered as to the status of both Jessup and Windsor. Had one of them been hit? Maybe, but one of them might just as easily have gone back to the car to radio for backup. In any case, Jessup and Windsor were beyond the Executioner's help for the time being. And they were both big boys who had known what they might be getting into when they'd pinned on their badges for the first time. They'd have to take care of themselves for the time being.

The gunfire from the backyard died down again. A deadly silence fell over the house yet again.

And then, the waiting game paid off.

The swing door blew open as if a tornado had erupted in the kitchen. Into the living room raced a grizzly man wearing full Redondo Beach Rebel colors. He was six foot six and couldn't have weighed less than 350 pounds. Yet he moved with the rugged grace of an Olympic sprinter. Using one of the Uzis, he sprayed the living room on full-auto. And like so many who gave into the anxiety induced "spray and pray" method, he burned lots of powder and hit nothing of value.

Bolan wasn't even sure the man had seen him or VanKrevlin when he blew the Rebel's face off with a well-placed .45-caliber round. The slug entered right below the nose and angled slightly upward. It appeared to take half of the man's brain with it as it exited the back of his head amid a mass of flying blood, tissue, hair, skin and bone fragments. The Rebel twisted completely as he was thrown backward. He slammed into the wall face first, then fell to the dirty carpet.

A short man with long stringy hair and an equally stringy mustache and goatee suddenly came through the swing door. He almost tripped over the big man's body but paused a second before he hit it. He'd have been better off tripping.

Bolan had just switched the Glock's partially-spent magazine for a fresh load, and he pumped three of the fourteen rounds into the man. The first two struck within an inch of each other over the heart. VanKrevlin added a .40-caliber round from his own SIG-Sauer. Then Bolan's third round took out the throat beneath the scraggly goatee, and the fourth drilled through the nose above it. The stringy-haired Rebel who had stopped in front of the body fell backward on the floor.

The thundering of footsteps came down the hall as a group of Rebels charged the living room at the same time. There were too many to make out individual shadows on the wall, but the noise and combined penumbra gave Bolan all the warning he needed. Raising the Glock to arm's length, he waited until he saw the first flash of color in the doorway and began pulling the trigger as fast as he could.

Screams, shrieks and moans erupted at the end of the hallway as the Executioner continued to fire, reaching for yet another magazine with his left hand as he worked the Glock's trigger. To his side, he could see VanKrevlin gripping his SIG-Sauer in both hands and throwing his own rounds into the kamikaze charge of the Rebels. The explosions were almost deafening in the small living room, and the Executioner felt the weapon in his hand growing warm. When he'd counted out thirteen rounds in his head, he reached for another magazine, then fired the fourteenth. Dropping the spent mag to the floor, he had the fresh load in by the time the slide closed again.

More shots erupted at the back of the house, barely audible between those going off in the living room. Four men made it over the bodies in the doorway only to die at the hands of Bolan and VanKrevlin. Another pair shot through the swing door from the kitchen, and the Executioner swung his Glock that way. A double-tap of .45 rounds struck a blond-haired man who looked more like a surfer than an outlaw biker, jackknifing him in two before he fell in death. His partner sprayed the room with another of the Uzis.

VanKrevlin caught the Uzi-toter in the knee with a .40-caliber S&W slug, and the man fell to his side just outside the door. But his finger never left the trigger, and the 9 mm rounds from the Israeli submachine gun continued to fly through the room. Bolan pulled the Glock over and down. A single semijacketed hollow-point slug shot from the barrel. It hit the man in the top of the head and spun down through the skull into the brain.

One such round to the head was more than enough.

A commotion in the hall. Feet running.

But this time *away* from the living room. A moment's reprieve in the battle.

"Still tired of waiting and doing nothing?" Bolan asked VanKrevlin as he rose to his feet.

"I wouldn't exactly call this doing nothing," the narcotics cop said.

"Stay here," the Executioner said. He looked up at the ceiling, then pointed to the staircase. "There's somebody up there. Watch for them."

Moving cautiously forward, Bolan held the Glock 21 downward in front of him at a forty-five-degree angle as he stepped over the bodies littering the floor. When he reached the hallway there were still Rebels at the end, trying to jam their way back into the bedroom and looking like a Keystone Kops movie as they bumped shoulders in the doorway. Dropping to one knee, Bolan began firing once more. He caught two of the Rebels in the side. One fell backward into the hallway, the other forward into the bedroom.

Bolan rose and leaped over the bodies in the doorway, landing on his feet in the hall. Dropping to one knee again, he let the rounds buzz over his head from a Smith & Wesson .44-caliber Special L-frame, then dropped the man firing the revolver with a shot to the face. Another Rebel tried to bring a 9 mm Kahr into play but a double-tap from the Executioner jammed him against the wall. More bodies danced and jerked as the big .45-caliber rounds exploded almost as fast as a full-auto weapon. One man, wearing a white T-shirt stained red with someone else's blood, turned to face the Executioner. He held a tiny .32-caliber North American Arms pistol in his fist, and snapped off two overeager rounds that flew high over Bolan's head. Before the soldier could return fire a loud explosion sounded behind the man and the front of his chest blew out. He fell to the ground to reveal a shocked Rebel holding a Desert Eagle much like Bolan's.

The biker stood staring down at his own gun in awe. In the confusion, he had shot his own man in the back.

Bolan shifted the aim of the Glock slightly and hammered two rounds into the man's chest. When he didn't fall fast enough, the Executioner added one to the head in classic two-and-one "Mozambique" style.

Suddenly the only men in the hall besides the Executioner were dead.

Bolan's barrage had jammed another doorway with bodies. But he knew some of the Rebels had escaped into the bedroom. He moved slowly down the hallway, his back to the wall, the Glock up and ready.

A loud commotion sounded at the front of the house. The soldier had no time to check it out, however, as an arm suddenly shot around the corner from the bedroom, a nickel-plated Colt Python in its fist. The arm fired blindly, missing Bolan by a good three feet.

Bolan didn't miss.

The next round from the Glock punched a hole through the hidden man's biceps. The follow-up penetrated the fingers wrapped around the Python's grip and hit the weapon's frame. A loud ding rang down the hall as bullet met steel, and the Colt went spinning out of the hand.

Behind him, in the living room, the Executioner heard voices. Backup cops had to have arrived. Which in turn meant either Jessup or Windsor had, as he'd suspected, gone back to the car to radio for help.

"Hey!" came a voice from the bedroom. "Don't shoot! We've had enough!"

Bolan hesitated. He hated leaving any of these animals alive to manipulate their way into a light or suspended sentence provided by the high-dollar attorneys the Rebels could afford. On the other hand, that's what cops did when bad guys finally agreed to give up—they let them. And if he didn't want to blow his cover as a cop, that's what he'd have to do now that the backup officers were on the scene. Besides, Cathy Underwood's statement that her brother wasn't home could hardly be taken at face value. Outlaw bikers, and their women, had been known to lie. Underwood might have been in the house and still be alive in the back. Bolan had killed a lot of dirty, hairy creatures in the past few minutes but none who really fit the full Wolfman description. And if Underwood was still breathing, the Executioner wanted to talk to him.

Footsteps behind him caused Bolan to glance over his shoulder.

"Police!" came a voice.

Bolan nodded at three blue uniforms. "They want to give up," he said.

A man wearing sergeant's stripes on his sleeves stepped forward carrying a 12-gauge pump-action shotgun. "Throw your weapons out! Now!" he shouted down the hall.

Two pistols and yet another Uzi came flying out into the hall. They struck the wall and the pistols fell to the floor. The Uzi came to rest on one of the dead bodies.

"Is that all?" demanded the sergeant.

"That's all. We swear!"

"How many of you are in there?"

"Three! Just three! We don't want no more trouble. I didn't want to—"

"Shut the hell up and listen!" growled the sergeant. "You can talk later. You're going to come out one at a time, hands clasped to your head, fingers interlaced and to the front where we can see them. If any of you make one wrong move—and by that I mean you even blink at the wrong time—we'll blow your ass to kingdom come." He paused for effect, then said, "You got all that?"

"Yeah! Sure! We don't want any trouble! We never did!"

The sergeant motioned over his shoulder and the other two uniforms joined him and Bolan. They, too, had shotguns.

"Okay!" the sergeant yelled. "The first one of you. Walk out slowly." The man with the stripes was an old hand, and now for effect he racked the slide of the shotgun. A terrifying sound that criminals the world over knew. It meant that sudden, bloody death in the form of double-aught buckshot was only a few pounds of finger pressure away.

The first man was bare-chested but had nearly enough tattoos to count as a shirt. He came walking out slowly, stepping over the bodies in the doorway. One of the patrolmen slammed him against the wall, slipped handcuffs on him with practiced dexterity, gave him a quick shakedown for weapons and then hustled him over and around the bodies littering the hallway into the living room.

"Number two!" the sergeant yelled. "Come out slowly, hands interlocked. Try anything, and you're dead!"

Methamphetamines were not the only drugs the next Rebel abused—he looked like a walking steroid advertisement. He wore a ragged cut-off sweatshirt that showed off biceps and triceps far beyond human capability without chemical help, and his chest was equally bloated beyond proportion. His features had been altered from the drug as well, and he stared out from under the low eyebrows of a Neanderthal. The second cop pushed him face forward into the wall but, because of the width of the man's back, he had trouble getting his arms close enough to handcuff. With an audible grunt, he finally got the job accomplished. The Rebel's face was pained with the strain on his shoulders as he was pushed out of the hall.

"Number three, you're on," the sergeant bellowed. "And if there's anybody else in there hiding, this is your last chance to live. When we come in after this, we're going to shoot anybody who hasn't spoken up no matter what they're doing."

"Man, it's just me left," came a voice from the other room. "I'm the last."

"Then come on out. Same drill."

The last man to leave the room had a short reddish-brown crew cut and short matching beard. The first thing Bolan saw was his eyes. The pupils were dilated and bore the half-dead, faraway look of the habitual doper. The man was flying.

And he wasn't obeying the sergeant's orders. He had his hands on his head, but his fingers were toward the back of his head.

The sergeant started to speak, but before the words could come out the man's hands began to move. Bolan's Glock barked twice, both rounds catching the Rebel in the sternum. As he fell to the ground, a tiny North American Arms minirevolver—formerly hidden behind his head—fell from his fingers.

The sergeant was visibly shaken as he stepped forward, picked up the tiny .22 Magnum pistol, and checked the man's pulse. Then, standing, he turned to Bolan. "Man, you are fast," he said admiringly. "I didn't even see this little thing." He held the minirevolver in front of his face. "You the cop from Houston?"

Bolan nodded.

"Any chance of hiring you away from them?"

Bolan smiled. "I'm pretty happy where I am."

"Well, that's good. Although by the time we're finished with the paperwork this is going to take—particularly with you being from out of town—you might as well be drawing an L.A. salary."

The two men walked into the living room, which was alive with cops, including Jessup and Windsor. The two prisoners had already been taken out to cars and were on their way to be booked. Cathy Underwood, now wearing a pink robe over the bra and panties she'd answered the door in, also wore handcuffs. She was crying. VanKrevlin stood next to her but when he saw Bolan he walked over. "She was upstairs," he said. "Nobody else."

The soldier was glad he hadn't shot at the noises above him. He walked over to the woman. "Your brother wasn't here," he said flatly. None of the men who had come out of the back bedroom had fit Underwood's description any more than the dead men littering the floors.

Hatred shot from her eyes as she looked up at Bolan. "No," she said. "Or you'd have killed him, too, you bastard!" Her eyes fell to one of the bodies on the floor. "You killed my old man!" Without warning she suddenly jumped forward and threw herself over one of the prostrate forms. "Skull!" she screamed. "Skull!"

Two uniforms grabbed the woman and jerked her back to her feet, doing their best to keep from getting any of the dead men's blood on them. Cathy, however, had stained the front of her pink robe crimson.

Bolan looked at her again. "Where's your brother?" he asked softly.

"Why? So you can go kill him, too?" she snapped.

"I don't want to kill him," Bolan said. "I just want to talk to him. And if you tell us where he is, he's got a much better chance of staying alive than if we have to find him."

Her face streamed with tears—tears she couldn't wipe away with her hands cuffed behind her back. She frowned, weighing the situation, then finally said, "He's at the beach. Lifting weights."

"Little Venice?" one of the patrolmen asked.

She nodded.

The cop turned to Bolan. "It's new. An outdoor muscle-head gym like the one at Venice Beach. Only at Redondo. And smaller."

Bolan nodded. It might be the best possible situation. He needed to talk to Sam Underwood, and that meant taking the man alive. He'd most likely be unarmed—it was hard to hide an Uzi in a tank top and gym shorts—and would be more likely to surrender peacefully.

The soldier looked at VanKrevlin. "Let's go," he said.

They started out the door.

"Hey, wait a minute," the sergeant yelled after them. "We've got paperwork that's got to be done."

"It'll wait," Bolan said. "This won't."

As he and VanKrevlin left the house, Jessup and Windsor fell in behind them.

5

Two crime scene investigation vans were arriving as Bolan, VanKrevlin, Jessup and Windsor sped toward the beach. VanKrevlin and Tim Saxon had been friends, and now that the gunfight was over the narcotics cop showed signs of depression. Windsor, who had been the man's partner, looked even more somber than usual. Jessup wore his usual face, which seemed devoid of all emotion.

As Windsor raced the car down the street, VanKrevlin tried to break the ice that seemed to have frozen the inside the vehicle. "The lab rats are going have their work cut out for them," he said, hooking a thumb over his shoulder. Lab rats was the term the chemists and other lab personnel who worked the actual crime scenes hated most.

No one responded. Then Jessup cleared his throat self-consciously. "I know he didn't think much of me, Windsor," the IAD man said, "but I'm sorry about your partner."

Windsor, true to form, didn't speak. But he nodded, and Bolan could see the pain behind the quiet detective's dejected face.

It was only a few blocks to Redondo Beach, and Windsor parked the car in a lot, flashing his badge to the attendant rather than paying the charge. The newly constructed concrete weight-lifting platform had been set a hundred yards farther down the beach, past the shops, coffee houses and cafés lining both sides of a walking street. The concrete slab was surrounded by a ten-foot chain-link fence topped with concertina wire in order to secure the equipment at night. It gave the place more the appearance of a penitentiary or war camp than an outdoor gymnasium. Bolan could see at least two dozen men, and almost as many women, moving through the forest of free weights and machines. The clinks and clanks of iron echoed across the sand.

VanKrevlin turned to face Bolan. "You've done pretty damn good running the show so far, Belasko," he said. "You got any ideas on how we should go about this?"

The soldier remained silent for a moment in thought. "Let's you and I go up there by ourselves. We'll bring Underwood back to the car, then take him downtown to talk to him."

Jessup cleared his throat again. "There are a lot of big guys up there," he said, nodding toward the lifting slab. "And my guess is that Underwood isn't the only Rebel. They're a pack, and they don't go places alone."

VanKrevlin snorted. "You were in the back of the house and didn't see our Texan friend here at work. Don't worry about us, Jessup. Worry about them." He opened the door as Bolan got out on his side.

A sidewalk rose and descended gently as they passed the shop area, doing their best to stay out of the way of in-line skaters and skateboarders who zipped past them going both ways. Here and there, a homeless man held out his hand, and they passed a group of youths in their late teens who looked like they were in the middle of a small-time drug deal. In their coats and ties, Bolan and VanKrevlin stood out among the more casually dressed Redondo Beach crowd, and the drug dealers halted in progress, making them as cops and waiting until they passed.

The soldier let a hard smile curl his lips. This was hardly the time to stop and go after kids selling bags of marijuana.

The clank of iron and the swishing sound of steel cable pulleys grew louder as they neared the platform. The shapes that had been indistinct from a distance now took the form of heavily muscled men and women. Most were dressed in gym shorts and tank tops or rag-cut sweats. Many of the women wore thongs, and a few had fashionable neon-colored tights. Bandannas and terry-cloth sweatbands encircled foreheads to keep sweat out of the eyes beneath the hot Southern California sun.

But even though they wore similar clothes, Underwood wasn't hard to spot. His appearance left no doubt as to how he'd gotten the nickname. His waist-length hair had been tied back in a ponytail that fell well below his belt in the back. His beard reached halfway to the belt in front, and grew high on his cheekbones, finally stopping just below his eyes. A thick matting, which looked more like an animal's fur than hair, covered his arms and legs outside of his tank top and shorts.

The hirsute man stood waiting his turn at the preacher curl bench as Bolan and VanKrevlin approached the gate to the slab. Underwood wasn't a big man—only five foot seven at most—but the barbells and machines there, and probably in prison, had made him almost as wide as he was tall. His training partner—who might be a fellow Rebel—was in the middle of a set, grunting and groaning the last few reps as Underwood urged him on with a string of profane accusations about his parentage, sexual preferences and manhood in general. The other man wasn't as hairy as Underwood, and as they neared Bolan saw the tattoo on his left biceps as it bulged through the curls. It depicted a cartoon demon on a motorcycle wearing a gray Civil War-style kepi. Above the picture were the words Redondo Beach. Below it was Rebels.

There were at least two Rebels. And maybe more.

Bolan led the way past an eight-station Universal machine to where Underwood stood. Fishing into his pocket, he started to pull out his badge case. Underwood looked up, peeking out between the hair on his head and that on his face. "Leave it in your coat, pig," he said. "I smelled you down the beach when you got out of the car."

The soldier looked the man in the eye. "We need you to come with us," he said.

Underwood's partner finished his set and stood, gasping for air. He stared at the two newcomers with hate-filled eyes but had no air with which to speak. This seemed to frustrate him, as if he had his own once-in-a-lifetime "pig" insult on the tip of his tongue but was impotent to verbalize it.

"Am I under arrest?" Underwood asked. He dropped into the seat his partner had vacated and rested his elbows on the barbell hooked into the uprights.

"No," VanKrevlin said. "But we need to—"

"Then fuck off," Underwood practically spit. He lifted the barbell from the rack and started his curls.

"We can do this the easy way or the hard way," Bolan said.

Underwood didn't answer. The veins bulged in his arms as the biceps contracted and then relaxed with each rep. When he got to eight, he set the bar back on the stand and looked up at Bolan. "You still here?"

"I'll take that as your preferring the hard way," the Executioner said. He reached out, grabbed the lobe of Underwood's ear and jerked him off the bench. A moment later, the biker was entangled in an arm bar and being walked toward the gate in the fence.

His partner had finally gotten his wind back and he lunged for the soldier. "You fucking pig!" he screamed.

Bolan twisted, slamming Underwood into his oncoming friend. The blow didn't hurt the man but it served its purpose, stopping him in his tracks. Now Underwood was between Bolan and the other Rebel, and the man with the tattoo stopped, wondering what to do next.

The Executioner experienced no such indecision. Keeping Underwood secured with his right arm, he reached around with his left hand and grabbed another the other biker's ear. Jerking the tattooed biker around to Underwood's side, he released the earlobe, quickly drew back his fist and caught the man with a solid left hook to the jaw.

The weight lifter dropped like a failed dead lift.

VanKrevlin shook his head in wonder. "You know, Belasko," he said. "I like riding with you. It's kind of like watching a Chuck Norris movie. Is everybody in Texas like you?" When Bolan didn't answer, he added, "I'm having fun just watching but if you ever need any help, feel free to ask."

"Watch my back, then," Bolan said. "There could be other Rebels here." He walked the cursing Underwood past other mystified weight lifters toward the gate. They were halfway there when the sudden roar of motorcycle engines in the distance caused him to stop.

Bolan looked through the fence to see at least twenty Harley-Davidsons jump the curb fifty yards away.

"Cavalry to the rescue," Underwood cackled. He pursed his lips and began making bugle sounds.

The motorcycles cut across the grass to the sidewalk, knocking skaters and pedestrians to both sides. All of the men sitting atop the Harleys wore Rebel colors. And all were armed with rifles or shotguns across the handle bars.

"I don't remember this ever coming up at the academy," VanKrevlin said.

"That offer still open?" Bolan asked.

VanKrevlin turned a white face toward him. "What offer?"

"About calling on you if I needed help?" the Executioner said. "Because now looks like a pretty good time to take you up on it."

BOLAN WATCHED as the Rebels closed in on them. He knew there was no way they could get to the car—the motorcycles were already between them and where Jessup and Windsor waited in the parking lot. And he also knew that if Underwood got away during the fight that was about to ensue, the man would disappear into the outlaw biker underworld. Finding him again would waste valuable time.

Time during which more cops would be assassinated.

So the Executioner twisted Underwood around to face him and used a straight left to send the man into the world of unconsciousness. Underwood dropped to the ground, and a second later VanKrevlin had him cuffed to a heavy knee extension machine.

"Securing a prisoner to a stationary object," he said as he stood back up. "Complete, total, and inexcusable violation of departmental policy."

"Call it extenuating circumstances in your report," Bolan said as both men drew their pistols.

VanKrevlin laughed out loud. "Report?" he said. "I hope I get around to writing a report."

The bikers roared closer. The Rebels at the head of the pack reached the sidewalk, knocking more people out of their way as they turned toward the weight lifting slab. Then a second tier split off, heading to the right side of the fence. The last few bikers went left. Their strategy was clear—they intended to surround the lifting slab, trapping Bolan and VanKrevlin inside the fence. They'd then fire through the chain links.

Far down the walkway, Bolan could see Jessup and Windsor getting out of the car in the parking lot. They hurried for the trunk where, Bolan hoped, shotguns and perhaps rifles were stored.

As the Rebels neared the slab, many of the weight lifters decided discretion was the better part of valor. Some sprinted out through the gates while others dropped to the concrete, searching for a place to hide amid the weights, racks, benches and machines.

"You suppose they just want to talk?" VanKrevlin asked, laughing nervously. Before he could answer the man on the lead Harley raised a pistol. The gun roared, and the bullet narrowly missed one of the innocent weight lifters who was fleeing for his life.

"Doesn't look that way," the Executioner said. "I'd say they got word of what happened at the house and that we'd gone looking for the Wolfman." Another round, fired from somewhere within the pack of oncoming bikes, zinged past them overhead. "I'd also suggest we take cover."

Bolan dropped behind a weight stand holding huge forty-five-pound Olympic weights. VanKrevlin found a similar place ten feet to his right. With their giant iron disks hanging from steel bars, the stands weren't bad protection. The iron would protect them from the bikers attacking from the front, like being in an armored car. But both Bolan and VanKrevlin would be partially exposed on both sides. The Rebels taking up positions to the left and right would have to fire through a mazelike forest of equipment but they still might find a hole through which to shoot. And bullets would ricochet even more than usual with that much hard steel around at odd angles.

The Executioner reminded himself that a warrior took what cover was available. He didn't waste time or energy wishing he had it better.

The lead Rebel in the party at the front got dramatic as he neared the concrete slab. Ten yards from the fence, he suddenly leaned to the side and laid down his bike. The roaring machine slid into the fence and the chain links sang as they swayed back and forth between the support posts. The biker was right behind, sliding on his side in black leather chaps like a base runner avoiding a tag at home plate.

The big difference was that he had a shotgun in his hand.

As the Rebel's heavy motorcycle boots struck the fence, he rose quickly to his knees and racked the slide on the pump gun. Pressing the stock to his shoulder, he held the barrel an inch away from the fence and pulled the trigger. A 12-gauge roar exploded, making the earlier pistol shot sound like a BB gun in comparison.

Bolan ducked as some of the lead pellets stuck the weights in front of him, flattening and bouncing off harmlessly. But at least one of the shots hit the fence just beyond the shotgun barrel and ricocheted back. The biker screamed and fell backward, holding his face.

Bolan steadied his arm on the stack of big Olympic plates and lined up the Glock's sights. One pull of the trigger put a bigger hole in the man's head than the shotgun pellet had, and ended his shrieks.

The rest of the motorcycles now slowed, coming to a halt as the men got off. Several were either stupid or more in love with their bikes than their lives. They stopped to lower their kickstands, and in doing so became stationary targets.

Bolan caught one of them in the chest, the .45 hollowpoint round drilling through a gold medallion hanging from around the man's neck. Fragments of golden shrapnel sparkled in the sun and blew to both sides while the rest of the medal was driven into the wound, enlarging it threefold. Both the bike and the rider toppled to the grass.

To Bolan's side, VanKrevlin now opened up himself, pumping out a trio of .40-caliber S&W rounds that took out another biker trying to park his machine. The others took the hint and let their precious vehicles fall, many even deciding to use them as cover rather than risk the deadly accuracy they were seeing come off the slab.

A tall, reed-thin man, bare-chested beneath his greasy cut-off denim jacket, aimed a .30-caliber carbine over his front tire and began pulling the trigger in fast semiauto fire. The light rifle rounds sounded like the bells of Notre Dame as they struck the weights in front of the Executioner. But they had no more luck penetrating the iron than the pistol and shotgun rounds had.

The plates were still vibrating from the blasts when Bolan leaned to the side, bringing the Glock up to eye level. He snapped off a shot that caught the rifleman squarely between the eyes, knocking him backward. Turning the pistol to the side, the Executioner let the sights fall on a pair of Rebels crouched behind a Harley with a gold gas tank and trim. Two more rounds sent the men sprawling over the bike, dead.

Pistol, rifle and shotgun rounds flew at Bolan and VanKrevlin from both sides. Bullets of all calibers, makes and configurations skimmed across the concrete and bounced back and forth between the steel stands, machines and weights. But the Rebels who had taken the flanks were farther away and unable to get a good picture through the maze of weight-training equipment. Some of their rounds came close, buzzing by the Executioner like angry hornets. But their nearness was more luck than accurate shooting.

Bolan changed magazines, watching VanKrevlin out of the corner of his eye as the L.A. detective aimed at a Rebel with rings and studs piercing his face. VanKrevlin's first round caught the man in the shoulder and spun him to the side. The second round struck just below the nose, blowing out two tiny silver rings hanging from his nostrils.

By then the Executioner had reloaded. Swinging his Glock into play, he added a round to the man's temple. That took care of the rest of the rings and studs in his ear and eyebrows.

The engagement continued with the Rebels employing a mixed bag of arms—M-16s and AK-47s blasted out rounds. Bolan and VanKrevlin stayed low behind their cover, leaning around or over the iron to snipe away at the Rebels. One by one, the outlaw bikers' numbers began to diminish. But the two men on the slab were still vastly outnumbered.

All around them, the weight lifters who hadn't escaped before the arrival of the bikers cowered behind whatever cover they had found. Moans of fear and groans of terror escaped the lips of both males and females. Here and there, a shriek of total terror pierced the air above the explosions.

Risking a glance down the sidewalk, Bolan saw that Jessup and Windsor had left the parking lot and taken up positions behind a row of parked cars. Both were firing AR-15s at the enemy's back from a safe distance. That was smart, and the Executioner didn't begrudge them their strategy.

He just wished both men were better shots. Only one round out of ten seemed to be finding its mark—so few that even the Rebels hadn't yet noticed the other two detectives.

A tall bulky biker, obviously stoned out of his mind, suddenly stood and beat on his chest like a gorilla. A second later, he led a one-man suicide mission toward the gate in the fence. In his hands he held a Streetsweeper shotgun, and the big scattergun roared with 12-gauge blasts each time his feet hit the ground. Buckshot blew through the weight-training area like a lead hailstorm, but all of it went high over Bolan's and VanKrevlin's heads.

Bolan steadied the Glock on the weight tree again and sent a pair of .45 rounds roaring from the barrel. They struck the man squarely in the chest, and he was dead on his feet. But whatever drugs pumped through his veins prevented him from knowing it, and although he slowed his pace, he continued to stomp forward and fire.

The Executioner wished for a moment that he had the Desert

Eagle, then pushed the thought from his mind. The fact was he didn't have it, and he might just as well wish for a rocket launcher or flamethrower. The charging biker jerked in reaction as one of VanKrevlin's rounds was added to the bullets Bolan had already put in his chest. But, like the monster who wouldn't die, who appeared in every cop's worst nightmares, the drugged-out zombie continued forward.

Bolan had gotten his fill of the man. Taking his time, he centered the white dot on the Glock's front sight between the two on the rear, then superimposed the picture over the charging biker's angry face. Squeezing the trigger, he let the recoil shoot down his arm and through his shoulder. The Glock barely moved and he watched the man's head explode above the sights.

The Rebel's oncoming momentum still carried him all the way through the gate. He finally fell, lifeless, onto the concrete less than two feet from where Underwood was cringing beside the knee extension machine.

Sirens sounded in the distance and for a moment the gunfire ceased. Then, just as suddenly, the air to the Executioner's side felt as if a freight train had just rushed past. A second later he heard a rifle round far louder than any of the others that had so far been fired.

Looking toward the spot from where the roar had come, Bolan saw a man lying prone on the ground. Far out on the grass, almost to the street where the Rebels had jumped the curb, he had set up a tripod and affixed a rifle to it. Bolan squinted, trying to get a make on the weapon. He couldn't be certain at this distance but it looked like a Browning High Wall. If that was the case, it would be chambered in either .40-65 or .45-70. Used primarily for long-distance silhouette shooting, the High Wall was a true elephant gun and with hard ammo, in either caliber, it could drill right through iron plates.

As Bolan continued to watch, the rifle jumped slightly and again a rush of air hit the side of his head. The same explosion came from the distance, but just before he heard it, another sound filled his ears from the rear. Glancing over his shoulder, Bolan saw a squat rack facing to the side of the slab. An Olympic bar loaded

PLAY
LUCKY HEARTS
GAME

AND YOU GET

FREE BOOKS!
A FREE GIFT!
YOURS TO KEEP!

TURN THE PAGE AND DEAL YOURSELF IN...

Play **LUCKY HEARTS** for this..

exciting FREE gift!
This surprise mystery gift could be yours FREE

when you play **LUCKY HEARTS!**
...then continue your lucky streak with a sweetheart of a deal!

1. Play Lucky Hearts as instructed on the opposite page.

2. Send back this card and you'll receive 2 brand-new Gold Eagle® books. These books have a cover price of $4.99 or more each, but they are yours to keep absolutely free.

3. There's no catch. You're under no obligation to buy anything. We charge nothing—ZERO—for your first shipment. And you don't have to make any minimum number of purchases—not even one!

4. The fact is, thousands of readers enjoy receiving their books by mail from the Gold Eagle Reader Service™ months before they are available in stores. They like the convenience of home delivery and they love our discount prices!

5. We hope that after receiving your free books you'll want to remain a subscriber. But the choice is yours—to continue or cancel, any time at all! So why not take us up on our invitation, with no risk of any kind. You'll be glad you did!

The Gold Eagle Reader Service™—Here's how it works:

Accepting your 2 free books and gift places you under no obligation to buy anything. You may keep the books and gift and return the shipping statement marked "cancel." If you do not cancel, about a month later we'll send you 6 additional books and bill you just $29.94* — that's a saving of over 10% off the cover price of all 6 books! And there's no extra charge for shipping. You may cancel at any time, but if you choose to continue, every other month we'll send you 6 more books, which you may either purchase at the discount price or return to us and cancel your subscription.

*Terms and prices subject to change without notice. Sales tax applicable in N.Y. Canadian residents will be charged applicable provincial taxes and GST.

If offer card is missing write to: Gold Eagle Reader Service., 3010 Walden Ave., P.O. Box 1867, Buffalo, NY 14240-1867

BUSINESS REPLY MAIL

FIRST-CLASS MAIL   PERMIT NO. 717-003   BUFFALO, NY

POSTAGE WILL BE PAID BY ADDRESSEE

GOLD EAGLE READER SERVICE
3010 WALDEN AVE
PO BOX 1867
BUFFALO NY 14240-9952

NO POSTAGE
NECESSARY
IF MAILED
IN THE
UNITED STATES

with three forty-five-pound plates at each end had been racked at shoulder level. And all three of the plates facing the Executioner had been perforated by the last rifle round. The entire squat rack still quivered from the massive shock, and the plates clanged like orchestra cymbals in the vibration.

"He's getting closer," VanKrevlin said, barely louder than a whisper.

Bolan didn't waste time worrying. Looking back to the sniper, he guessed the man at roughly 250 yards. Far out of the Glock's range. His eyes shot to the men he had downed around the fence. The closest was the biker who had made it all the way inside the gate but he'd carried the Streetsweeper, and a shotgun would be of even less use to the Executioner now than the Glock. Many of the men just outside the fence had dropped rifles. But in order to get to them he'd have to run twenty yards in clear view, then slow through the gate, and again to pick up a weapon. The gate would frame him like a picture, and that's where the Rebel sniper would hold his sights. The Executioner knew that.

Because that's what Bolan would have done.

Another mammoth rifle explosion sounded, and this time the Executioner felt the wall of air pass on his other side. What the sniper was going for was clear—sighting in his weapon. He was getting the big rifle aligned with the weight tree in front of the Executioner, and just as soon as he had it zeroed, he'd begin popping rounds right through the forty-five-pound weights.

The sirens grew louder as the police neared the scene. But they weren't near enough, and they wouldn't get there in time to be of any help.

Bolan glanced down the sidewalk to Jessup and Windsor. Both men appeared to have seen the sniper and were firing his way. But Bolan could see their rounds skimming the grass in a wide circle around the Rebel on the ground. He sighed in disgust. If he were a betting man, he'd put his money on the fact that neither of the AR-15s had been sighted in recently, either. To add to the problem, both Jessup and Windsor jumped slightly each time they pulled the trigger. Neither was comfortable with the long guns.

Bolan set his jaw firmly as he turned back to the sniper. He could rely on no one—not Jessup, Windsor, VanKrevlin nor the oncoming patrol cars with the blaring sirens. No one was going to get him or VanKrevlin out of this jam except him. He could come up with some plan, or die, as simple as that. The Executioner was on his own.

Bolan heard engines roar to life in front of him and to both sides. The bikers heard the sirens, and now they took off on their motorcycles, more intent on escape than rescuing Underwood or killing the men trying to take him. Suddenly he and VanKrevlin were alone.

Except for the man on the grass. The fight had changed. It was no longer an engagement between two armies.

It was a duel.

The big iron plates no longer serving as decent cover, the Executioner rose to his knees, his head high over the top of the plate tree. If the sniper's bullet was to get him, he saw no benefit in making it pass through the iron plates first. Resting both elbows on top of the weight tree, he sighted down the barrel, putting the white dots on the sniper. Before he could squeeze the trigger, another windstorm blew past, this one so close it singed his cheek. Again, the roar of the high-powered rifle came a second later.

Shaking it off, Bolan took a deep breath and let half of it out. He squeezed the trigger, keeping his eyes open and watching the bullet clip into the grass a good ten feet in front of the prone Rebel. As far as he could tell, the sniper didn't even notice. Raising the Glock higher, he sighted an inch over the spot where the man lay. But again, the pressure of a high-powered round blasting past inches from his face caused him to pause. And, once again, this time the round burned slightly on the other side of his face.

The Executioner took another deep breath, let out half and squeezed. This time, his round struck just behind the sniper, kicking up a patch of grass and dirt.

The sirens screamed in the distance, but they were still at least two blocks away. The last rifle round had been the last "test" shot for the sniper. He was doing the same thing Bolan was only adjusting for windage rather than range. The Rebel now had the Executioner dead on, and the next round would hit home.

It was now or never. Whoever pulled the trigger next was going to live.

This time, Bolan held the Glock's sights a half inch over the tiny target when he squeezed the trigger. He watched closely but saw no point of impact either high or low. A second later, the rifle jumped in the sniper's hands again. But this time there was no air pressure anywhere close to the Executioner. And the loud clang of the bullet hitting iron sounded far on the other side of the weight-lifting slab.

The explosion came next, as expected. Then the sniper rose from his prone position to his knees. For a few seconds, he knelt there, looking down at the slab. Then he set down his rifle and lay on his side as if taking a nap.

The Executioner stood and raced to the gate. Behind him, he could hear VanKrevlin's footsteps pounding after him. He leaped over the dead biker in the gateway, then sprinted past the dead Rebels and their abandoned bikes, running toward where the sniper lay in the distance.

The first of the squad cars arrived as the Executioner neared the man on the ground. Raising the pistol in his hand in case his last round hadn't killed the sniper, he slowed to a walk, the Glock held at a forty-five-degree angle to the ground and ready to snap up into action at the slightest movement.

More police cars pulled to the curb, lights flashing and sirens screaming. In his peripheral vision, Bolan saw Jessup and Windsor jogging down the sidewalk toward him. A dozen blue uniforms exited the cars on the street, the men grabbing shotguns and rifles before sprinting across the grass to join him.

Bolan came to a stop three feet from the sniper and looked down. The man was clean-shaven and wore mirrored sunglasses. He was dressed in the Rebel uniform of dirty, faded jeans, black motorcycle boots and the sleeveless denim jacket which bore his colors. One thing, however, was different. The T-shirt beneath his jacket read Hot Lead, Hot Sun and Cold Women. I Survived Desert

Storm. On his forearm was a readily recognizable tattoo—the emblem of the 75th Ranger Regiment.

The man had exhibited good marksmanship, and now Bolan saw why. He'd had good training.

The Executioner let the Glock fall to arm's length. Unlike so many of the world's criminals, terrorists and other scum who had fallen to his guns over the years, this man's face had not frozen in death with an expression of either pain or horror. The fact was, the Rebel sniper looked peaceful. He looked as if the Executioner had released him from some living hell of his own creation, and Bolan glanced once more to the tattoo. At one time, this had been a man of honor, and the Executioner couldn't help wondering what had happened to steer him so far onto the wrong path after the war. But he'd never know, and there was no sense dwelling on it.

Bolan shoved his weapon back into its holster as the other police officers ground to a halt around the body.

"Son of a bitch!" one of the uniforms said in amazement. "You do that from all the way down there? With that Glock?"

Bolan didn't answer as he turned back to the lifting slab. But as he did, he heard the same voice say, "Can you believe that, Greg? Right through the bastard's throat with a *pistol!*"

Jogging back to the concrete platform, the soldier walked to where Underwood was still handcuffed to the equipment. His punch had sent the man into a temporary sleep.

But one of his fellow bikers had made that sleep permanent. Two rounds had passed through the low-cut tank top, and both shirt and shorts were drenched in blood. More blood shone wetly off the thick masses of hair coating his arms and chest.

Wolfman Underwood wasn't going to tell the Executioner anything.

THE INTERCOM in Senator Owen Killian's office buzzed. Dropping the pen in his hand, he reached for the receiver on his desk. "Yes, Janet?" he said.

"There's a Mr. Domnick on the phone," Killian's secretary said in her breathy voice. "He says it's urgent."

Killian bristled, the name putting the brakes on the sexual fantasies he usually had about Janet whenever she spoke to him over the phone. Domnick. It was the name he had given to Clayton Rudd, to be used only if he found it necessary to call Killian at the office, and only if an extreme emergency came up. But this wasn't an extreme emergency—Killian would bet his seat in the Senate on that. Rudd had called too many times using the Domnick name, and they had all been *perceived* emergencies at worst.

"Put him on, Janet," the senator said wearily.

"Will do."

A clicking sounded in Killian's ear and a moment later Rudd's voice said, "Hello?"

"This had better be important," Killian said.

"It's a matter of life or death," Rudd responded.

"Whose?"

"Mine."

Right, Killian thought. "Go on," he said.

"We've got a problem," Rudd said. "One of the Houston cops is on to something."

The senator gripped the phone tighter. Men like Rudd were the only weak links in his plan. They were a necessary evil in order to get the bloody work done but many of them were loose cannons, and Rudd was about as loose as a cannon could get without falling completely apart. Killian sighed inwardly. He supposed a man had to be at least a little strange to be capable of out-and-out cold-blooded murder. He knew he could never pull the trigger or plunge the knife. He didn't have any trouble orchestrating such things, however. "Who is this cop?" he asked.

"Guy's name is Belasko," Rudd said. "Just transferred in from Administration to work the task force."

"That's a strange career change, isn't it?"

Rudd coughed before answering. "Yeah, usually. But it seems Belasko was some hotshot investigator a few years ago. Wife died, and he wanted something routine while he got his head back on straight. Maybe a drinking problem or something. Hell, I don't know."

"Well," Killian said, "tell me what you do know."

"I know the asshole came close to killing me the past night, that's what I know," Rudd said. "I went by to take care of that Radio Shack wimp who saw my face—the little puss finally came back from wherever he was hiding. And when I went in there's this big bastard all dressed in some kind of black assault suit and he's browbeating the hell out of the guy and his skinny-assed girl-friend. Shots were fired. The guy's good."

"Why?" Killian asked. "What was he doing at...what was the Radio Shack man's name?"

"Buxton," Rudd said.

"What was this Belasko doing at Buxton's, dressed like that, and intimidating him?"

"Senator, I told you, I don't know. But my guess is he wanted a description of me and knew Buxton could give it. In any case, he's on to something. Nobody moonlights on his own time just for the fun of it. All dressed up like it's Halloween with a ski mask and everything."

Killian could feel the blood pulsing through his head at the temples. Something was very wrong with this picture. "None of this makes sense," he said. "If he had a ski mask on, how can you be sure he's really a Houston cop?"

"At first I didn't know who he was," Rudd came back. "Fig-ured he was just some lowlife scumball pulling a home invasion. But I found out differently this morning."

"How?"

A sharp intake of breath came on the other end of the line. "What, you don't think I know how to do my job?" Rudd said in-dignantly.

Killian turned his face away from the receiver so the other man couldn't hear his own breath of exasperation. Rudd was the strangest mix of conceit and neurosis he had ever encountered. But he did many things well, and if he said he was sure the man in the ski mask was this Belasko fellow, then that's probably who it was. Should he pursue this and risk loosening the cannon further?

Rudd kept him from having to make the decision. "He rammed

the side of his head into my shoulder. Almost knocked him out, and it's a good thing, too. He'd have killed me if he hadn't."

He paused a moment, and Killian heard a strange squishing coming over the line. What was it? Ah, yes. That stupid rubber ball Rudd was always fiddling with.

"Anyway, Belasko had a bump the size of a baseball in the same spot the next morning. And he's the same size and shape. Believe me, I know it was him."

"I believe you," the senator said. "Did Belasko see you?"

"No, hell no. I was in the hallway and he never got a look at my face."

"You're sure of it?"

"If he had, I would have found that out at the meeting."

Killian saw no reason to question that, either. But Rudd was irritating. He was a subordinate, and it was easy to see why he'd been forced to leave the Army. He knew the story Rudd had told him about his general discharge was true—he'd checked into it to be sure. But the fact was the officers at Fort Sill had wanted to get rid of him for a thousand other reasons, as well.

Finally Killian said, "Be very careful around this man."

"That's like telling a man who's hanging off a building to hold on," Rudd said with the same tone of disrespect that irritated Killian further. "You got another one for me?"

The senator bristled, at first thinking Rudd meant another stupid remark. But before he said anything he realized that wasn't what the man had meant at all. Rudd was changing the subject abruptly, as he did so often, and that was another indication of his instability in Killian's eyes. But he answered the question anyway. "Yes, you have a major job in Texas the day after tomorrow."

"What do you mean by major?" Rudd asked.

"Check the Web site, Clayton. You'll see."

"How's the time line look for the whole program?" Rudd wanted to know.

Killian sighed. Another subject change. "I've told you many times Clayton, this thing can't be hurried if it's to be done well. But when you see what I have in mind for you you'll also see that

I'm speeding up things. When I say *major,* I suppose I mean we're all going to make a *major killing* the day after tomorrow."

"I'm just tired of where I'm stuck," Rudd said. "I don't like hick work."

Before me, you didn't have work at all, Killian thought. But it was never wise to push unstable people's sensitive buttons too hard. "That job is only temporary, as you well know. Check the Web site for your instructions. You'll see what I mean."

"Yeah, sure. You haven't forgotten what job you promised me, have you?"

Try as he could, Killian couldn't keep all the irritation out of his voice this time. "No, I haven't forgotten. But if you ask me one more time, I might." As soon as he'd said the words, he knew it had been a mistake. Not that Rudd didn't deserve them, he did. But they wouldn't help Killian's own cause.

There was a long pause on the other end of the line. "That wouldn't be very wise, Senator," Rudd said. "If I don't get what you promised, I'd have no reason to live anymore. Men with no reason to live do drastic things. Sometimes they even make sure people who fucked them over don't have any reason to live anymore, either."

The senator bristled but caught himself before he spoke. "Relax, Clayton. I know it's taking longer than you'd like. Imagine how I feel." He reached down and took a sip from the glass of water on his desk. "But you don't have to wait on the situation with Belasko. I've decided what you should do."

"And that is?"

"Kill him. There's no point in taking any chances."

On the other end of the line, Rudd laughed out loud. "Now, how'd I know you were going to say that?"

"I'll enter some instructions on the Web site. We'll make it look like another police assassination." And we'll make it look like we're trying very hard to make it look like it's *not* one of the other police assassinations, he added in his mind.

"Okay."

"Very good, then," Killian said. "Now, please don't call me anymore. That's what the Web site is for."

"Only if I need to again," Rudd said and hung up.

Senator Killian set the receiver back in the cradle. For the thousandth time since he had created the Web site to communicate with Rudd and the other men he'd employed, Killian wondered if it had been a good idea. No one knew about the site but them. They each had their own post board and entry codes, and none of them even knew how to get onto the others' boards. They particularly didn't know how to get into Killian's own personal site where he kept his records and plans. He had to communicate with them somehow, and this was far safer than most ways. Still, it worried him sometimes.

Killian leaned back in his chair and clasped his hands behind his head. Rudd. Miserable little bastard. He grunted out loud, recalling the man's question about the promise Killian had made him. Rudd had been referring to the senator's promise that he would become the director of the U.S. National Police Administration once it was formed. Well, Rudd didn't know it but that position had been promised to all twelve of the men killing cops for him. And none of them were ever going to sit in that chair. The very thought of someone like Rudd directing a national agency was ludicrous. They were all uncultured hillbilly killers. And when the time came, they would have to be eliminated in order to erase the trail.

But the senator reminded himself once again that right now they were necessary. And they were all good at what they did. The day after next, they would have a blast if everything came off as planned. Even if only one or two of the strikes were successful, it would still shake the world. He should have all of the support in the Senate he needed after that. Even the men and women who opposed him would be afraid to go against him when he called for a federal police force.

Killian looked at his watch. He'd been working on a speech when he'd been interrupted. He was speaking to the District of Columbia Christian Ministers' Alliance that afternoon on the need for stronger federal law enforcement. A cake-and-coffee reception. And, in addition to his speech, he was supposed to give the invocation.

The senator picked up his pen and looked down at the blank sheet of paper on his desk. Yes, that was what he'd been getting ready to do when the phone had rung—write the prayer. What should be the prayer's theme? It should tie in with his speech, of course. Perhaps he should appeal to God to change the hearts of men and end the violence plaguing the cities. The preachers would just love that. He would make eye contact with all of the ministers right before he began to pray, then close his eyes tightly as if he were in pain. And he'd let his voice quaver, ever so slightly, as he called on the Almighty to put an end to the mayhem.

"O Heavenly Father," Killian said out loud. "Blah, blah, blah, blah, blah. Amen."

The senator began to write, but even as his mind formed the words, he knew no God would listen to such a prayer. If there was a God, he had turned his back on this world long ago, leaving it to those strong enough to take it.

And Killian was one of the strong. Strong enough, at least, to become the first President of the United States with his own national police force at his command.

Like Senator Richard Lane had said, strong enough to become the first American dictator.

The task force meeting was about to begin when Bolan walked into the suite the next morning. No official seating had been assigned around the big conference table but people were creatures of habit, and they were taking the chairs to which they'd grown accustomed.

Ronnie Vogt had saved Bolan's place, and even had a cup of coffee waiting for him. The soldier set his briefcase on the floor next to the table and slid into his chair. "Good morning," he said.

The heads along the table nodded. Bolan then turned to face Vogt when he felt the man's eyes boring into him.

"It looks better," Vogt said.

For a moment, the soldier didn't know what he was talking about. Then he remembered the bruise on his temple. It still hurt slightly but not so much that he noticed it. "Yeah," he said. "Doc said it would be okay. No concussion."

"They do X rays?" Vogt asked.

Bolan nodded. "Yeah. No problem. Just going to look a little nasty for a while."

"I think it's sexy," came a voice from across the table. When Bolan looked up, Cohlmia was grinning at him. "And I still think I know how you got it."

Burnett took his place at the head of the table and said, "Okay. I suppose you've all heard about the Illinois cop beaten to death yesterday."

There was a murmur around the table. Some of the men nodded. Others shook their heads. Bolan remained silent. He had gotten word of the new assassination from Brognola during his flight back from Los Angeles. Again, there were few leads to get the Illinois investigators started. All Bolan knew for sure at this point was that it hadn't been Sam Underwood.

"State trooper," Burnett said. "Found just outside of Evanston on the highway. He had stopped a car for speeding—just ten miles over the limit. No particular reason to think it was anything more than that. They've got the whole thing on videotape from the camera in his vehicle. Trooper gets out, walks up to the car and you see this mist shoot out the window. Turned out it was pepper spray. Then the guy —he's wearing a Richard Nixon mask—gets out with a Louisville Slugger and proceeds to methodically beat him to death." He paused and shook his head. "Takes his time, picking out targets. He knew there was a camera on him, and he'd point to the target—like the nose—as he looked back at the patrol car, then bash it in. I understand it's enough to make a twenty-year homicide investigator puke."

Stan Carmichael, a detective from Deer Park if Bolan remembered correctly, spoke up. "They get a make on the car tag?"

"Sure," Burnett said. "And just as you might guess, the vehicle was stolen. The tape shows the guy driving away in it, right after he gives the camera the old middle-finger salute. They found the car a few hours later parked in the library parking lot at Northwestern University."

"Prints?" Cohlmia asked, but her tone of voice said she already knew the answer. The men behind these assassinations hadn't been that careless so far, and there was no reason for them to start now.

"Nothing left at the scene to have prints on it," Burnett said.

"And none in the car. The bat was there, but it was wiped clean. They didn't find the pepper-spray dispenser, so they have to assume he took it with him."

A. K. Spencer, who had been sick the first day Bolan had joined the task force said, "So again, the guy knew police procedure. Besides wiping down the car for prints, he knew there'd be a camera watching him."

Burnett nodded. "The Illinois investigator I talked to said they've run the tape a hundred times. Even blew up stills. When this guy is first stopped, you can see the back of his head and he doesn't have the mask on. Then, just as Trooper Jones—that was his name, Steve Jones—passes the left rear bumper where the frame between the rear window and the back windshield block his view, you can see him slip the Nixon mask over his head."

Carmichael frowned. "This guy not only knew about the camera, he knew about the blind spot."

Bolan recognized the term. It was that moment Burnett had just described, when the officer's view was blocked while approaching a vehicle. And there wasn't any way around it except to not approach.

"These guys don't just know a lot about police procedure," Cohlmia said. "They know cops."

There was a moment of silence while everyone in the room thought the same thing but didn't want to be the one to voice it. Finally A. K. Spencer did. "It's beginning to sound like maybe they are cops. At least some of them."

Several heads nodded slowly, but not everyone around the table wanted to admit the killers might be brother officers. "Hell," Alexander said. "Maybe they just watch *Cops* on TV."

"Maybe," Burnett sighed. "But unless some officer on *Cops,* or some other police show, said something about the blind spot, it seems a little far-fetched. But wherever they've learned it, it's right. And they know how to hide their tracks."

A secretary came out of the other room, picked up one of the pots on the four-burner range and began circling the room filling the cups. Her high heels clicked along, sounding almost as loud as gunfire in the silent room.

"Okay," Burnett said. "So much for that. Maybe this one ties into ours and maybe it doesn't. We'll stay in touch with Illinois." He cleared his throat. "Item two. LAPD no longer thinks the poisoning murder of their officer is related to our crimes or any of the others around the country. I got a call this morning from a Detective VanKrevlin. It looks like Thurman was killed by his ex-brother-in-law, and there's some kind of drug deal involved." He turned and looked Bolan in the eye. "He wanted to give a special thanks to you, Belasko, for all the help you gave them."

The soldier waited. Burnett was smiling, and it didn't look like he actually knew Bolan had gone to L.A. It was apparent that whatever VanKrevlin had said could have been interpreted as help Bolan had given him over the phone, and that was obviously the conclusion the task force coordinator had come to on his own. Otherwise, he'd have already asked the soldier about it.

"This VanKrevlin went on and on about how great you are, Belasko," Burnett continued. "What'd you do, pay him?"

There were a few chuckles around the room. Bolan smiled and shrugged. "What can I say," he said. "I make great phone calls." He glanced down at the papers on the table in front of him. But again, he could feel Vogt's eyes on him.

The daily rundown began, with the task force members going around the table to give their reports. The secretary who had been filling the coffee cups finished her rounds and disappeared again.

As the reports continued around the room, casting no new lights on any of the killings, Vogt leaned closer to Bolan. "You didn't tell me you called L.A.," he said. "I thought you went to the doctor's office."

"Not all day," Bolan whispered back. "I've known VanKrevlin for years. I called him when I got home."

The reports of interviews and other leads were roughly halfway done, and Spencer was speaking, when a phone rang in the other room. It was answered, and the secretary's soft voice drifted into the meeting room. A moment later, the same woman who had poured the coffee came clattering in on her high heels. "I'm sorry to interrupt, Deputy Burnett," she said, "but there's man on the phone who wants to talk to someone about the Kenard case."

Burnett pursed his lips in slight disgust at the interruption which, if it was like every other lead on this case, was bound to come to nothing. "Did he say who he was or who he wanted to talk to, Amy?"

The secretary shook her head.

Burnett nodded to Don Macy from Morgan's Point. "You're closest to the door, Don, why don't you field it?"

Macy got up and left the room.

Spencer continued talking about canvassing the area around the second cop killing. He had learned nothing of value that the Executioner could see.

That frustrated Bolan. He wasn't a cop, and he was tired of playing cop. It was time to don the blacksuit again and go after these monsters who were killing the police. But until he got some kind of lead to go on, the best thing he could do was just what he was doing. Continue portraying a cop and wait for his chance.

Macy came back in and said, "Excuse me, did somebody talk to a Jack Crenna about some kind of squeeze ball or something?"

Next to him, Bolan saw Vogt's face redden. "Yeah, uh, that was us. He's the old guy that heard the footsteps run past his window." He stood and coughed. "It's one of those Szaball hand exercisers. He found it in his yard the next morning after the supermarket hit. It's really a long shot. That's why I hadn't mentioned it." He gave Bolan a quick look that reminded Bolan how silly he had thought the whole lead was before, then said, "I'll go talk to him."

Spencer went on with his report, then sat down. Chuck Larson—the other cop who had been out the first day with the flu—stood.

Vogt came back in just as Larson was finishing. Burnett held up a hand as Bolan's partner crossed the room and said, "Anything?"

Vogt shook his head. "Nah, he's just a lonely old man and wanted to know if the Szaball had helped. I don't know why he didn't just ask for me or Belasko to begin with." When he got to the table, he set down two fresh cups of coffee, one in front of the Executioner.

The reports began to wind down and then the meeting broke

up. Some of the investigators drifted out while others broke into groups to discuss the cases. Bolan and Vogt had gathered their papers and started to leave when Burnett called to them from the head of the table. "You two got a second?"

"Sure," Vogt said. He and Bolan left their coffee cups and briefcases on the table and walked over to where the deputy still sat.

Burnett looked up at Bolan. "What in the world did you tell that guy in L.A.?" he asked. "He couldn't get over how great you were."

Again, it looked like VanKrevlin's praise could be interpreted as being in reference to things he'd said over the phone. But there had been too much of it for a mere phone call, and he needed to cover his tracks. So he laughed, feigning embarrassment. "I didn't tell him anything to speak of," he said. "And I didn't know he was going to call you. It's one of those inside deals where he's just trying to make an old friend look good. Van and I went to a two-week FBI Homicide Investigation school together in Denver a few years ago. Did our best to drink all the Coors in Colorado, and got to be good friends."

Burnett laughed. "Been there, done that," he said. "But he could have saved his breath for your chief—it's not me who writes your paycheck." He grew more serious, then added. "Now, what's this squeeze ball thing?"

Behind the three men, the room was clearing out as the rest of the cops and deputies hit the streets.

Vogt coughed again. "Uh—"

"I'll tell him, Vogt," Bolan said. "My partner thought I was crazy then, and he's embarrassed now. It's a Szaball. Rice ball covered in rubber. They're made in Miami and used to strengthen the hands."

"Yeah...okay...I know what you're talking about now," Burnett said.

"Jack Crenna—the old man who heard the footsteps—found one outside his window the morning after the Kenard killing," the soldier said. "I just thought there was a chance the killer could have dropped it when he ran past. I admit it's a long shot, but we don't seem to be coming up with much better."

Burnett shrugged. "Can't hurt to hang on to it," he said. "You never know, and you're right. We don't have anything better to go on." He began gathering up his papers, and Bolan and Vogt walked back to the table. The soldier waited while Vogt grabbed one of the coffee cups he'd just brought over. "Think I'll take one with me for the road," he said. "You want yours?"

Bolan shook his head.

The coffee had evidently gone cold while they talked to Burnett, because rather than sip it Vogt took two large gulps as they left the suite and started toward the car.

They were halfway across the lot when Vogt suddenly coughed, choked, dropped his coffee cup and briefcase, and fell to the ground clutching his belly.

BOLAN KNELT next to his partner on the asphalt. By now, Vogt had vomited all over his shirt, tie and coat. Mucus and thin lines of blood trailed from his nostrils, and he had rolled to his side in a fetal position. Bolan didn't know what it was or how it had happened, but he had seen such symptoms before.

Just like Officer Thurman in Los Angeles, Vogt had been poisoned.

Grabbing the man on the ground, the soldier hurried him to the car. There was no time for an ambulance, and the nearest hospital was almost ten miles away. Stretching Vogt out in the back seat, Bolan left the hotel parking lot, ran the red light at the intersection and headed up the on ramp to I-10.

In the back, Vogt made gurgling noises broken up by moans and gasps.

The morning traffic rush hadn't ended yet, and a half mile later Bolan's speed was cut down to thirty miles an hour. Cutting off the highway onto the shoulder, he floored the accelerator and sped past honking horns and hands upraised in obscene gestures. Remembering the red light in the back seat, he twisted, grabbed it off the floor where it had fallen when he laid Vogt inside and stuck the magnetic base on the roof of the car. The siren switch was under the radio, and he flipped it on.

With lights flashing and siren wailing, Bolan raced along the shoulder of the highway. In the back, Vogt was going into convulsions, alternately moaning, gasping, and then quieting as his body stiffened as if already in rigor mortis. The soldier glanced at his wristwatch as he cut back onto the highway and darted around a slow-moving farm truck. Even with the lights and siren he wasn't going to make it.

Stomping the accelerator, Bolan sped up, hitting the brake suddenly when a minivan—oblivious to the lights and noise—decided to change lanes and cut in front of him. He pulled onto the median, barely missing the rear bumper of the van and ripping the grass to shreds with his skidding tires. As soon as he was around the vehicle again, he cut back into the fast lane.

Which still wasn't fast. Bolan glanced over his shoulder to see that Vogt's face had turned apple red. He twisted the wheel back onto the shoulder and raced past the morning traffic. Ahead, he saw a car stalled on the side of the road, a man kneeling next to it using a tire tool and jack. Leaning harder on the gas pedal, he edged past a Honda Civic, this time scraping the front fender as he cut back into the right-hand lane ten feet in front of the car with the flat tire. He heard a frightened "What the—" as he raced past the man with the jack.

Bolan turned again, this time seeing that the red was gone from Vogt's face and his skin had turned a ghostly white. He glanced once more to his watch as they topped a rise. No, he wasn't going to make it. Ronnie Vogt was going to die right there in the car. From poison put in the coffee he'd drank.

Poison, Bolan knew, that had been meant for him.

Then, as they topped the hill and an exit appeared just ahead, the soldier saw the one-story gray brick building. Several signs were stacked on top of one another like branches of a tree but were unreadable at the distance. Of recent construction, the building had the look of a doctor's complex. On the other hand, it had the look of many office complexes that had nothing to do with medicine. It could house real estate, insurance, or any other sort of businesses. And he wouldn't know if he didn't take the exit.

Bolan glanced over his shoulder once more. Vogt was now an ashen gray and vomiting blood. He wasn't going to last all the way to the hospital. The Executioner twisted the wheel violently, crossing three lanes in front of furious drivers to whom the lights and siren meant nothing. If the gray brick building didn't have a doctor in it, maybe one of the others along the access road did. In any case, he had to chance it. Vogt wasn't going to make it all the way to the hospital. And if he was wrong, the Houston detective would be dead anyway.

Bolan hit the off-ramp at sixty miles per hour, his tires screaming as he leaned on the brake. The car fishtailed slightly as he neared the yield sign at the end of the ramp. Looking both ways, he saw no traffic for half a block and blew through the sign, twisting the wheel again, to the left this time, and pulling toward the stacked signs. At the speed he was going he couldn't read what they said. But two letters caught his eye.

M.D. followed at least one of the names on the bottom sign.

The tires squealed again as Bolan turned into the parking lot, barely slowing as he neared the closest entrance. There were no open parking spots nearby so he pulled to a halt behind a Chevrolet in front of the door and slammed the transmission into Park.

A moment later, he had the door open and was pulling Vogt out of the back. The Houston detective was jerking spasmodically. The blood still ran from his nose, and his skin alternated bloodshot and ashen. Carrying the man in his arms, Bolan sprinted through the door into the hallway.

The first office he came to announced W. W. Kruse, M.D. Obstetrics and Gynecology. He rammed the door open with his shoulder to find himself in a waiting room full of women. Rushing to the desk, he looked past the counter to see a receptionist wearing a light floral print dress. "Detective Belasko, Houston PD," Bolan announced. "This is Detective Vogt and he's been poisoned."

"You should take him to a hosp—"

"We don't have time to take him to a hospital!" Bolan shouted at the woman. "Get the doctor!"

An elderly man wearing a white lab coat had heard the commotion, and stuck his head into the reception area from somewhere in the rear of the complex. "Problem, Grace?" he asked.

Bolan repeated what he'd told the receptionist.

"I'm Dr. Kruse," the man said as he came through the door to the waiting area. "Let's get him next door to Dr. Blankenship. He's an internist. I'll get a gurney and—"

"We haven't got time for a gurney and we don't need one," Bolan said. He nodded toward the door he'd just come through. "Open it!"

The doctor did, standing back while Bolan carried Vogt back into the hall. Kruse directed them to the left, and led the way into a back door of the other doctor's office. They entered a hallway, walked past what appeared to be a lab and into a file chart room where several desks were located.

"Gina," Kruse said to a woman sitting at one of the desks. "We've got an emergency. Get Dr. Blankenship immediately."

The woman jumped up and ran out of the room.

A moment later a middle-aged man, balding on top with a fringe of gray-white hair around the ears, hurried in. He held the end of the stethoscope around his neck in his hand. "Bring him this way," he said and turned an about-face.

Bolan carried Vogt into an examining room and laid him on the table. The detective had gone limp in the soldier's arms. His eyes were closed and his breathing was shallow. Bolan jammed an index finger into his neck. The pulse was there. Barely.

"I'll stay and assist," Kruse said. He turned to Bolan as Blankenship began taking vital signs. "Any idea what he's ingested?"

Bolan stared at the man on the table. "I'm not certain," he said, "but I think it got put in his coffee."

Blankenship lifted the phone on the wall, punched a button and began barking orders to his nurses.

"Please," Kruse said, taking Bolan's elbow, "come out into the hall with me, won't you?"

Bolan followed him out.

"This is not my specialty by any means," Kruse said, "but I'd say your friend is very close to death. Very close." He spoke in a quiet, professional voice, careful not to be heard in the examining room. "If we don't know what substance to treat, I doubt we can find out in time to save him."

Bolan took a deep breath. Officer Thurman in Los Angeles had been killed with nicotine sulfate, and a little voice in the back of his brain was screaming at him, telling him that was what Vogt had ingested. But the Thurman murder wasn't related to the other police assassinations. Was it? It didn't appear to be, but the voice in his head nagged on. If they were related, even if the same man hadn't done both poisonings—and Sam "Wolfman" Underwood had been dead before Vogt drank the coffee—perhaps they had learned how to make the poison in the same place. If that was the case, and Bolan told the doctor, Vogt still might have a chance. But if he was wrong, and the hunch was incorrect, it would mean the man's death.

The answer was simple when he thought about it. It was just like his decision to take the exit for this building instead of going on to the hospital. It was a gamble. But again, even if he was wrong, Vogt was about to die anyway.

"Try treating him for nicotine sulfate."

A nurse elbowed her way past them carrying an IV drip and several syringes and vials.

Kruse frowned. "Are you sure about that?"

"No," Bolan said. "It's a guess. But it's an educated guess, and the only one I've got."

Kruse nodded, and Bolan could see that the man understood and required no further explanation. He was a doctor, and in their own way doctors were like soldiers and cops; they were men of action who handled emergency situations, and they understood hunches, guesses and those little voices that spoke inside their heads.

"All right then, Detective," Kruse said. "I'm going in to assist Dr. Blankenship. You can either wait here in the hall or in the waiting room."

Bolan nodded. He leaned back against the opposite wall as the door closed in front of him. With nothing to do but wait, he ran back over what had happened at the task force meeting. Vogt had gone to the phone to talk to Crenna. When he came back, he carried two cups of coffee. One for him, one for Bolan. Bolan had already had his fill and ignored it. Had Vogt drank any then? He didn't think so, but he couldn't remember for sure—it had been an insignificant detail and not worth making note of at the time. Then Burnett had called them over.

He reached up, scratching his head. That's when it had to have happened. That's when the poison had to have been added to the coffee. The pot itself hadn't been spiked or others would have been poisoned, too. The two cups had been in plain sight until he and Vogt had gone to talk to Burnett, leaving them on the table with their briefcases. He did remember Vogt taking a gulp or two right before they'd left. Had the Houston detective picked up his own cup then or the one in front of Bolan's chair? Again, Bolan couldn't remember. Probably his own. But what had he said? "Do you want yours?" Maybe that meant he had lifted Bolan's coffee off the table to hand it to him, planning to get his own cup as soon as he did. Then when the soldier declined, he might well have decided one cup was as good as the other and just drank from the one already in his hand.

Or had he just not paid any attention to the cups from the start?

Suddenly Bolan realized it made no difference. Whoever had decided to poison him would have taken no chances. He would have poisoned *both* cups to make sure.

Hurrying back into the file room, Bolan lifted the phone on an empty desk. He punched 9 to get out, then tapped in the number of the task force suite. When Amy answered, he said, "This is Belasko. Is Burnett still there?"

"Yes, sir, he was just leaving but I think I can catch him."

"Do it. Fast."

Bolan heard the phone being set down. A moment later, the Harris County deputy said, "Belasko? You tore out of here in a hell of a hurry. What's—"

"Burnett, go back in the conference room and see if the cup of coffee is still on the table where I was sitting."

"What? You want your coffee?"

"I'm at a medical complex a couple miles from you," Bolan said. "Vogt's been poisoned."

"Poisoned? Belasko, what is—"

"Burnett, just go get the coffee before it gets thrown out, okay?"

"Okay." Again, Bolan heard the phone being set down. Thirty seconds later, Burnett was back on the line. "I've got it."

"Get it over to your lab and have it analyzed. I'm particularly interested in seeing if it has nicotine sulfate in it, but have them check for any foreign substances."

"You think someone *here* poisoned Vogt?" Burnett asked, his voice incredulous.

"It had to be someone there," Bolan said. "No other way it could have gone down. They were after me but they got Vogt."

"Why would they be after you?"

"It's a long story and I'll tell you later. But somebody there put poison in both of our coffee cups."

"You know what that means?" Burnett asked.

"Yeah. The killers, or at least one of them, is a cop. And he's on the same task force that's looking for him."

THE EXECUTIONER returned to the hallway, resuming his position outside the door. Inside he could hear movement, conversation and the beeps and hums of medical equipment. Now and then a nurse—there appeared to be three of them working on Vogt along with Kruse and Blankenship—hurried in and out of the examining room. But he had no idea how it was going or if Vogt would live to see another sunrise.

Bolan was a man of action and waiting—unless in the line of duty—didn't come easy for him. He would've preferred to be in the examining room, helping, doing something, doing anything. But he knew he would just be in the way. So he would wait, unpleasant as it might be. It was the flip side of both courage and self-discipline. Some men had to learn to force themselves into dangerous action.

Others had to learn when to force themselves to stand by.

A half hour later, Kruse and Blankenship both came out into the hall. Blankenship shook his head, and at first the soldier thought it meant that Vogt hadn't pulled through. But what Kruse said next told him that Blankenship's gesture had been one of simple disbelief.

"That's one tough cop," Kruse said.

"It was touch and go for a while," Blankenship added. "And he's still not completely out of the woods. But I'd guess he's going to make it."

"When can I see him?" Bolan asked.

"Right now if you want to," Blankenship said. "In fact, he's asking for you. But he's weak, and it'd be better if you didn't wear him out."

The soldier walked between the two men in the white coats and entered the examining room. Vogt still lay on his back. His coat, shirt and tie had been cut away and lay in frazzled heaps on the floor in the corner. A tube ran down his throat, and he had IVs in both arms. His face was as white as the walls except for around the eyes where the skin had taken on a grayish-brown hue. When he saw Bolan, his eyes flickered, drawing him closer.

Bolan took up a place next to the Houston detective. "Don't try to talk," he said.

Vogt shook his head, the movement obviously exhausting. "Have...to..." he croaked out around the tube.

Bolan frowned. "What do you need to say?"

Vogt was breathing hard, his chest heaving up and down. "Jack...Crenna..."

It hit the Executioner like one of his own right crosses to the jaw. Whoever had poisoned Vogt had been at the task force meeting. He had heard everything said there, and that included the conversation about Crenna and the Szaball. If he had indeed dropped the exerciser as he ran away from the Kenard murder, the old man was as good as dead.

Unless Bolan could get to him first.

"Go...get..." Vogt croaked out.

But by then Bolan was out the door.

CLAYTON RUDD LEFT the meeting, forcing himself to whistle and telling himself his worries were just about over. Within an hour, Mike Belasko would be dead. The next day, the talk around the table would be about the poisoning, and everyone there would be a suspect, including him. But that was no problem if he could stand up to the heat. They had no more reason to suspect him than any of the other two dozen people in the room. Just the same, it didn't help his nerves and he reached into his pocket for the new Sza-ball. It wasn't there, and he was damn glad it wasn't. What if he'd taken it out of his pocket unconsciously at the meeting?

Rudd walked to his black Chevy Blazer, telling himself he didn't need the ball and that he didn't need to worry. Nobody could prove a thing. All he had to do was get through a simple routine interview in which he told them, no, he hadn't seen anyone acting suspiciously and no, he couldn't think of a reason anyone in the room would have wanted to kill the two men, and no, he didn't do it himself. Depending on who conducted the investigation, they might even try the hard-nosed approach. But he'd been grilled by better men than them. His mind flew back momentarily to his last few days in the Army. He'd withstood those interrogations, and he'd withstand this one, too. Eventually they might even try to force everyone into a polygraph exam. But by then, it should be too late to make any difference to him. He'd be using his real name—Clayton Rudd—again, and be sitting behind a big desk in Washington, D.C. Burnett and the others would never make the connection between him and the man who'd once been part of their rinky-dink task force.

Rudd smiled as he got into the Blazer. There was just one final detail to take care of, and then he'd ditch the rest of this shift and get started planning this big job for Killian. The task force never knew where he was, and his own boss didn't even keep tabs on him since he'd volunteered for this assignment. He couldn't have asked for a better gig than this one. As a member of the task force, he was kept up to date daily on everything that went on. If anybody even got a clue, he could be out of town before they pinned it on him. But so far, none of them seemed to be able to find their own ass with both hands.

Except Belasko. He was different.

Rudd glanced at his watch. By now, Belasko and that squirrelly little partner of his should be dead.

Two down, one to go. Jack Crenna. Bye-bye, Gramps. He had lived too long anyway. As soon as the old man was dead, it was on to the big Killian job. He'd already looked at the senator's instructions on the Internet post board, and he had some preparations to make before he left town for the job.

Rudd started the engine and pulled away from the motel. Two miles from the Drury, he pulled into the parking lot of a discount store and parked the Blazer at the side of the building. Then, boldly walking through the field of vehicles, he found a green Chevy Impala with the doors unlocked. After a quick look around, he cracked the steering column with his collapsible baton, used the blade of his pocketknife to start the engine and pulled the vehicle around to where the Blazer was parked.

No one paid any attention to him as he transferred his suitcase to the Impala.

Rudd pulled the Impala out of the parking lot. He had a purchase to make, and he didn't want it to be too near the Drury or the house where he was heading. So he drove four miles out of his way, pulling into a bicycle shop on the edge of downtown Houston. He chose a slick, moderately expensive bicycle with detachable wheels, picked up a plain white helmet and paid the salesman in cash. By removing the wheels and switching his suitcase to the back seat, the bike fit easily into the trunk of the vehicle. Fifteen minutes after he'd stopped, he was on the road again, heading back once again to the supermarket where'd he'd killed Kenard.

Rudd pulled into the same gasoline station where he'd changed clothes two nights earlier, got out of the car and pulled out his suitcase. He entered the men's room and locked the door behind him. It was morning rather than night, and broad daylight required a different kind of cammo than his navy blue night garb. Removing his sport coat, slacks and tie, he left on his white shirt and donned a pair of black shoes and a black tie.

Digging into the suitcase once more, Rudd grabbed the blue denim-looking Thunderwear holster. The rig consisted of a belt that ran around the body just below the waistline, over the shirttail but beneath the pants. At the front were two large pouches that could effectively conceal even large-frame handguns. From the suitcase, Rudd chose a matched pair of Colt Commanders with ambidextrous safeties and slide releases. Stuffing them into the pouches, he checked himself in the mirror. No problem.

Finally, from a side pocket of the suitcase he pulled out the *Book of Mormon*. Then, shoving the clothes he'd worn to the meeting into the suitcase, he hauled the case back to the Impala and returned it to the back seat.

Crenna hadn't been much of a problem up until now—just an old man, sick in bed, who'd heard Rudd running past his window after the shooting. As far as the task force was concerned, that running might or might not be related to the shooting death of Kenard. But now it was a different story. The old son of a bitch had found the ball he'd lost, and even though he knew it couldn't bear prints and that there was no way to trace it back to him, it was still just a little too close to home.

It needed to be taken care of. He never used a ball at work, but there was never any telling when somebody might bump into him off-duty and see him with one. It might still not draw any special attention—the exercisers were everywhere these days—but it was still something he didn't want to, or intend to, deal with or even worry about. Better to just whack the old man and be done with it.

Rudd chuckled as he got into the Impala and turned the key. According to what Vogt had said, the old fart had arthritis and was about a half-step out of the grave anyway. Hell, he'd be doing the old man a favor. Getting him out of all that pain.

Rudd drove six blocks past the old man's house before turning into an alley and parking. He scanned the passageway, making sure there were no curious eyes. Satisfied, he got out of the Impala, opened the trunk and removed the bicycle frame and wheels. A few minutes later, he had the bike put together again and with the *Book of Mormon* in hand, he was pedaling back toward Crenna's house.

BOLAN HAD LEFT the car in the middle of the parking lot, blocking two vehicles, when he carried Vogt into the doctors' complex. Now a young man and a middle-aged woman stood there waiting, ready to read him the riot act as he raced through the door toward the vehicle.

One look at the Executioner and they stepped back quietly, letting him pass.

Bolan jumped behind the wheel, started the engine and squealed out of the parking lot back onto I-10. He glanced at his watch. If the cop killer had left the task force meeting and driven directly to Crenna's house, he'd had plenty of time to get there by now. If that was the case, the old man was already dead. Bolan would have to pray that something had detained or sidetracked the assassin.

But who was he? Or could it even be a she? He visualized Cohlmia for a moment. And there was another woman besides her on the task force. Bolan hadn't actually seen the figure shooting at him that night at Buxton's house, except when the killer had been knocked to the floor in the kitchen. Even then, it had been dark, he had been only half-conscious from the blow to his temple, and the picture had lasted only a few brief seconds before the shadowy form took off through the backyard.

Could it have been a woman? No. His instincts told him it wasn't. The figure on the floor of the kitchen had been male. And Buxton had described a man only slightly smaller than the Executioner himself. Neither Cohlmia or the other female cop even came close to that description.

Bolan navigated the complex series of Houston highways, then turned off into the neighborhood where Kenard had been killed in the supermarket parking lot. Nearing a stop sign, he looked both ways and started to pull through, then noticed the black-and-white squad car just behind him in the rearview mirror. His badge would prevent a ticket or other problems from running the sign, but he couldn't afford the time it would take to explain. It would be faster just to stop, then go on. He hit the brakes and rolled the vehicle to a halt.

Bolan waited while a Mormon missionary—*Book of Mormon* in hand—rode by in front of him on a bicycle. He glanced into the rearview mirror again. The cop had his right turn signal on. Good. That should be the end of him.

The soldier turned left, careful to break no traffic laws that might cause a detainment. He passed the Mormon, his eyes still in the mirror as he watched the patrol car turn in the opposite direction. Driving on, he drew near Crenna's house on the side street that ran past the edge of the supermarket. Scanning the street, he saw no cars parked along the curb. If the killer was there, he hadn't parked his vehicle in front. He drove past the house. Quiet. A quick glance to the mirror again told him the black-and-white that had been behind him at the stop sign had disappeared.

But something else he saw bothered him, bringing an uneasy feeling to his soul.

Bolan felt his eyebrows lower in concentration. Something was wrong. But he couldn't put his finger on exactly what it was. He pulled past Crenna's house and turned into the same alley through which the killer had run the day he'd killed Kenard. Again, there were no vehicles parked in the area. Just large white trash containers and empty cardboard boxes.

Coming to a halt in the alley, Bolan parked next to the supermarket's back wall. He reached over the seat and pulled his briefcase into the front. As he had been all along while masquerading as a Houston cop, he wore the Glock 21 in a belt slide holster on his right hip. But now he wanted more firepower than the .45 could afford, and opening the latches, he pulled both the .44 Magnum Desert Eagle and the Beretta 93-R from under the false panel in the bottom of the case. There had been no room inside the briefcase for the 93-R's shoulder rig or the Eagle's Concealex holster, so he jammed both weapons into his belt beneath his jacket.

Exiting the car, Bolan started across the alley to the back of Crenna's house. Out of the corner of his eye, he saw the Mormon missionary on the bicycle pedal by the entrance of the alley and disappear around the side of the supermarket. The Executioner had just reached the edge of the alley and was stepping onto the grass in Crenna's backyard when it hit him.

He had seen Mormon missionaries the world over. They always dressed the same, just like the one he had just seen pedal by. They always rode bicycles like this man had, and they always carried the *Book of Mormon* with them. They had always worn a plain white bicycle helmet as well.

The fact was, they always looked exactly like the man he had just seen. Except for one thing.

The Executioner had never seen one of the Mormons working

alone. They always rode in pairs. He supposed there could be exceptions but if there were, he had never seen one, and the coincidence made him uneasy. He thought back to the man on the bicycle. There was something else about him. Although Bolan couldn't have identified him, there was still something vaguely familiar about the quick flash of face he had seen.

Bolan glanced back down the alley, but it was empty. Reaching under his jacket, he wrapped his fingers around the grips of the Desert Eagle stuck in his belt. Then, moving quietly and cautiously, he left the alley, stepped over a small fence and began crossing Crenna's yard toward the back door.

Until he heard the sudden explosion of a gunshot inside the house.

Then he ran.

7

Rudd neared the house, keeping his eyes straight ahead as he pedaled. In his peripheral vision, he watched the unmarked Houston PD car pass him, then slow as it neared the alley behind the supermarket. He had seen the car when he rode by the stop sign but hadn't really taken notice of it—he had been far more interested in the black-and-white patrol car right behind it. Were they together? It didn't look like it. Not now at least. The cruiser had gone the other way after the stop.

But when the unmarked car had passed him he'd caught a quick glimpse of the man behind the wheel. And that quick glimpse caused the hair on the back of his arms to stand up.

Belasko? How could that be? By now, he and Vogt should both be dead. What had gone wrong?

Rudd peddled on, straining to see the man through the driver's-side window as the car turned into the alley. Maybe it wasn't him after all. He couldn't be sure. But if it was, it meant he had not drunk his coffee. Why? Had he seen Rudd drop the solution in with the eyedropper? No. If that had been the case, the big Houston detective would have confronted him then and there.

Rudd quit pedaling, gliding along on the bicycle as he neared Crenna's house. There were any number of reasons the man might not have come back for his coffee. The most likely was that after he and Vogt had gone over to talk to Burnett they had simply forgotten all about the cups on the table. No. They wouldn't have forgotten. They had left their briefcases right next to the cups.

A cold chill shot up Rudd's spine to the top of his head. Part of him knew he was overanalyzing things. It didn't matter why the man hadn't drunk the poison as long as he didn't see Rudd putting it in his coffee, and if he had, Rudd would already know about it. Maybe they had just decided they didn't want any more coffee. They'd had enough and left it there.

Rudd began pedaling again and realized he was working the spine of the book in his hand as if it were a Szaball. Okay, fact number one: the man was alive. Fact number two: he was there. At Crenna's house. Why? Had he come interview the old man again? Had Crenna said more during the brief phone conversation he'd had with Vogt than Vogt had mentioned when he'd returned to the meeting? If so, why wasn't Vogt there, too? Maybe Vogt had the coffee but his partner hadn't. But if that was the case, wouldn't he be with Vogt now? He wouldn't just leave the man dying and go off on a routine interview, would he?

Nearing the front lawn of the house, Rudd slowed once more, trying to sort things out in his mind. They knew about the Szaball Crenna had found in his yard. Vogt had told the whole task force about that. But did they know more? Did they know about him? Did they know that one of their own task force members was actually named Clayton Rudd instead of the name they knew him by, and that he was responsible for many of the cop killings?

Rudd's thoughts swirled in his head with questions he couldn't answer. But they didn't matter—at least not compared to the real question and that was whether this was a trap. Had the man come, knowing that the killer who dropped the Szaball would go after Crenna?

Question upon question upon question flew through Rudd's muddled mind, and he decided to ride past the house. If it was really him in the car, he might have parked in the alley. Maybe he could get a better look and make sure. Rudd used the back of his wrist to wipe sweat from his eyebrows as he steered the bicycle past the house with one hand. Maybe he was just imagining things. Maybe what he'd seen wasn't even a Houston PD car. The car had a radio antenna. But lots of cars had radio antennas these days. For all he knew, the driver might be some insurance or real-estate agent.

Rudd was almost convinced that he had imagined the whole thing when he reached the mouth of the alley and saw the detective get out of the car. There was no mistaking it this time. Big, square-shouldered and rugged-looking. It was him.

It took all of Rudd's willpower to pedal past the alley and disappear around the corner of the supermarket. He came to a halt as soon as he was out of sight and leaned against the bricks along the wall. He forced himself to consider his options. The man hadn't noticed him—of that, he was sure. He could ride on, circle to the Impala and come back for Crenna another time. The cops weren't going to put the old man under protective custody just because he'd found a rice-filled rubber ball. But what if his phone call had been to tell Vogt he had more information, and that's why the detective was there now? Had he seen Rudd run by that day, and was just now working up the courage to give his description?

The last thought made up Rudd's mind for him. His attempt to poison Belasko had failed, and he still needed to kill the detective as well as the old man. There they were, both in the same house, and no witnesses. He wouldn't get a better chance, and once it was over he wouldn't have to worry about it anymore.

Stepping onto the pedals once more, Rudd rode quickly back across the alley and dropped the bike just outside Crenna's front door. He hurried up the steps and started to knock, then tried the knob. Unlocked. Sticking the *Book of Mormon* under his left arm, he reached down into the Thunderwear holster and drew his right-hand .45-caliber Colt Combat Commander. He was grinning at how easy it was all going to be as he opened the door.

Crenna wasn't in the living room, but Rudd heard shuffling footsteps somewhere in the back of the house. That meant the detective had already knocked at the back door, and the old man was heading there to answer. Rudd would simply creep silently back that way, wait behind Crenna until he opened the door and let the detective in, then shoot them both before they even knew he was in the house.

As quickly as he could without making any noise, Rudd crossed the worn carpet of the living room, finalizing his plan as he went. Shoot the cop first, he told himself. He passed a bookshelf that had been turned into a shrine for some old lady. Photographs of the woman, some with Crenna, others by herself, filled the shelves. Rudd moved on. Put two in his chest, then two more in his head to make sure. Then he'd probably still have time to lay down and take a nap before the old fart who'd found his ball had figured out what was going on.

Rudd passed the bookshelf-shrine and moved into the dining room. A door was set in the wall to the side. He could see part of a hallway that had to lead back to the bedrooms and the kitchen. More confident how, the smile on his face grew as he started to turn into the hall.

The smile disappeared when he saw what was waiting for him.

DESERT EAGLE IN HAND, Bolan lowered his shoulder against the door. It gave way at the same time the second gunshot met his ears. Racing through the opening into a utility room, he saw the door into the rest of the house just to his left. He pivoted that way and turned right into the kitchen.

The dishwasher door was open, and the racks holding dishes, glasses and coffee cups had been pulled out of the machine, blocking half of the small kitchen. As a third shot blasted from the living room, the Executioner hurdled over the obstacle and turned into the hall.

A low moan escaped someone's lips as the explosions died down. Bolan turned the corner into the hall and crouched as the house went quiet. Slowly he made his way down the corridor. The moan sounded again, then weak words drifted toward him.

"Please...Belasko...help me...."

Bolan didn't know who had said the words, but it wasn't Crenna. He remembered the old man's voice, and remembered that it didn't sound nearly as old as he was. What this voice sounded like was someone else *trying* to sound old.

Dropping to one knee, Bolan took his time as he edged an eye around the door frame. He stopped as soon as he saw Crenna. The old man lay on his back on the floor. The carpet around the him was soaked with dark blood, and an old World War II-era Government Model 1911A1 pistol lay a few feet from his outstretched hand.

But Crenna was still alive—at least for the moment. Bolan could see his chest heaving up and down. His breathing was labored, and a red mist of spittle blew from his mouth with every exhalation. Lung shot.

The Executioner moved back behind the wall. What had happened was obvious. Crenna had a gun, and had met the intruder with it. The first two rounds the Executioner had heard had been from that old war relic. He hadn't had time to look, but he'd be surprised if the living room walls didn't show bullet holes where the arthritic old man's rounds had missed their target.

The third gunshot had come from the killer. It was the one that had found its mark in Crenna's lung and dropped him to the floor.

Slowly, Desert Eagle ready, Bolan inched his eye back around the corner. He moved farther out to see the rest of the room. Each inch he moved increased his range of vision. But each inch exposed his head more, as well.

Suddenly Bolan caught a quick glimpse of the man he had taken for a Mormon missionary crouching near the front door. The man held a gun in both hands and was half hidden behind the edge of the divan. The Executioner caught only a flash-sight of the man's face but again it looked familiar.

Before Bolan could focus more specifically on the man's face a barrage of pistol fire blasted into the hallway just over his head. He threw himself backward, away from the flying lead and splinters of wood and plaster from the wall. Then the same voice, stronger and sarcastic, and no longer trying to sound old, said, "Come on, Belasko, help the old bastard." The taunt was followed by another round of fire.

The Executioner was forced halfway back to the kitchen to

avoid the rounds that penetrated the thin wall. More chunks of plaster blew from the walls, and a framed photograph of Crenna and his wife fell off the wall, the glass shattering at Bolan's feet. Angling the Desert Eagle by guesswork, the soldier sighted at a spot on the wall and squeezed the trigger. A mammoth 240-grain semi-jacketed hollowpoint round flew from the Eagle and drilled through the wall, into the living room.

The house became quiet once more. Bolan knew his shot hadn't hit the man posing as a Mormon missionary. He had been shooting blind and hadn't expected it to.

He just wanted the man to know he was still in the game.

The Executioner waited but no return fire was forthcoming. Quickly, drawing from the experience of more battles than he could remember, he considered the situation. What would the man do next? Whoever he was, he knew Bolan's face, and he knew his alias. How he knew those things was easy to figure out.

The killer was a fellow member of the task force.

But did he think Bolan knew his face and name as well? If he did, he couldn't afford to leave this house with the Executioner still breathing. The man had gone out of his way to disguise himself as a Mormon, and if he suspected the disguise had successfully hidden his features, he might flee out the front door any moment. He would know that all of the task force members would be suspects in the poisoning, and might think he could fade the heat long enough to complete whatever master plan of which he was part.

And there had to be some bigger plan. There had to be some greater end to all this than just seeing how many cops could be killed. Whoever was behind all this—group or individual—whoever was sending assassins out to kill police officers, had to have some agenda.

Another barrage of bullets smashed the walls in the hallway, and they told Bolan more than the killer probably knew. The man had been firing .45s. Not only were the explosions louder than 9 mms or .40s, one of the ejected brass casings had bounced into the hallway after being ejected from the weapon. And Bolan had counted the other man's rounds. Seventeen. More than twice as many as a standard Colt-pattern .45 auto, and three more than the high-capacity Glocks or ParaOrdinance pistols held. The Executioner had also listened closely during the pauses in fire and had heard no tell-tale sounds of a magazine exchange.

What that told him was that the phony Mormon had at least two pistols with 8-round or higher magazines. Now, as the noise died down once more, the distinctive sound of a steel mag being slammed up the butt of a weapon met his ears. Bolan's guess was that the man had a pair of Colts, either full-size 1911s or one of the more compact models. And he was using the newer 8-round magazines. Reloading after seventeen shots meant the killer had left one in the chamber during the magazine change. The sound of another magazine being inserted, then a slide ramming home, confirmed Bolan's suspicions.

The Executioner's eyes narrowed as he considered his options. He could outwait the man, counting shots again, then move during the next reload. That would be the best plan of attack if the pseudo-Mormon was bent on seeing this to the bitter end. But he also had to consider Crenna, and each second that dragged on meant the old man on the floor was closer to death.

Another thunderstorm of fire blew his way as the Executioner made his decision. He waited for it to die down, then pulled the Glock from his holster. He had carried the Beretta and Desert Eagle in his briefcase with no room for holsters or extra ammo. With a deep breath, he raised the Glock in his left hand and began pulling the trigger, firing as fast as his finger would move. Dust and chunks of plaster flew from the wall as the rounds penetrated it on their way to the living room. The wooden door frame, already in ruins from the cop killer's assaults, finally splintered entirely off the wall. Bolan angled his shots well over where Crenna lay on the floor, and as soon as the slide locked back on an empty chamber he jammed the weapon into his waistband and sprinted forward.

Bolan dived forward onto his belly as he reached the doorway. He slid along the carpet, the Desert Eagle gripped in both hands, the barrel pointed at the end of the couch but ready to swing either way in case the enemy had changed his position. He came to a halt next to where Crenna still lay gasping for air on the floor.

But other than Bolan and Crenna, the room was empty. The front door stood open and the storm door was swinging back on its spring.

"He's...gone...." Crenna gasped.

Through the open door, the Executioner saw the man in the white shirt and black pants pedal past the opening on the bicycle. He raised the Desert Eagle. But as his sights found their target, a car drove by right behind him on the street. He knew the hand cannon would penetrate easily through the fake missionary, and he was forced to stop his trigger pull halfway back.

Bolan rose to his knees and knelt over the old man. Crenna had taken only the one shot through the chest. A red mist shot from the hole every time he choked for air. He still had a chance if he got medical help. Reaching down, he ripped the old man's shirt down the front, then tore a fistful of the soft flannel away from his body and jammed it into the hole. "Hold this," he told the man. "Direct pressure."

Crenna nodded. Then he looked up and smiled. "Remember... that...old commercial...?" he asked the soldier.

Bolan had already grabbed the phone and was dialing 911. "Don't try to talk," he said. "I'm calling for help."

Crenna grinned up at him. "On my way to join Elsie," he said.

Bolan gave the operator the address and a description of the wound, then dropped the phone. He was still going after the killer, but he stopped to check Crenna's wound one last time. Pressing the old man's hand tighter over the cloth, he said, "They're on the way. Hold this until they get here."

"The old...commercial...dammit," Crenna panted.

"What?" Bolan asked as he rose back to his feet.

"...and my...Timex is...still ticking." The old man grinned.

Bolan dashed out of the back door toward his car.

TIRES SQUEALING, the Executioner backed out of the alley and twisted the wheel in the direction he'd seen the man on the bicycle heading. Three blocks ahead, still on the same street, he could see the dark figure pedaling as fast as he could. He floored the accelerator and the sedan shot forward. In less than ten seconds he had dropped the man's lead to two blocks. So far, the phony Mormon hadn't seen him.

Bolan drew the Desert Eagle from his belt with his left hand, guiding the car with his right. He raced on, planning to run the stop sign at the end of the next block. But as he neared, a motorcycle suddenly appeared in the intersection and he was forced to slam on the brakes. The tires screamed to a halt, and ahead he saw the killer jerk his head around at the commotion.

The element of surprise was gone.

As soon as the motorcycle had crossed in front of him, Bolan floored the gas pedal again. A trail of rubber thirty feet long marked his passage as he resumed pursuit. A few seconds later the fake Mormon's lead had dropped to a block and Bolan leaned out the window, the Desert Eagle outstretched in his hand. Curling his arm around the windshield, he sighted at the bicycle. He wanted the man alive. Dead men could tell him nothing, and by now the Executioner knew the story of the assassinated police officers didn't start and end with this one man. Aiming low at the rear tire of the bicycle, he had prepared to squeeze the trigger when his own front tires hit a bump. The sights on the big Magnum gun shot up and over the fleeing man's head, right onto the second-story of a house ahead.

Bolan pulled the weapon back inside the car. An expert shot could do remarkable things with a pistol. But an expert shot with any sense recognized the possible from the impossible.

Ahead, the man on the bicycle suddenly turned sideways, his right arm extended behind him. Bolan heard two quick explosions as the man pulled the trigger. One of the rounds flew harmlessly past the sedan. The other struck the windshield on the passenger's side, blasting through the glass into the seat next to him and sending cracks across the glass.

The Executioner dropped lower behind the wheel, leaning harder on the accelerator as he drew within two houses of the bicycle. The cop killer fired one more round, hurriedly over his shoulder, then suddenly turned into a driveway.

Bolan hit the brakes, fishtailing down the street past the driveway before he could get the car stopped. But as he flashed past, he saw the bogus missionary ride up to the fence between two houses, leap off the bike and vault the barrier. When the car had finally ground to a halt, the Executioner jumped out and raced after him.

The abandoned bicycle lay on its side, the front wheel in the air and still spinning, as Bolan sprinted past it. Through the fence he saw the man in the black slacks and white shirt vault another fence at the rear of the property. Bolan raised the Desert Eagle, but again the man had dropped to the ground before he could fire. Propping his free hand on the top of the fence, the Executioner swung his legs over the steel links and continued pursuit.

The yard the man entered was littered with swing sets, a jungle gym and other children's toys. Bolan raced toward the fence. On the other side he saw his prey sprint up the slick surface of a child's slide just inside the wooden fence separating the front yard from the back. When he reached the top he leaped over the solid barrier and dropped out of sight.

Bolan cleared the chain links in the back, then followed the man's path, hurdling an inflated plastic wading pool with rubber ducks floating in the water. Reaching the bottom of the slide, he started up. He was halfway to the top when the trap about to be sprung occurred to him.

Bolan shifted his weight slightly as he neared the top of the slide. Then, instead of leaping over the fence as the cop killer had done, he thrust upward and lunged out for the roof of the house three feet to the side. As he'd known it would, an explosion sounded from the ground directly behind the fence. He twisted in the air to see the man holding the upraised Colt Commander, a look of shock on the half-recognized face.

Hitting the canted shingles on his back, the Executioner felt air rush from his lungs. But he ignored the pain, twisting again to get the Desert Eagle around to fire. The man on the ground turned to flee a heartbeat before the .44 Magnum round left the barrel, and the big hollowpoint passed an inch behind his back before drilling into the grass just beyond him.

A good twelve feet from the ground, Bolan rolled off the pitched roof and dropped to his feet on the grass. He felt as if someone had beaten him across the back and kidneys with a two-by-four. The escaping man with the Colt Commander was a half block away now, and running full speed. Bolan started to raise the Desert Eagle, then saw the children standing in the yard just beyond the running man. They had frozen in place directly in the line of fire and stared, openmouthed, at the oncoming man with the gun.

Bones, muscles and tendons screaming protest, Bolan ran on. For a moment he feared the man he was chasing might stop and take one or more of the children hostage. But the fleeing form turned the corner ahead of them and disappeared.

The Executioner raced on, remembering the trap the man had set for him at the fence and slowing as he neared the corner. Three feet before the edge of the house, he threw himself forward onto his shoulder, half expecting another shot to be fired. But the only noise was the excited chattering of the children, and he rolled back to his feet, the Desert Eagle before him.

The man dressed like a Mormon missionary seemed to have disappeared.

Bolan ran on, his eyes darting between the houses as he neared the end of the block. A man across the street stood holding a garden hose. The unusual excitement in this quiet neighborhood had caused him to turn away from his flower bed, and he now stood watering the concrete of his driveway. His eyes were frozen on a spot ahead, and when the Executioner followed that gaze he saw an alley between the two streets.

Racing that way, the Executioner heard a car engine turn over. He couldn't be sure but it sounded as if it were parked roughly halfway down the alley. Cutting across the street, he dashed into the narrow corridor, raising the Desert Eagle to shoulder level.

The green Impala roared to life as Bolan stopped just inside the mouth of the alley. Through the windshield, behind the wheel, he could see the masquerading Mormon as the man threw the car into gear. But again the fates where against him. Though the man looked him squarely in the eye, the sun reflecting off the glass distorted his features and rendered them unrecognizable. For a moment, time seemed frozen. Then dirt and gravel shot backward, away from the tires, and with a mighty roar of the engine the car shot toward him.

Bolan aimed down the barrel of the mammoth Desert Eagle, dropping the sights on the driver. He'd have preferred taking the man alive, but that no longer seemed an option. It was either this or let him get away. He would have to hope that when he learned who the murderous member of the task force was he would also find leads to whoever else was behind the cop killings.

The Executioner squeezed the trigger and the massive Magnum

pistol roared. But just as he did, the car dipped into a pothole in the asphalt alleyway. The high-speed round hit the thick glass at an angle and skidded off. Bolan fired again, lowering his aim, and this time the car came up out of the hole and the round crashed through the grille.

But it had done no serious damage. The Impala raced on, forcing the Executioner to dive to the side to avoid being run down.

Bolan rolled to his feet as the vehicle hit the end of the alley, firing a rapid string of rounds that hit the trunk and back windshield. The glass exploded, but the car barely slowed as it squealed its way into the turn and shot off down the street.

The soldier ran after it, taking up a stance in the middle of the street. As the car sped away, he fired a final round and saw it take out the left rear taillight.

Then, suddenly, two black-and-white squad cars rounded the corner in front of him. He heard another engine and turned to see a third Houston PD vehicle grind to a halt to his rear. A split second later he was surrounded by blue uniforms who had taken cover behind doors and engine blocks and aimed shotguns and pistols his way.

"Drop the weapon!" one of the cops roared.

"I'm a Houston detective!" Bolan shouted back. Slowly he started to reach into his jacket for his badge case.

"Drop the damn weapon!" the same voice screamed. "That ain't no Houston PD gun in your hand!"

Bolan let the Desert Eagle fall slowly to the end of his arm. Then, turning slightly, he tossed it onto the grass of the yard next to him. His jaw set firm in determination, he watched as the Chevy Impala turned the corner a half mile away and disappeared.

HOUSTON DETECTIVE Mike Belasko was under suspension. But that didn't have much effect on the Executioner. It was time for him to give up that identity.

Bolan drove swiftly along the highway, cutting in and out of the lanes. In addition to his vehicle, Houston's Internal Affairs Division had taken both his Glock and the Desert Eagle until they could complete their investigation of the shooting. He had been confined to desk duty until the investigation had been completed.

Among other things, IAD was particularly interested in why he had used the unauthorized .44 Magnum gun.

The suspension would have been nothing more than a joke to Bolan, had it not been that he wanted to be at the next task force meeting. He needed to see who showed up, who didn't, and particularly who might show up and act strangely.

Or who might show up and try to kill him again.

So Bolan had simply turned the shortcomings of bureaucracy against itself. Aaron Kurtzman had hacked back into the Houston PD computer files and authorized annual leave for him over the next two weeks. Task force coordinator Archie Burnett, however, had gotten a different memo from the Harris County sheriff advising him that Houston Internal Affairs had completed their investigation, ruled the shooting good and Bolan would continue work with the task force as usual. Since Burnett was with Harris County, he couldn't have cared less what went on with Internal Affairs within the city of Houston, and had no reason to check into the matter further.

The soldier had rented a car that morning—a Pontiac Bonneville—and now he urged as much power out of the unmarked car as he could get, glancing occasionally at the open map on the seat next to him. Only one man who had been present at the task force meeting the day before had been absent that morning. A. K. Spencer. Spencer had an excuse—it was his regular day off. But Bolan was still suspicious. The Chambers County deputy sheriff had also been absent when the Executioner first arrived—out with the "flu." And a quick computer check by Kurtzman had shown that Spencer had been either off duty, on annual leave or sick days when many of the other police assassinations took place.

But more than such circumstantial evidence, Bolan trusted his instincts, and those instincts now told him he had finally found the man he'd been looking for. Among other things, Spencer fell into the broad description Buxton had given of the gunman at the supermarket. And the deputy hadn't looked like a man just getting over the flu when he'd returned during Bolan's second day on the job. Perhaps most of all, the Executioner remembered the small cut he'd had on his face—a cut he attributed to shaving. There had been no reason for the mark to register in Bolan's brain then, but now that he remembered it he also recalled a small, yellowish-green bruise sticking out from one side of the Band-Aid on the man's face. His skin looked like it had been scraped. But not with a razor.

Bolan saw the exit sign ahead and changed lanes. The fact was, the mark on Spencer's face looked exactly like one that might be left if a gun barrel had scraped across his chin. A gun like a Desert Eagle. And Bolan remembered doing that very thing to the man in Buxton's house that night. He had been only half-conscious at the time but his memory of the small, then-insignificant event was distinct.

The bottom line was that the cut on Spencer's face hadn't come from shaving any more than Bolan's own injury had been sustained by a fall in the shower.

Bolan drove on, seeing signs announcing Winnie, Stowell and Beaumont farther on. He passed both pastureland and rice fields, then he took the exit ramp and left the highway. Another of Kurtzman's early-morning tasks had been to get him Spencer's home address. And the deputy sheriff was listed as living in one of the newer apartment complexes within the town.

Fast food restaurants, motels, gas stations and other travel-related establishments lined the street onto which the Executioner found himself. Winnie might not be able to boast more than five thousand full-time inhabitants, but almost ten times that number passed through the town each day. Glancing at the map again, Bolan cut away from the industrial main drag and entered a residential area.

The Intracoastal Apartments were made up of a dozen identical redbrick buildings with wood-shingled roofs. Each looked to house eight apartments—four downstairs, another four on the second floor. The soldier slowed, passing buildings marked A, B and C before parking in front of D. He didn't want to get too close and take the chance of Spencer seeing him through a window. According to Kurtzman, the deputy lived in apartment E-3.

Bolan got out and walked up to the apartment house in front of him, quickly making mental notes. An open-air hallway, decorated with plants and flower beds, ran through the center of the building. The front doors faced the courtyard. Quickly he circled the iron stairs leading up, noting that apartments 1 through 4 were downstairs. Apartment 3 was at the end where he'd parked. Which meant Spencer had the lower-level apartment on the southeast end in the next building.

Bolan got back into the car and drove past Building E, his face shielded by the sun visor. He didn't expect to come across a green Impala—that car had been reported stolen, then found abandoned earlier this morning. But parked near apartment number 3, among numerous other vehicles, was a black Chevrolet Blazer. In the bottom left-hand corner of the windshield he saw the small sticker that read Texas Sheriff's and Peace Officers Association. A large seven-point star was in the center. That, in itself, would have told him the vehicle was Spencer's. But he wanted to make sure. He couldn't afford to follow the wrong car.

Bolan drove on, circling the complex, then taking up the same spot he'd parked in earlier. Reaching into the back seat, he pulled his briefcase into the front, opened it and pulled out the cellular phone. Plugging it into a small portable scrambling device, he tapped in the number for Stony Man Farm once more. When he had Kurtzman on the phone, he gave the computer man the license number on the Blazer. Seconds later he was assured that the vehicle was indeed listed to A. K. Spencer of Winnie, Texas.

Bolan was just hanging up when Spencer suddenly emerged from his apartment carrying a suitcase. Dressed in blue jeans and a navy blue T-shirt, the deputy walked swiftly to the Blazer, unlocked the tailgate and tossed the bag inside. Then, leaving the tailgate door open, he walked back toward the apartment again.

The soldier reached into the briefcase and pulled out the electronic tracking device. Roughly the size of a half-dollar coin, it could be fixed to anything metal using the rare earth magnets inset at the back. He had planned to hide it under Spencer's bumper. And he still planned to do just that, but he was going to have to be quick about it. Wherever the man was going, he was about to leave.

Exiting the Pontiac, Bolan stayed low behind the row of parked cars as he hurried toward the Blazer. As soon as he'd passed Building D, he could see into the courtyard of Spencer's building. The door to the apartment was wide open. A second later Spencer appeared carrying another suitcase in one hand, a key ring in the other.

Bolan dropped behind the cars, holding the tracker between his index and middle fingers as he crawled to the back of the Blazer. As he reached the bumper, he could hear Spencer's footsteps nearing the vehicle. Reaching up, he jammed the tracker behind the bumper and felt the magnets grab hold. But the footsteps were almost upon him now. There was no way to get back to his own car without being seen.

Parked next to the Blazer was a rebuilt Dodge Charger. Bolan didn't hesitate. Rolling beneath the vehicle, he caught a flash of blue denim rounding the front of the Blazer. Not a foot away from where the Executioner lay, Spencer walked past and threw the other bag into the rear of the vehicle, then closed the door. A moment later, he was backing the Blazer out of the lot.

Bolan rolled out from beneath the Charger but stayed low, watching over the trunk of the old car. He waited until the Blazer had turned out of the complex and disappeared into the traffic before jogging back to his own car.

TRAFFIC WAS HEAVY and the drive to the airport took longer than Bolan would have liked. But with the tracker firmly in place, he wasn't worried. He had called Grimaldi as soon as he'd gotten back to the car, and the pilot already had Spencer's vehicle pegged on the screen in the cockpit. Now it was simply a matter of getting into the air and following the man.

No, he wasn't worried about losing Spencer. But right now, he had another problem.

For several miles, as the Executioner had neared the airport, he had noticed a dark green Nissan in his rearview mirror. It looked like a man behind the wheel, but with the sun at the angle it was Bolan couldn't even be sure of that. What he was sure of, however, was that the car had had plenty of opportunities to either pass him or fall farther behind. But it hadn't. It stayed roughly ten lengths behind him, and always kept two to four other vehicles between them. It changed lanes shortly after he did each time, as if the driver didn't want to be caught flat-footed if he suddenly took an exit.

In other words, it looked like a tail. A fairly good tail by someone who knew what he was doing, but a tail nonetheless. So who was it? Houston Internal Affairs? Bolan doubted it. He'd kept his eye out for them ever since they'd arrived at the scene of the shooting and had seen no signs that they were following him. They'd set a hearing for him in two weeks, and seemed more interested in the Desert Eagle than anything else. Well, they already had his gun. For the time being, anyway.

Bolan glanced at the Nissan again. Did Spencer have a confederate on these cop killings? A partner who might have seen the soldier plant the device and decided to follow him? Possible. But improbable. He had searched the parking lots thoroughly before getting out to plant the tracker, and had seen nothing.

Bolan changed lanes twice for no reason and watched the Nissan do the same behind him. The truth was, he didn't have any idea who might want to follow him at this point.

But he intended to find out.

Following the signs to the airport, the soldier turned away from the hangar where Grimaldi waited and toward one of the hourly parking garages. He stopped at a red-and-white-striped electronic arm, took the ticket that came out of the machine and drove on as soon as the electronic arm moved up and out of his way. In the rearview mirror he could see the green Nissan in line behind a red panel van.

Bolan drove up the ramp to the second level, stopping at a stop sign, then turning left into the semilit garage. Quickly he parked in a No Parking zone and jumped out. Keeping his back to the wall, he stayed in the shadows and moved to the edge of the opening. From where he stood, he was ten feet from the stop sign. But unless someone looked closely, he wouldn't be noticed.

Drawing the Beretta, he held it down at his side against his leg and waited.

The panel van pulled up to the stop sign, stopped, then turned past without noticing him. A few seconds later, the Nissan appeared.

Bolan started moving just before the dark green car came to a halt. By the time the vehicle had stopped, he had the driver's door open and the sound suppressor on the end of the barrel jammed under the chin of the driver.

The man behind the wheel was caught completely off guard. He froze, his eyes glued downward to where the suppressor smashed into his neck. His face was a ghostly white, and at first the Executioner thought the blood had drained as the fear rushed in to take its place. Then he saw who the man was, and realized terror was only one reason the man was so pale.

He had also recently been poisoned.

Finally Ronnie Vogt found his voice. "Well, Belasko, you gonna shoot me or what?" he asked quietly.

Bolan stuffed the Beretta back into his shoulder rig and stepped back. "Find a place to park, Vogt," he said. "I'll explain things to you as we drive."

8

"You're supposed to be in the hospital," Bolan said as he got behind the wheel of the Pontiac again.

"You don't ever do what you're supposed to do," Vogt said as he waited for the soldier to unlock his door. "Why should I?"

Bolan hit the electronic button and the passenger's door clicked. "So, where'd you pick me up?" he asked.

"I parked outside the task force meeting and waited."

"You followed me all the way to Winnie?"

"Winnie?" Vogt sounded surprised as he took the passenger's seat in Bolan's car. "That's where you went? Hell, no, you lost me on the highway. I spent an hour trying to figure out where you might have turned off and finally gave up. I'd pulled off and was coming up the ramp to go home when you suddenly whizzed by again, going back toward Houston." He shook his head. "Pure blind luck."

"You may not feel all that lucky when you find out what you've gotten into," the soldier said as he started the engine. "Why'd you follow me in the first place?"

Vogt shrugged. "There were things about you that didn't add up. I mean, first off you show up and, before you're even introduced you disarm that dope dealer in the booking room like something out of a Bruce Lee movie. Then the next day you look like somebody took a sledgehammer to your head, and you've got this story that you slipped in the shower. It didn't make sense to me. Call me crazy, but I just can't picture you slipping on a bar of soap."

Bolan guided the car down out of the lot, paid the man in the ticket booth for an hour's parking and turned toward the private plane hangar. Vogt, he knew, was searching for concrete reasons why he'd suspected his new partner led a double life. The truth was, the Houston detective was simply utilizing the instincts he'd developed over the years—instincts, similar to Bolan's own, which simply told him when something wasn't quite right.

"Then you take off to go to the doctor," Vogt added, "and the next thing I know you're in L.A."

The Executioner didn't ask how the man sitting next to him knew that. He knew he wouldn't have to. Vogt was grinning so wide he'd bust if he didn't tell Bolan how he'd found out about the quick trip to California.

"I've got a friend in L.A. homicide," Vogt said. "After Burnett read your praises from LAPD yesterday, it sounded as if you'd done more than just give them some tip over the phone. So I called out there, and my buddy did some checking. You were there, and word is you left more than a few bad guys in your wake." He paused a moment and the smile faded. "But you're going to catch all kinds of heat for not sticking around to clean it all up on paper. My friend says they're drafting a letter to the Houston chief right now."

Bolan turned onto the access road leading to the hangars, thinking briefly of Aaron Kurtzman again. "Tell your friend not to worry. I've got my own friend who can handle the letter."

"You don't seem too concerned," Vogt said. He went silent for a moment, as if he weren't sure whether he should ask the next question. Finally, he said, "That's because you're not really even a Houston cop, right?"

Bolan shook his head as he pulled up to the hangar. "No. I'm not a cop. Houston or anywhere else."

"So," Vogt said. "What are you? Fed?"

"Not exactly."

"Spook? CIA? Defense? What?"

Bolan turned to him. "Ronnie," he said, "I've told you all I can about me. Just keep in mind we're on the same side, working toward the same goal—to get rid of whoever it is killing cops." He looked hard at the other man, noting the pale skin and dark shadows under the eyes. "You should still be in bed. Take this car when I leave and go home."

Vogt shook his head. "No way. I want this guy—and all the other guys like him—as bad as you do. I didn't sneak out of the hospital just to go home and get in bed."

Bolan studied his face again. The whites of his eyes still held a yellowish tint. The man was sick. But he was earnest. "All right," he said. "But listen to me, and listen well before you decide you really want to go. First off, like you said, I'm not a cop. Which means I don't play the game the same way you do. And if you go, you go with my rules."

Vogt nodded. "You're saying you bend the law a little. We all have to do that."

"No," the Executioner said, shaking his head back and forth. "I'm not saying I bend laws, I'm saying I break them. Demolish them sometimes when they stand in the way of justice."

The Houston detective frowned. He hadn't expected so blunt an answer. "Well," he said, "you said we'll be going by your rules. If your rules aren't the law, what are they?"

"Right and wrong," Bolan said simply.

The pale man frowned, obviously wondering exactly what Bolan meant. "In other words, you take the law into your own hands?"

"Sometimes."

Vogt continued frowning. "You're saying you play judge, jury and executioner?"

The soldier had to smile at the choice of expressions. "When I have to," he said. "But I don't have time to explain it all to you or try to justify it. Can you play by my rules or not?" He reached out and placed a hand on the door handle.

Again, Vogt frowned hard, trying to decide what to do on the limited information he had. And he knew he would get no more. After a few seconds of deep concentration, he finally said, "Back in the booking room, you took that gun away from the drug dealer with your bare hands. You could have killed him with your bare hands, too, couldn't you?"

The Executioner didn't respond.

Vogt already knew the answer and went on. "And it would have been justifiable homicide. Clear-cut. But you didn't kill him. Why?"

"I didn't have to."

The pale face brightened slightly. "Yeah," Vogt said. "I can play by your rules. In fact, they sound an awful lot like my own."

The two men got out of the car. Grimaldi had pulled the plane out of the hangar and was warming it up as Bolan tossed his suitcases on board, and Vogt followed him into the plane. The soldier went directly to the lockers on the wall. Opening one, he pulled out a spare Desert Eagle, checked the magazine and chamber, then opened his suitcase and got out a holster for it. Replenishing the ammo he'd used up over the past couple of days, he led Vogt to the front of the plane as Grimaldi taxied to the runway.

"Jack, Ronnie Vogt. Vogt, Jack," he said.

Grimaldi glanced over the top of his aviator sunglasses and said, "You don't look too good, Vogt. Heard you drank some coffee that didn't agree with you." Before Vogt could reply, the pilot turned to Bolan and tapped the screen in front of him. "Your pigeon's flying north," he said. "I-45 toward Dallas."

"How far ahead is he?" Bolan asked, studying the screen.

"Not that far. We can be on top of him in a few minutes."

Bolan nodded. "Get a visual, then drop back. We don't know where or how far he's going. And we won't until he gets there. We could be up a long time."

"You're the boss, Sarge," Grimaldi said as the plane got clearance and took off.

Bolan pulled the cell phone out of his briefcase again and called Kurtzman. "Bear, I need you to intercept any correspondence concerning me from LAPD," he said. "Do whatever you need to do to keep Houston from knowing I was even in L.A." He took a breath. "I don't think I need the Houston cover any longer, but I want to keep it available just in case." His eyes fell on Vogt, who had taken the seat directly behind him. "And while you're at it, Bear, hack into the hospital medical records and give Ronnie Vogt an official release as of this morning. Then put him on sick leave with the PD." He hung up.

The plane rose in the sky and flew over Houston, cutting toward I-45 where Spencer's Blazer was still beeping on the screen.

Behind the soldier, Vogt coughed. "It's that easy?" he asked.

"What?" Bolan said.

"Covering your tracks. I mean, you—or whoever it was you called—can just hack into the computers and change things?"

"Pretty much," Bolan said.

Vogt laughed. "If I do a good job for you, you suppose you could make me a captain?"

"We'll see," he said. "Now, Jack was right. You don't look too well. I'd suggest you get some sleep."

"I'm not tired," Vogt said.

"That doesn't matter. Do it anyway."

He turned to Grimaldi. "You've got the screen?" he asked.

The pilot nodded. "I'll wake you up if anything interesting happens. Sweet dreams."

Bolan closed his eyes. He had learned long ago that each mission would mean many nights without sleep, and that the wise warrior learned to catch catnaps whenever the opportunity presented itself.

CLAYTON RUDD bore down on the new Szaball in his left hand as he left I-45 and took U.S. Highway 75. Beneath the rubber coating, he felt the rice grind back and forth. Like his nerves were grinding inside his head and chest. They were getting bad again. And the ball wasn't working the way it had.

Rudd passed a sign announcing Sherman, Texas, as the next large city. But his mind was not on the highway or the city or even the job he was about to perform. As it seemed to do these days when his nerves acted up, it was drifting back over the years to the time he'd spent in the Army.

Rudd switched the ball to his right hand and took the steering wheel with his left. He had never planned to make the Army his career. It had simply been a stepping-stone to what he'd wanted to do with his life ever since he could remember. Be a cop. But he had thought a stint in the service would be just the ticket on his résumé to help him land a position with one of the major police departments or even one of the federal agencies. It would be especially impressive, he had figured, if he could get into one of the special combat units. Green Berets, Rangers—he didn't care which. He'd just wanted it in his file.

And he'd come awfully close to pulling it off. But not quite.

Ahead, the flatlands of central Texas seemed to stretch into eternity as Rudd continued to reminisce. He remembered the day he'd been notified that his application to Ranger school had been approved. He'd been the happiest man at Fort Sill. But since he had never been good at making friends, he had celebrated alone at the NCO club, then moved on to some of the seedier strip clubs around the base in Lawton, Oklahoma. The dancers had the effect on him they strived for, and by midafternoon he had given into his urges and gone to see Ruth.

That had been his downfall.

The wife of a young lieutenant, Ruth had been to bed with half of the enlisted men at Fort Sill, and rumor had it she was also working her way through the Lawton "townies." It was the best known secret on base that Ruth's arms—and legs—were always open to lonely GIs.

Rudd felt the rubber beneath his fingers grow warmer as he worked the exerciser. Back and forth. Back and forth. He changed hands and squeezed again. He'd been a fool to go to Ruth's house like he had. He should have known her husband could come home at anytime.

He felt his breathing rate increase as he remembered what had happened. Blood rushed to his face as he switched hands with the ball again. Ruth had tried to talk him out of it. But Rudd had been drunk and wouldn't listen to reason. And she hadn't tried very hard. A "quickie" she had finally agreed. Right there on the living-room couch. But it had turned into three times before the front door opened and her husband stopped in the doorway.

Which was when Ruth suddenly screamed rape. Even the lieutenant had known it was not rape. Rudd had seen the sad look his face. And when he'd gotten dressed to leave, the man had just stood there, even stepping aside to let him out the door. Rudd had been convinced the lieutenant would keep his mouth shut out of shame. And he had.

But his crazy wife hadn't.

Sweat broke on Rudd's forehead as he pushed the Blazer down the highway. In some insane attempt to save a reputation she didn't have, Ruth had coerced her husband into taking her to the MPs and that was the day Rudd's life, for all practical purposes, had ended. By 1900 hours he'd been in the guardhouse and charged with rape. Ruth might like screwing around, but she also liked being married to an up-and-coming officer, and that meant sticking with the lie to the bitter end. The only thing that saved Rudd from life in a federal penitentiary was Ruth's long-overdue nervous breakdown. Suddenly he had found himself being escorted out of his cell to the MP office. They'd told him he was one lucky son of a bitch. They'd told him he didn't deserve it, but he was getting a break. A general discharge, they said. All charges would be dropped.

They had assured him a general discharge was nothing like a dishonorable discharge. It was just what it said. General.

The highway went into a long sweeping curve. Rudd guided the Blazer around one of Texas's mammoth ranches—bigger even than some of the northeastern states. He remembered signing the document, not knowing it would haunt him from then on. A general discharge, he would learn, was *not* general. Everyone who saw it interpreted it as being something he got because he'd done something nefarious, but they didn't quite have enough evidence to prove it in a court-martial. At least that's the way every police department and other law-enforcement agency to which he'd applied had viewed it. The bottom line, he not only wasn't going to Ranger school, he was never going to achieve his life's dream of being a police officer, either.

Rudd woke up from his daydream and saw that he was nearing Sherman. He squeezed the ball again as he felt a tear trickle down his cheek. "Stop it, you weak little bastard!" he screamed at the inside of the car. Then, in a calmer voice, he said, "Things are finally about to turn around."

Rudd saw the Motel 6 sign ahead and slowed as he neared the off-ramp. A few moments later, he parked outside the lobby and walked in to the front desk. He had no intentions of spending the night there, but he needed a base of operations. He was tired of changing clothes in gas station rest rooms. He paid the desk clerk in cash, showing him one of the driver's licenses he had stolen from the evidence room back home. He had changed the picture himself, and hadn't done a particularly good job. But a desk clerk wasn't a cop, and he paid no attention. Rudd signed the registration card accordingly.

His room was on the ground floor, but the parking space in front of it was taken. Rudd pulled in a couple of doors down and got out of the Blazer, still squeezing the ball in his right hand. Walking back to the tailgate, he started to transfer the exercise ball to his left but it fell from his hand, hit his toe and rolled under the car.

Rudd cursed as he squatted, peering beneath the chassis. The damn thing had rolled halfway under the car. He dropped and squirmed between the tires, cursing again as dirt and tiny flakes of gravel stuck to his shirt. Grabbing the Szaball, he was crabbing back out from under the Blazer when his eyes fell on the round, half-dollar-shaped object affixed to the inside of his rear bumper.

He froze in place, still half under the vehicle.

Rudd recognized the tracking device immediately. He knew what it was, and although he didn't know how or when the man had done it, he knew exactly who had put it there.

Belasko.

Sweat beaded his forehead and soaked the armpits of his navy blue T-shirt. He squeezed the exerciser furiously, transferring it back and forth from hand to hand. Rising to his feet, he twirled a 360-degree turn. Where was the big bastard? How had he followed him? And what was he planning to do?

Rudd forced himself to calm. If he had any real evidence, the big detective would have arrested him that morning at the task force meeting. Which meant he was still fishing. He didn't know anything. He just suspected. And cops couldn't arrest people on suspicion. They had to have probable cause.

So what should he do?

The idea hit Rudd quickly and, because it was so simple, so easy, and yet so foolproof it made him laugh out loud. He was still squeezing the ball when he knelt again at the bumper of the Blazer. By then he had quit laughing but a smile still curled his lips.

At least to Rudd it was a smile. Many people would have seen the expression more as a sneer, and to others it would have been a snarl.

OWEN KILLIAN KNEW it was rude to have his secretary place his phone calls for him, then tell the contacted party, "Please hold for Senator Killian." It implied that his time was more valuable than theirs. But it kept people in their place.

The intercom light on his phone lit up and the familiar buzz filled the office. Killian lifted the receiver. "Yes, Janet?"

"Chief Baxter on line two," the secretary purred.

Killian thought about the woman as he punched the appropriate button. He had not slept with her yet, and would not. At least not until he was in the White House. The pendulum of tolerance for such things had swung the other way, and the public was far less willing to overlook sexual infidelities in their leaders than they had once been. He'd wait. She'd still be there. She'd all but said so.

"Hello, Chief," Killian said, pressing the phone to his ear. "Everything ready?"

Jeff Baxter, the owner of the Baxter Executive Protection and the man who provided Killian's bodyguards, said, "Hello, Senator. Yes, sir. We'll have two men waiting for you in the lobby. They'll take you to the plane. And I've arranged for two more guards once you touch down in Los Angeles. They're from Apex Security out there. Good firm. Owner's a friend of mine."

"Very good," Killian said. He thought about the complexity of providing his own security. Even top firms like Baxter's, who were licensed in the District of Columbia, rarely held credentials in all of the places he traveled. This required coordination between companies, and the client never knew for sure what was waiting for him on the other end. Sometimes they were professionals, other times they were little more than wino security guards in plainclothes. It would be nice once he was in the White House, and the Secret Service could handle the bodyguard work.

Killian caught his mistake as he hung up the phone. What was he thinking? By the time he took his seat in the Oval Office, there would be no more Secret Service. The men who provide his security would have some name like the Presidential Protection Section of the National Police Administration. The senator sat back and clasped his hands behind his head, a rush of adrenaline washing through him. This night would be a pivotal point in seeing to it that the National Police Administration became a reality.

Killian gathered up the notes he had just made and moved away from his desk to the computer hutch. He logged on to the Internet, then typed in the web address known only to him and eleven other men. When the screen appeared, he typed in the code that would take him to the first of the dozen post boards. Only one other man had that code. His name was William Marshall, and he was a former NYPD officer who had served a term in prison for graft. He had been a member of the bomb squad, and had taken a huge payoff to cover up evidence of a bomb a Mafia Family had used to destroy members of a street gang who were infringing on their territory. Killian had given Marshall a pardon when he'd been governor of New York, then helped him secure a private investigator's license. Angry at the entire system, Marshall had been an easy mark for Killian to recruit to his cause. The disgraced cop didn't mind killing other officers one bit. In fact, he enjoyed it. And his knowledge of demolition had been proved—not only how to build simple yet highly destructive explosives, but also how to acquire the necessary components without leaving a paper trail.

The senator checked the latest post from Marshall. Everything was set for his role in the little drama. Marshall expected no problems.

Killian logged out and moved on to the second of the post boards, typing in another secret code word. Evan LaFond lived in

Detroit, where he had been turned down by the Detroit PD and every other law-enforcement agency to which he'd ever applied. The reason? He couldn't pass the MMPI or any of the other psychological tests. He was a schizophrenic who kept himself in check with medication and had spent his entire adult life one step out of a mental institution. The fact that he'd never quite crossed the line had meant he could still qualify to rattle doors as a hospital security guard.

LaFond, too, was ready to go.

The senator typed in a few words of praise for the man's past performance. LaFond was very much like a puppy who had to be rewarded with a biscuit each time he performed. Killian shook his head in amazement as he left LaFond's board and moved on. Eleven of the twelve men who had been killing police officers for him wanted to be cops and, for one reason or another, couldn't be. That was the bait that had hooked them. He dangled the National Police Administration directorship in front of all of them like a carrot, and he had to keep a short leash on some of the more unstable ones, keeping his fingers crossed that none of them would crack before his plan was complete. But as soon as the strikes were complete, he'd set them on one another until they were all dead. If one of them did break first and talk, it would be the word of a man with either a criminal record or a past history of mental problems against that of a United States senator. Who was the public going to believe?

No one, that's who. A United States senator controlling an army of assassins who killed cops so he could form a Gestapo-like federal police force, then win the presidency? Preposterous. It had all the earmarks of a paranoid delusion.

The fact that it happened to be the truth would go unnoticed.

Killian grinned as he moved into the post board for his man in Phoenix. Phoenix was fine, as was Philadelphia and Kansas City. His man in Seattle had experienced some anxiety because he had been the last stop on Marshall's list when the bomb expert delivered the components. But he was the kind of man who found a way to experience anxiety over something no matter how smoothly things went. He was okay now. Marshall had arrived, put together the explosives for him and shown him how to set the timing device.

Killian typed in the address for Clayton Rudd's post board, and his good humor faded slightly. Of all of the men on his team, Rudd worried him the most. He wondered why. Rudd, while he was nuttier than a fruitcake, was the only one of the twelve who had never had serious mental or legal problems. The only reason he had been turned down by police agencies was the general discharge from the service. Killian started to hit the button to pull up Rudd's board, then changed his mind and sat back in his chair for a moment.

Rudd being on the team had been nothing but accident. The senator hadn't sought him out the way he had all of the others. He had met Rudd two years after the Army discharge, when the disgruntled man had finally given up on being a regular police officer and applied to Baxter Executive Protection. Killian had just retained the firm, and happened to be in their offices when Rudd found out that they weren't going to hire him, either. It had obviously been the lowest moment of Rudd's life. The man learned that he was not only never going to be a police officer, but he couldn't even get a job as a rent-a-cop.

Killian had changed his life for him. He had used his influence and contacts to set up the A. K. Spencer identity, then pulled a few strings along the "good old boy" network and gotten him a job as a deputy sheriff in Texas. Like all the others, Rudd had been promised the directorship once the National Police Administration became a reality.

So why did Rudd worry him the most? Killian wondered. Was it the man's many unauthorized calls to the office, each a breach in security? Was it Rudd's insubordinate attitude? The other ten men were all the grateful little puppy dogs that they should be. Rudd sometimes acted as if it were Killian who should be grateful. Maybe it was that damn squeeze-ball thing Rudd carried with him all the time. When the senator had first met the man, he had been about to squash the thing to pieces right there in Baxter's waiting room. He said it was for grip strength. The senator knew it was for nerves.

Killian hit the button and logged on to Rudd's site. As usual, the man was waiting until the last second to post his reply, and hadn't yet done so. That might have been the reason Rudd troubled him more than the others. At least it had to be part of it. While the man did excellent work, he was always the last to post, leaving Killian to wonder what was going on.

Jumping off Rudd's board, Killian went on down the list until he'd finished. Everything was set. Only one other member of the team hadn't posted, and Killian had hardly expected him to. He was dead—the only casualty of Senator Owen Killian's race to the White House, and certainly an acceptable loss who even deserved what he had gotten. Underwood was the only man who had tried to mix the senator's plans with his own private agenda, and Killian supposed he should have expected it. The dead man was the only member of the team who had never had aspirations of being a police officer. He was just a criminal, a two-time felon, who hated cops.

Killian rose from the computer hutch, gathered up his notes and walked to the paper shredder. A few moments later, all evidence was gone. He took a seat at his desk and, rather than have Janet place the next call for him, he punched one of the lines and tapped the numbers himself. Another feminine voice answered the phone with "Merritt Avionics, may I help you?"

"Hello, Juliet," Killian said. "Owen Killian, here."

"Hello, Senator!" the woman said back. "How are you today?"

"Juliet, if I was any better, I'd be twins. At least I'm not bad for an old man."

Juliet giggled, the way he'd hoped she would. "You're not old, Senator. Just...distinguished. And sexy. Those eyes of yours... ooooh!"

Killian laughed, making sure the sound was low, husky, masculine. "You're too kind, Juliet," he said in the same voice.

"Just stating the truth, Senator," the woman said. "You calling to check on your plane?"

"I am indeed."

"Let me switch you to Ray. Hold on."

A pair of clicks sounded in Killian's ear, then a male voice said,

"I've got the mechanics going over her, doing their final inspection, Senator. She'll be up and running in plenty of time for you."

"Thank you, Ray," Killian said. "I appreciate it." He started to ask if the man had filed a flight plan yet, then stopped. He didn't really need to know, and it was the kind of question that might stick in the man's mind, coming back at some later date to haunt him. Besides, it didn't matter. Flight plans were often changed after the plane was in the air. And he would have ample reason to do so tonight—reason that would cover his tracks later.

After all, he was not only a senator, what would be hitting the news later concerned one of his pet projects. No one would ever question why he had suddenly decided to zigzag his way across the continent instead of taking a more the direct route to the West Coast.

After a few more meaningless sentences of small talk, Killian hung up. Sitting back in his chair, he put his hands together, steepled his fingers and stared at the ceiling. He was about to fly to Sacramento, ostensibly to meet with the governor there to lend his support to a gun control bill about to go before the California state legislature. But the real reason was so he could watch the fireworks. Owen Killian knew himself well, and knew one of his characteristics was more than a small amount of vanity. Nothing wrong with that. It was directly linked to confidence. But the fact was, he wanted to see at least some of the results of his handiwork. He had put in months of work on this project—work that could never be shared with or appreciated by anyone but himself. Not even his staff knew of it, and they never could.

The least he could do was to treat himself to a few of the sights.

The phone buzzed again and Killian picked it up. "Yes, Janet?"

"The Baxter men are here, Senator."

"Thank you, dear," he said. "Ask them to wait."

The senator gathered up a few items from his desktop and tossed them into his briefcase, then stood. He walked to the rack in the corner and pulled his trench coat off the peg. His luggage was already packed and waiting in the outer office. He'd have Janet fetch one of his aides to carry it. He never liked using the bodyguards for such work. He preferred they kept their hands, and minds, free for other things.

Rudd crossed his mind one final time as he walked to the door.

He stopped, his hand on the doorknob. Maybe he couldn't put his finger on exactly why Rudd bothered him even more than the rest of the men. But he did. And there was no reason to put up with it after this night. Rudd, he decided, would be the first of the eleven men left who would be killed. He'd send Marshall down to Texas to do the job. After all, Marshall liked killing cops even more than the rest, and he'd be happy to take care of a deputy sheriff named A. K. Spencer.

Without another thought on the matter, Killian opened the door and walked out.

"HE'S SLOWING DOWN, Sarge," Jack Grimaldi said, shaking Bolan's arm. "Better wake up."

The Executioner came awake instantly. "Where are we, Jack?" he asked.

"Just outside of Sherman, Texas," Grimaldi answered.

Bolan rubbed his eyes and looked at the screen. Spencer's car, or rather the tracker fixed magnetically to it, showed up as an encircled X on the screen. As long as the tracker was still charged and working, the X blinked on and off, once each second. When it was in motion, meaning the vehicle to which it was attached was moving, it also beeped with the blinks. It also contained a heat-sensitive feature that made other autos within one-hundred feet show up as dark shadows on the screen. Bolan could see that traffic had thickened on the highway below.

"He's maneuvering to the right hand lane," the soldier said.

Grimaldi glanced at the screen and nodded. "Looks like it."

"My guess is he plans to take the next exit." Bolan grabbed the cellular phone and hit the speed dial to Stony Man Farm. When Barbara Price, the mission controller answered, he said, "Get Aaron, Barb. Quick."

Price knew what quick meant and didn't bother to answer. Bolan heard a series of clicks, and then the familiar voice of Aaron Kurtzman said, "What do you need, Striker?"

"Wheels," Bolan said. "On the ground in Sherman, Texas."

"Want me to call ahead and arrange a rental?" Kurtzman asked.

"No time, Bear. Check and see if we've got anybody in the area who's blacksuit trained." Besides fielding counterterrorist strike teams, Stony Man Farm also provided top-flight training to selected police and military personnel the world over. These men and women arrived at the Farm in blindfolds, received their training and did a tour there, then left with their eyes again covered, never knowing exactly where they'd been or who had trained them. Stony Man kept tabs on their careers from then on, and they occasionally assisted on missions when necessary.

"I don't have to check the computer," Kurtzman said. "And I can do better than just blacksuits trained." He paused, then said, "How about a former full-time blacksuit?"

"What are you talking about?" Bolan said.

"Remember Gypsy Reinhardt?" Kurtzman asked.

"Of course," Bolan said.

"He retired last month. Living on his family's ranch near Luella."

"You'll excuse me, Bear, if I can't pinpoint Luella on the map right now."

"A few miles southeast of Sherman, Striker."

"See if you can reach him."

"I dialed the number while we were talking," Kurtzman said. "Hang on."

In the background, the soldier heard the Stony Man computer genius identify himself. A moment later, Kurtzman came back on. "I'm linking you in direct," he said.

Bolan heard a raspy voice with a Texas accent he recognized immediately. "Howdy, Striker," Reinhardt said.

"Howdy back at you, Gypsy," the soldier said. "We're going to have to call you out of retirement for a few hours."

"You ain't gonna have to twist no arms, Striker," Reinhardt said. "Pigs and chickens been the only excitement I've had since I left the Farm for the farm."

"He's turning off the highway," Grimaldi said. "Pulling in someplace. I'll cross-check the coordinates on the map." In the corner of his eye, Bolan saw the pilot hit several buttons on the computer, then squint at the screen. A second later Grimaldi said, "Looks like a Motel 6."

"I'll explain all this when I see you, Gypsy," Bolan said into the phone. "But right now, you know the Motel 6 right off the interstate?"

"Sure," Reinhardt said.

"I need to be there, on the ground with wheels, ASAP. Is there a place to jump nearby where you could pick me up?"

There was a pause on the other end, then Reinhardt said, "You can land right out here at my place. It'd be faster."

"Give us the coordinates," Bolan said.

Reinhardt did, and he passed them on to Grimaldi. The pilot altered course slightly.

"Drop down till you see the house," Reinhardt said. "Skim down low, and there's plenty of flat pasture land just to the north. That old worn-out flyboy Grimaldi the one chauffeuring you?"

Bolan smiled, remembering that Reinhardt and Grimaldi had been good friends. "He's the one," Bolan said.

"Well, tell the old fart not to scare my cows," Reinhardt said.

"I'll tell him, and we'll see you in a few minutes."

"I'll have the truck warmed up and running," Reinhardt replied. "Soon as I see you, I'll head out after you and be waiting when you come to a halt."

"Affirmative," Bolan answered.

"One more thing."

"What's that?"

"Want me to call ahead to the Motel 6? Tell them to leave a light on for us?" The retired blacksuit began humming the familiar Motel 6 theme song, then hung up.

RONNIE VOGT HAD SLEPT through the conversation with Reinhardt but woke up when the wheels touched down on the pasture four minutes later. As they bounced across the bumpy landing field in a whirl of dirt, tumbleweeds, flying prairie grass and cactus, he said, "Where are we?"

"Just south of Sherman," Bolan answered as the plane slowed. He unbuckled his seat belt, moved past Vogt and grabbed his equipment bags.

True to his word, Reinhardt pulled up next to them as in a new red Dodge Dakota pickup as Bolan and Vogt deplaned. The Texan was grinning through the window, and Bolan returned the smile as he tossed his bags into the bed of the truck, then got in next to the man. Vogt took the back seat.

Reinhardt had aged a little since Bolan had seen him last. And, in the absence of the vigorous daily training the blacksuits underwent, he had put on a pound or two. Still, he was in far better shape than ninety-nine percent of the men his age, and probably ninety percent of men *any* age. The white Western shirt tucked into his faded jeans didn't hang over the large rodeo belt, and the seams at the shoulders looked ready to either burst or pop the pearl snaps that held the garment together. Hand-tooled Western boots completed his outfit, and upside down, in a wire rack attached to the roof of the Dakota, was a big brown cowboy hat.

As soon as Bolan and Vogt closed the doors, Reinhardt spun the tires of the Dakota, kicking up almost as much dirt and foliage as the landing Learjet had. He cut across the pasture toward a ranch road that Bolan assumed led to a highway. "I'm guessing we're headed toward the Motel 6 near Sherman," he said.

The soldier nodded. He opened one of the cases he'd brought along and produced a small laptop. Opening it on his knees, he punched in a series of codes and a tracking screen, identical to the permanent one fixed inside the plane, appeared. The circled *X* still flashed every second, but it had quit beeping, which meant the Blazer was no longer moving.

The Dakota flew off a short embankment as they left the pasture and landed on a dirt road. Reinhardt cut the wheel and they skidded into a ninety-degree turn. "I'm also guessing you're in a hurry," he said.

Bolan nodded.

Reinhardt guided the Dodge through a series of twisting curves that finally emerged onto a blacktop road.

Bolan cleared his throat, then introduced Ronnie Vogt. Reinhardt, he told the Houston detective, was a former member of the same organization he represented. By now, Vogt knew any further questions would be fruitless, so he just nodded. Bolan quickly ran down the situation to the retired blacksuit and explained about the tracker on the Blazer.

Reinhardt nodded as he pushed the pickup down the county road toward Sherman. "I see why we need to get there fast," he said. "Those trackers are great when you're in the sky and your mark's out in the open. In town, they can lose you. All it takes is a little road construction or another change that hasn't had time to get entered into the computer and show up in the screen."

"Exactly," Bolan said. As they passed a sign announcing the Sherman city limits, he said, "You armed, Gypsy, or you need something?"

Reinhardt laughed. "Got my old Beretta in the glove compartment there," he said. "Several extra mags. There's an M-16 behind the back seat, 120 rounds." He glanced at Bolan. "We going to need more than that?"

"What are you carrying now?" he asked.

Reinhardt shrugged. "Nothing serious. Just the .38 in my boot and my neck knife," he said.

"I think you'll be okay, then," Bolan said.

Reinhardt glanced over his shoulder at Vogt. "Don't take this personal," he said, "but I gotta ask a question of my old compadre here."

Looking back at Bolan, he said, "Is it okay to talk in front of him?"

"First names only," Bolan said.

"Okay." He asked what was happening and was told about Vogt's poisoning.

"You don't look all that chipper, bud. You going to be okay if the feces hit the oscillator?" Reinhardt asked.

"I'll be okay," Vogt said. "Getting better every minute."

Taking several back roads, they skirted the south edge of Sherman, finally emerging on the access road that ran parallel to the highway. "Motel's a mile that way."

As they passed a Wal-Mart, Bolan glanced at the screen in his lap, noting that the *X* had still not moved. "Let's do a drive-by and get a visual on the Blazer," he said. "Then find a parking place as close as you can without burning us, Gypsy."

Reinhardt nodded as he guided the Dakota along the access road to the motel. Coming up to a four-way stop, he waited for another vehicle, then pulled into the parking lot. Bolan and Vogt didn't bother ducking in their seats. The Dakota's windows were tinted enough that no one more than three feet away could see through them. They circled the two buildings that made up the motel, and found the Blazer parked in a slot between rooms 34 and 36.

"He has to be in one of these along here," Vogt stated.

"He doesn't have to be," Bolan said. "He's switched vehicles before. If he had one waiting on him here, he may have already taken off." He stopped, staring at the rooms around the Blazer as they drove on. "One way or another, we've got to find out if he's still inside."

Reinhardt drove through the parking lot, hit the access road again and passed a Denny's restaurant. "Well, unless I'm mistaken he knows both of your mugs by sight, right?"

The Executioner nodded.

Reinhardt pulled into a convenience store. "Then I'd say that leaves me." Pulling up in front of the store, he left the truck running as he got out and clicked his heels across the concrete. A minute later, he came back out carrying a square paper bag. Setting it on the seat between him and Bolan, he reached in, twisted his hand back and forth couple of times, and pried a can of Coors beer out of the plastic ring connectors. With the other hand, he steered the pickup as he backed out of the parking spot.

As soon as they were back on the access road, Reinhardt popped the top on the can and took a gulp. Then, without further ado or ceremony, he simply poured the rest of the can over his shirt. "Kind of hurts a Texan like me to waste good beer," he said. Then, turning to Bolan, he grinned. "Which is why I bought this Colorado Kool-Aid instead of Lone Star."

Bolan knew what Reinhardt had planned and approved. There was no reason to say anything. That was once of the best things about working with men from Stony Man Farm. They knew how each other thought.

"Be sure to park far enough away that he won't see the truck," the soldier said. "We're going to be using it the rest of the night, and it stands out like a sore thumb."

Reinhardt glanced at him, a look of mock pain on his face. "Now that hurts, Striker," he said. "Especially for a man who was trained by Leo—" He had started to say the name, but caught himself.

Bolan turned to face the front. "You just had to get this thing in fire engine red, Gypsy?"

"Yep," the man said. "Always wanted a red truck. And I *thought* I was retired."

In the motel parking lot once again, Reinhardt found a spot just beyond a huge eighteen-wheeler that had stopped for the night, pulling the Dakota in behind it. All three men got out, and Bolan and Vogt took up positions between the tractor and trailer through which they could see the doors along the building. The Executioner glanced at his watch. It had been only a little over thirty minutes since Spencer had checked into the motel. Was the man still there? He didn't know. But he hoped they were about to find out.

Reinhardt walked across the parking lot with the too formal stride of the drunk who didn't want anyone to know he'd been drinking. He passed between the Blazer and a blue Suburban, and walked up to room number 36. Although he knocked firmly, Bolan was pleased that he didn't pound too loud. If he overplayed this drunken cowboy role, all they'd get was a lot of unanswered doors.

A moment later, the door opened to the end of a security chain. Bolan saw an elderly face peek through the opening. Whether it was male or female, he couldn't be sure. Reinhardt spoke briefly, then the door closed again. The retired blacksuit moved on to room 34.

Reinhardt knocked and waited. There was no response. He knocked again, a little louder this time. Again, he waited but nothing happened. Bolan thought he was about to move on when the former blacksuit suddenly brought his fist back and hammer-fisted the wood so hard it sounded as if it might break. He repeated the blow three more times, then screamed, "Dammit-to-hell, Martha, if you're in there I'm gonna skin your ass and that polecat sombitch's too! Open the door or I'll kick it in. I swear to hell I will!"

There was a brief pause, and then the door suddenly swung back. An arm with a Colt Combat Commander at the end of it shot through the opening, the barrel stopping an inch from Reinhardt's nose. The form of a man appeared behind the gun.

A. K. Spencer.

Spencer wore the dark blue T-shirt and blue jeans Bolan had seen him in earlier that morning. He seemed to be speaking quietly. But even at the distance he was at, Bolan could see the look of a man ready to kill in his eyes.

Reinhardt had thrown up his hands as soon as he saw the gun, and now he staggered back a step, swaying slightly, playing his role with award-winning proficiency. The Executioner could see him talking with great animation, no doubt apologizing profusely for mistaking this room for the one hiding Martha and her illicit lover.

The conversation was short. The door closed, and Reinhardt staggered off along the side of the building. When he was out of eyesight of the window to room 34, he looked across the lot at the eighteen-wheeler, then pointed toward the front of the motel.

Even though he knew the man couldn't see him, Bolan nodded his understanding. Spencer might be watching through the closed curtain, and Reinhardt didn't want him to see him go behind the big truck and then emerge in the Dakota. The Executioner and Vogt got back in the pickup, and Bolan drove it to the front of the motel. He scooted across to the passenger's seat before Reinhardt got back behind the wheel.

The soldier was curious. "How'd you know the room wasn't empty?" he asked.

"Heard him inside," Reinhardt said. "Then I saw the curtain move. It could have been anybody—lot of folks are just scared to answer the door at motels nowadays. I just followed my hunch." He turned to Bolan as he threw the transmission into Drive and drove slowly toward the other side of the motel lot. "Was it this Spencer guy?"

"Yes," Bolan said.

Reinhardt nodded. "So, what do we do now?" he said.

The Executioner glanced over his shoulder. "Find a spot to park on this side of the building," he said. "We can tell when he leaves by the tracker, and I don't want him seeing us pull out after him."

"We wait?" Reinhardt asked.

"We wait," Bolan stated.

9

Clayton Rudd shut the door and locked it. The look in the drunk's eyes told him he had scared the living shit out of him. The man wouldn't be back looking for his philandering wife. On the other hand, there was no sense in taking chances, and so he replaced the security chain in the slot. Who knew what some drunken cowboy might do? And besides, if there was one looney-toon out, there might be more. Had to be a full moon.

Rudd tossed the Colt onto the bed closer to the door, picked up the Szaball and walked back to the desk. He had just set up the laptop and plugged it into the phone when the pounding on the door started. Now he sat back down and logged on, typing in the address of the Web site where he'd link to his personal post board. He had already reviewed the instructions and knew what to do. And that clown with the Brooklyn accent had shown up early that morning at his apartment with the C-4 plastique and other things with which he'd put together the bomb. Rudd didn't know anything about explosives, and he didn't want to. In truth, they scared the hell out of him. But the man—who might as well have had former

NYPD stenciled on his forehead—had shown him how to set the timer, and it looked easy enough. Now, he would make one final check of the post board to make sure nothing had changed. That had never happened before, and he didn't expect it to this time. But there was a first time for everything, and he just couldn't be too careful.

The site appeared, Rudd typed in the code for his personal board, and the new page showed up on the screen. The mission was still a go. He hit the Reply button, and typed in the fact that he had read and understood the assignment. The board would automatically post the time so he didn't bother with that. He considered telling Killian about the tracking device he'd found on the Blazer, then decided not to. He'd already handled it. Signing his post with a simple "AK," he logged off and unplugged the laptop.

Rudd had no intention of coming back to the room after he'd carried out the night's mission. So he closed the small computer and stuck it back into the soft-sided carrying case. There was another case on the bed, this one a briefcase with hard leather sides instead of soft. Such construction was important to the next phase of his mission. Rudd flipped open the catches and lifted the lid. Inside was another briefcase of the same color and makeup—just small enough to fit into the first. He pulled it out, opened the lid and looked down at the contents.

The C-4 plastique looked like the Play-Doh he'd played with as a kid. How the hell could this stuff, which looked no more dangerous than a child's modeling clay, blow up something? He supposed he'd have learned all about it if he'd gotten to go to Ranger school. But that hadn't happened, and now he no longer cared. All he wanted to do was get it where it needed to go, set the timer then get the hell out of there.

Rudd closed the case, inserted it back into the larger one and looked around the room. The bed was unmade, the sheets wrinkled as if he had slept on them. He had already paid for the room, had made no telephone calls, and there should be no reason to suspect the man who had checked into the motel of having anything to do with what would happen later. Even if someone did question his presence, the false ID he'd used would lead to a dead end.

But he'd wiped down all the surfaces he'd touched since coming into the room anyway.

Having already changed into a navy blue blazer, light blue slacks, a white shirt and tie, Rudd now stuffed the plastic garment bag in which he'd brought the clothes into a small satchel with his T-shirt and jeans. He stuck the computer case under his arm, grabbed the briefcase with the C-4, then lifted the satchel with the other hand.

A quick look out the edge of the curtain told him the parking lot was quiet. Exiting the door, he walked to the Blazer and put all of his luggage on the back seat. Finding the tracking device behind his bumper had put him on extra alert, and he walked the length of the building both ways, glancing into each vehicle as he passed. All were empty. Whoever had planted the tracker wasn't in the parking lot.

Getting into the Blazer, Rudd started the engine and gave it a moment to warm up. As he waited, he saw a red-haired woman who looked like a hooker come out of the room at the end of the building. She got into the yellow Camaro parked in front of the door and backed out of the parking space.

Rudd found himself laughing out loud. A hooker. She was in for an interesting evening.

He had spotted a Wal-Mart at the highway exit just before this one, and it should be busy this time of night. Perfect place to pick up some wheels for the evening. Throwing the transmission into Reverse, he backed out of the parking space, twisted the wheel and took off down the access road.

BOLAN HEARD THE QUICK BEEP and looked down at the screen in his lap. "He's on the move," he said. "Get ready."

The Dakota was already running. Reinhardt threw it in gear.

The beep on the tracking screen grew louder. "Coming our way," the soldier said. "Wait for him to pass and let him have a block or so before we pull out after him."

They had parked at the end of the lot farthest from the access road, backing into a space in front of the last room on the opposite side of the building from Spencer. As he had told Reinhardt, the red Dakota was too easy to spot, and too easy to remember, and he wished they had some less flamboyant vehicle. But he could hardly blame that on Reinhardt.

He'd thought he was retired.

A canary yellow Camaro came around the side of the building and stopped at the edge of the road, waiting for two cars to drive by. The beep from the tracking screen grew louder still. Spencer's Blazer had to be right behind the Camaro.

Bolan and the other two men waited. The Camaro took off down the road, headed north toward downtown Sherman. But the Blazer didn't appear. And the beep began to grow more faint.

The soldier's eyebrows lowered. "Something's wrong," he said. It didn't take him long to figure out what.

"Pull around the building," the Executioner ordered. "He found the tracker, and he stuck it on that Camaro."

Reinhardt did as he'd been told, cutting a hard left turn around the building. He slowed as he drove past the rooms.

The Blazer was gone.

Bolan suppressed a curse. What had caused Spencer to look behind his bumper and find the tracker? He had no idea, and probably was never going to find out. But that's exactly what had to have happened.

"What do you want—" Reinhardt started to say.

The Executioner had nothing to go on now but luck, experience and gut instinct. He had no idea what Spencer had planned. But on each of the missions the man had either had another vehicle waiting for him or stolen one to use. If wheels had been planted for him like the motorcycle seemed to have been in Oklahoma City, it could be anywhere. But if he planned to steal a car, now there was still a chance. In the past, the cop killer had favored large parking lots, both for the initial theft and then to dump the vehicles after he was finished with them.

Bolan turned to Reinhardt. "Gypsy, what's the biggest parking close by?"

Reinhardt had known the soldier too long to question the question. He frowned. "Big Homeland supermarket a mile north. Wal-Mart a mile back south—we passed it on the way in. Then there's a Target store and a shopping mall over—"

"Wal-Mart the closest?" Bolan asked.

"Yep."

"Let's kick it," the Executioner said.

Reinhardt hit the accelerator, speeding out of the parking lot just this side of laying rubber and drawing attention. "Any particular reason?" he asked as they started down the access road.

"We might as well try something," Bolan responded. "And even on the highway instead of the access road Spencer may have seen the Wal-Mart when he drove past on the way in, too."

The Dakota zoomed on, being delayed for a moment by a slow-moving Cadillac. Then Reinhardt grunted his annoyance and pulled around the vehicle, barely getting back into the right-hand lane before an old Buick hit them head-on.

Vogt, still sick and knowing he couldn't contribute much, had stayed pretty quiet most of the night. But now the Houston detective let out a nervous breath and said, "I survive an attempted poisoning just to get killed in a car wreck?"

Reinhardt grinned into the rearview mirror. "You play in the big leagues," he said, "you gotta take your chances and sometimes your lumps."

They reached the Wal-Mart and pulled in. "Start on this side," Bolan said. "Drive up and down the lanes and see if you spot the Blazer."

"Okay, but he's going to make the Dakota if he sees it," Reinhardt warned.

"I know," Bolan said. "That's why you're going to let me out. Slow down." He reached for the door handle.

"What are you—" Vogt started to ask.

"Just hang loose there, Vogt," Reinhardt said. "You'll figure it out as we go." He came almost to a halt as he hit the first row of parked cars, and Bolan leaped from the rolling vehicle.

RONNIE VOGT WASN'T sure what he'd gotten himself into, and he wasn't sure he shouldn't have just stayed in the hospital. He knew the man who called himself Belasko was a good guy, and he knew the man was on the right side.

But he took chances. Both with his life and the law, too. Now, unless he missed his guess, the man was going to steal a car. And they'd be riding around the rest of the night in a stolen vehicle. Vogt could forget his job, retirement and pension. Of course he wouldn't have to worry about money. He'd have room and board, and three meals a day free in the penitentiary.

"Keep your eyes open, Vogt," the man who'd been introduced as Gypsy told him from the front seat. "If Spencer's here, he's probably already parked and gone looking for his wheels. We're going to have to be fast to make our own switch."

Vogt stared out the tinted window as they drove up and down the lanes. Twice, they got stuck behind other cars waiting for parking spaces and both times Reinhardt tapped his horn and pulled around the cars, narrowly missing the vehicles backing out. He got two return honks and one middle finger for his effort. They spotted the Blazer near the back of the busy parking lot on the seventh row. It was empty.

"Damn," the driver said. "He's out and running. And with this much traffic coming and going, it'll be a miracle if we see him." He drove past the parked Blazer. Both men scoured the lot with their eyes, looking for Spencer. It was like looking for the proverbial needle in a haystack.

"He's got to have equipment with him, right?" Vogt said suddenly.

"Yeah, I'd suppose," Reinhardt agreed.

"Well, he wouldn't take it with him when he goes for the other car, would he? I mean, he'd get the thing up and running, then come back for his stuff."

Reinhardt turned in his seat, the big grin Vogt had seen so many times already on his face again. "You know, there's hope for you," he said. He pulled the Blazer to a halt. "Hop out and take a look. But don't let him see you. Wait." He reached up to the rack on the roof of the pickup and pulled down the cowboy hat. "Here. Take this."

Vogt took the hat and was surprised when it fit. Although he'd been born and bred in Texas, he had never owned a cowboy hat. He resisted the temptation to check himself out in mirror—both because there wasn't time and he was afraid he'd be disappointed in what he saw. He felt slightly silly as he got out and started for the Blazer.

Vogt was still a car away when a year-old silver Lexus pulled up behind the Blazer and stopped. The driver got out. Spencer.

The Houston detective was too close to suddenly jump behind the vehicle parked next to the Blazer without drawing Spencer's attention. He was afraid even changing his course might catch the man's eye. So, turning to look to the side, he kept walking, hoping the hat and the angle hid his features and that Spencer's mind would be preoccupied. Holding his breath, he walked right past the man, so close either one of them could have reached out and touched the other.

Vogt kept walking toward the front of the Wal-Mart. He risked one quick look over his shoulder and saw Spencer transferring a briefcase from the Blazer to the Lexus. Not knowing what to do next, he turned back and continued toward the front of the store. He stopped when a Honda Civic turned down the row of cars and came to halt at his side. The window on the passenger's side came down, and Vogt saw Reinhardt riding shotgun.

"Need a lift, cowboy?" the man said.

Vogt got into the back of the Civic and they drove away.

"WE'LL HAVE TO BE CAREFUL," Reinhardt said as the Civic followed the Lexus out of the parking lot. "Even a car as mundane as this one is going to get spotted if he sees it too many times. Especially if he's on the lookout for a tail."

Bolan let the Lexus get half a block ahead before he turned after it onto the access road. "He'll be watching for a tail," the Executioner said confidently.

Vogt was crowded against the window. The rest of the area was crammed with equipment bags and a black ballistic nylon assault rifle case that he guessed contained the M-16 Gypsy had said was behind the seat in the Dakota. "What makes you think he'll be looking for a tail?" he asked.

Reinhardt turned and rested his arm on the back of the seat. "If you were getting ready to kill somebody, and you found a tracker on your car, you'd be looking for one," he said. "By the way, gimme back my hat."

Vogt took off the brown cowboy hat and handed it over the seat.

Bolan tailed the Lexus, taking note of the fact that the left tail-light was slightly brighter than the right. Such knowledge might become invaluable in heavy traffic, and it looked like Spencer was heading for the interstate again. The soldier stayed as far back as he dared, walking that fine line between being spotted and losing his mark. Regardless of how it might look on television, in movies and in detective novels, one-car tails were rarely very successful for any length of time. Ideally it took a minimum of four vehicles with radio communication to tail another vehicle.

No, this was hardly the ideal way to follow Chambers County Deputy A. K. Spencer. But in all the years he'd fought against the evil in this world he couldn't remember being in one situation that was ideal, and the Executioner wasn't sure he'd know how to act if he ever did chance upon one where they odds were all in his favor.

The Lexus took the ramp up to the highway and Bolan lagged behind, letting a Volkswagen get in front of him before following. He kept his eyes glued to the taillights. But his mind split, wondering just who Spencer really was.

Was the man just a cop gone bad? Someone who had been lured into committing multiple homicides by money? Or was he a mole, a plant put in position by some foreign government or terrorist organization years before and left waiting until he was needed? That didn't seem logical. Small-county deputy sheriff positions hardly merited the effort or expense of inserting an enemy agent.

Had Spencer—if that was even his real name—fallen prey to some perverse political ideology? It had happened to cops before. They saw so much of life's depravity, and watched so many criminals walk free from an imperfect criminal justice system, that they were often easy prey for militant extremists from both the far left and the far right. They got to the point where anything—even anarchy—seemed better than the hypocritical status quo that set child molesters free because their Miranda rights hadn't been read to them, or let rapists walk because some unscrupulous defense attorney made the victim look like a whore on the witness stand.

Bolan didn't know what made Spencer tick. At least not yet. But before the night was out, he intended to find out.

The Lexus stayed on the highway, heading for downtown Sherman.

In the front seat, Reinhardt had put on his cowboy hat. "Got any ideas where he's going?"

The Executioner shook his head. "No. Not yet, anyway."

They continued to follow, but a mile later the Lexus suddenly cut from the left lane to the right and shot off a downtown exit ramp. Bolan watched it go, knowing the man behind the wheel had made the sudden move on purpose to watch for a tail. If he followed suit, Spencer would see them. Bolan had no doubt the man's eyes were glued to his rearview mirror even now as he drove down the exit ramp.

Bolan slowed the Civic and pulled into the right hand lane but drove past the exit.

In the back, Vogt leaned forward. "What are you doing?" he asked in an anxious voice. "We're going to lose him."

"Maybe," Bolan said. "Maybe not." He slowed the car further as the Lexus glided through a yellow yield sign at the bottom of the ramp, then turned onto the same access road they'd been on before. A moment later it took a right at the corner onto one of the city streets. As soon as it had disappeared behind a gas station on the corner, the Executioner pulled onto the shoulder and stomped on the brake.

The Civic's tires screamed in protest as the car ground to a halt. He threw the transmission into Reverse, turned and put an arm over the headrest, and shifted his foot to the accelerator. The tires screamed again, this time going the backward. Cars passing in the right hand lane honked their horns as Bolan drove the car in reverse along the shoulder, the wheels bouncing and protesting as they hit potholes in the asphalt. Just beyond the exit ramp, he stomped the brake again, threw the transmission back into Drive and squealed off down the ramp.

A two-ton flatbed truck was gliding down the access road as the soldier reached the yield sign. Pressing harder on the accelerator, he inched the Civic past its nose, missing the front bumper by inches. The move got him another honk as he twisted the wheel around the corner.

As soon as he'd made the turn, Bolan stared ahead down the street. Traffic wasn't heavy in the early-evening hours, but it wasn't light, either. The streetlights were good and the moon was full. Enough illumination that he could identify the makes and models of the various types of vehicles as long as they weren't too far away. But he didn't see the Lexus. Flooring the gas pedal once more, he cut in and out of lanes, racing down the street toward downtown Sherman. It had not been a full minute yet since the Lexus had left the highway. But already there had been dozens of places where Spencer might have turned off. If he had, they weren't going to find him again this night.

They'd been lucky at the Wal-Mart store, but that kind of luck wasn't likely to come their way again.

Bolan sped on, hoping he wouldn't pass any local police cars that could detain him. Then, three blocks farther, he saw an indistinct form of a vehicle ahead. He couldn't make out its shape. But the taillights were unmistakable.

One was bright. The other wasn't.

The Executioner slowed the Civic, not wanting to draw attention in case Spencer was still watching his rearview mirror. Little by little, however, as they neared downtown Sherman, he closed in on the Lexus. By the time they had entered the center of town, he was less than a block away and only an old Ford pickup with a camper shell separated them. Bolan stayed behind the camper as all three vehicles stopped at a red light. When the light turned green, the Lexus made a left onto Travis Street, and pulled into a parking lot next to a two-story concrete building with glass windows circling the second floor.

"That's the Sherman police department," Vogt said from the back seat.

Bolan turned after the Lexus but drove past the building, noting the brick front entryway. He slowed, watching the rearview mirror, hoping to see Spencer emerge before they got too far away. He wasn't disappointed. As the soldier pulled to a halt at the stop sign at the next intersection, the deputy came around the corner from the parking lot lugging a briefcase. Two other cars had pulled up to the four-way stop, giving Bolan an excuse to wait. He did, and saw Spencer disappear into the building.

Reinhardt turned in his seat to face Bolan. "You don't suppose he's just going to go in there and start shooting cops, do you?" the retired blacksuit asked. "That briefcase looked heavy. Might have a subgun inside."

Bolan drove through the intersection, turned into the driveway of another city government building and backed out onto the street. There was no other immediate traffic and he stopped, keeping his foot on the brake as he stared down the street to the brick entryway. "I don't think so, Gypsy," he said. "There's more to all this than that." He had known for some time now that these police assassinations had been leading up to something bigger, some far more dramatic and climatic event, and now his gut instinct told him this was the night, and what Spencer was doing was part of it. Whatever it was, it had to be something that raised the stakes and furthered whatever goal the mastermind of this whole thing was working toward.

"Maybe we better warn them," Vogt said. "I'd hate to have him go in there and kill a bunch of fellow officers when we could have stopped him. I don't want to live with that on my conscience."

"Neither do I," Bolan said. "But that's not what's going to happen."

"How do you know?" Vogt asked.

Reinhardt had known the Executioner long enough to answer for him. "He just knows."

Ronnie Vogt nodded. He didn't full understand what the man meant yet. But he was beginning to.

RUDD FELT BETTER than he had earlier in the evening. He still had the Szaball with him, and he worked it with his right hand as he pulled into the parking lot next to the Sherman police department. But he wasn't squeezing it as hard as he had been. Whoever had been tracking him—and he still suspected it was Mike Belasko— was now following a yellow Camaro. That hooker, or whoever she was who had come out of the room down the building from his, was going to have some explaining to do before the night was over.

Rudd pictured the detective in his mind as he parked the Lexus in the lot and exited the vehicle. The poisoning hadn't worked. But as soon as he got back to Houston, he'd take care of the man in a more direct way. Easiest thing would just be to find out where he lived and go waste him. Shoot him in his sleep. His wife was dead—Rudd knew that—so he probably lived alone. It shouldn't be that hard.

Grabbing the briefcase from the back seat, Rudd walked across the lot to the sidewalk in front of the police department. It was only a few steps to the brick entryway, and he pushed his way through the glass door and into the lobby.

A black woman in a blue uniform sat at a desk behind a plate of glass as Rudd approached. He gave her his best smile, and she returned it, as he reached into the inside pocket of his sport coat and pulled out the badge case. "Detective Sellers, Dallas PD," he told the woman. "I wonder if I might talk to one of your investigators about a case we're working on?"

"Let me see who's back there," the woman said, lifting a phone to her ear. A moment later, Rudd heard her say, "Buzz, got a Dallas detective here wants to talk to somebody." There was a brief pause, then she said, "Okay" and hung up. She reached under her desk, and a second later a buzz sounded from the doorway at Rudd's side. The door popped open.

"Come on back," the woman said as she got up from behind the desk. "I'll show you where he is."

Rudd followed the woman down a short hallway into an office with four desks. Three were empty, which didn't surprise Clayton Rudd. The Sherman PD was made up of around sixty commissioned police officers and twenty-four civilian personnel. The night shift would be light. Just the way he wanted it. Night almost always meant relaxed and informal when it came to police work. For one thing, the brass was rarely around during the evening.

"Buzz Yount, this is Detective... Sorry, what did you say your name was again?" the woman asked.

"Sellers. Brad Sellers," Rudd said.

Yount was sitting in his chair, his feet crossed on top of his desk, finishing up the remains of a sandwich. "Take a load off, Sellers," he said around a mouthful of meat, cheese and bread. "I'd ask you if you've eaten and offer you some, but it's too late." He stuck the rest of the sandwich into his mouth, crumpled up the paper that had wrapped it and threw it into the trash can next to his desk. Several chews, a swallow and a drink from the paper cup on his desk later, he said, "What can I do for you?"

Rudd pulled a paper from inside his coat and unfolded it, then tossed it on the desk in front of Yount. It contained a forensic artist's sketch of a wanted man—a man who had actually been apprehended in Houston two years earlier and was now in prison. But Yount would have no reason to know that. "It's a long shot," he said, "but one of our snitches heard this clown might be in Sherman. Look familiar at all?"

Yount had a piece of lettuce stuck to his chin. He reached up and brushed it off as he lifted the drawing with his other hand. "Face doesn't ring any bells right off hand," he said. He squinted at what was written beneath the picture. "Guy's name's Preston?"

Rudd nodded. "Clifton Leroy Preston," he said.

"What do you have on him?"

"Killed a ten-year-old boy," Rudd said. "Cut his throat."

Yount's face hardened. "No wonder you came all the way up here on nothing more than a snitch rumor," he said. "I would, too." He looked up from the desk. "Can I keep this?"

"Sure. Got plenty of them."

"I'll ask around," Yount said. "See if any of our people on the day shift recognize him or if anybody's got a snitch who knows him. You staying in town?"

Rudd shook his head. "Gotta head back tonight," he said.

"You got a card so I can call you?"

Rudd had anticipated this question and had considered having fake business cards made up in the name of the Detective Sellers. But he didn't want to leave anything around with his prints on it. He doubted anyone would put a random business card together with what was about to happen at the Sherman police department—if that card even survived what was about to happen—but he couldn't be too careful. He patted his jacket and shook his head. "Got away without my card case this afternoon," he said. He laughed at himself. "Sometimes I'm lucky to remember my gun."

Yount returned the laugh. "Hell, there are days I'm lucky to remember my ass," he said.

"Just call the main Dallas number, ask for Homicide, and they can connect you."

Yount nodded. "Anything else I can do for you?"

"Sure is," Rudd nodded. "You can point me toward the nearest men's room before I embarrass the hell out of both of us."

Yount stood and escorted him into the hall, then pointed toward the end. "Last door to the right," he said. He held out his hand. "I'll be in touch if we come up with anything."

"Thanks." Rudd shook the man's hand.

Walking down the hall, Rudd passed several darkened offices. He was disappointed when he entered the men's room. He had hoped there would be some kind of utility closet or other place to stash the briefcase. There wasn't. And if he left it out in the open, someone would find it before the night was over. Maybe they'd just take it up to the lost and found but more likely they'd open it to see if there was any ID inside so they could get it back to the owner.

Sticking his head back out the door, Rudd saw that the hall was empty. Quietly closing the door behind him, he tiptoed out and walked quickly into the first darkened office he came to. In the half-lit room, he could see only one large desk. Hurrying behind it, he rolled the chair quietly back on its rollers and knelt. The chair well was deep beneath the desk. At least deep enough that a man could sit at it and not have his shins bump up against the briefcase if it was pushed to the far end of the opening.

Quickly Rudd unsnapped the outer briefcase, withdrew the inner one and opened it as well. Setting the timer was no harder than twisting the dial, and he closed the case again and jammed it as far into the hole as it would go. Lifting the outer briefcase, he crept back to the doorway. The hall was still empty and he stepped outside and walked back to where he'd left Yount.

Rudd stuck his head inside the door. "Thanks again," he said. "Hope to hear from you."

"I hope you do, too," said Yount. "You get used to a lot of things in this business. But never child killings."

Rudd nodded and left. He said goodbye to the black woman at the front desk and exited the building the same way he'd come in.

BOLAN LIFTED HIS FOOT off the brake and let the Civic creep back to the four-way stop. He cruised past the Sherman PD again and stared at the entryway. He could see nothing through the doorway.

A bank stood directly across the street from the police station, and several drive-through lanes, closed for the night, ran along that side. Seeing the night-deposit slots in the window next to the building, the Executioner pulled in, stopping as if he were in the process of making a deposit. The three men waited.

"You have any idea what he's up to?" Vogt asked.

"Not yet," Bolan answered, but that wasn't the entire truth. In reality, a vague thought had been playing around the corners of his mind. If he was right, and whoever was behind all this had indeed decided to raise the stakes, they might have decided to take out a lot of cops all at once instead of one or two at a time. There were several ways to do that. But one seemed the easiest, and therefore the most likely.

"Why would somebody getting ready to kill a cop go to the police department first?" Vogt asked. "I mean, why draw attention to yourself. Make yourself remembered?"

Bolan didn't answer. He continued to watch the entryway.

"What are we going to do when he comes back out?" Vogt wanted to know.

"It all depends," the Executioner said.

"On what?" Vogt asked.

Reinhardt was getting tired of the Houston detective's questions. He sighed. "It depends," he said, "on what Spencer does. And the answer to your next question is that we don't know what Spencer will do next yet, but we'll do what is necessary." He paused. "Okay?"

In the rearview mirror, Bolan saw Vogt frown. "I'm not sure I followed all that," he said.

"You don't have to follow it," Reinhardt told him. "Just take it from me. The guy sitting behind the wheel here is the best of the best. He knows what he'd doing. All you have to do when you ride with him is follow and not get in his way."

Before the conversation could continue, Spencer came back out of the building, swinging the briefcase in his hand as he walked. He glanced their way, and when he did Bolan reached through the window and opened the night-deposit drawer into the building. Spencer turned his eyes back to the sidewalk. He walked on to the parking lot, opened the door to the stolen Lexus and tossed the briefcase inside.

Reinhardt turned to Bolan. "Did you see that the way I did?" he asked.

Bolan nodded. "The briefcase was heavy when he carried it in. It was light on the way out. Whatever he had in it, he left inside the building."

"What do you think it was?" Vogt wanted to know.

"Well," Reinhardt said, "it wasn't his laundry." He drew the Beretta that had been in the glove compartment of his Dakota from his belt and pulled the slide slightly back, checking to make sure a round was chambered. Then, turning back to the Executioner, he said, "We take him down now?"

Bolan shook his head. "Let him get away from the station. I want him alive if possible, and I don't want the Sherman cops getting in our way."

The Lexus pulled out of the parking lot. Bolan gave it a half block, then followed. They drove back to the street they had taken from I-75 and turned back toward the highway. "I'm going to pull around and in front of him at the next stoplight," the Executioner said. "Block him from going forward at least. Get out of the car as fast as you can, guys. If we can surround him fast enough, he won't have time to go for a weapon."

Reinhardt nodded. Over his shoulder, he said, "Vogt, hand me that fancy deer rifle, will you?"

Vogt handed the black nylon rifle case over the seat. Reinhardt unzipped it and pulled out a CAR-15, a shortened version of the M-16.

Ahead Bolan saw a light turning yellow as they neared. He changed lanes, pulling in directly behind Spencer. The man might notice them, and might even recognize Bolan's face at this distance. But it was now a chance he had to take. As the Lexus slowed at the light, Bolan suddenly pulled out into the oncoming lane and raced around it, jerking the Civic to a halt at a forty-five-degree angle in front of Spencer's vehicle. Reinhardt was already out of the car and Vogt was opening the door by the time the Executioner slammed the transmission into Park. He threw open the door, drawing the Desert Eagle as he leaped from the still-rocking vehicle.

A split second later, the Executioner had the big .44 Magnum pistol leveled over the roof of the car. In his peripheral vision, he could see Reinhardt to his left with the CAR-15 aimed into the Lexus. To his right, Vogt gripped his Glock in both hands and pointed it the same way.

"Freeze, Spencer!" the Executioner yelled.

For a moment, the man Bolan knew as A. K. Spencer sat motionless, his eyes staring straight ahead as if he were unaware of the three men holding him at gunpoint. Then, ever so slowly, he turned to face the Executioner. With dead eyes he seemed to stare right through the big man.

Then his lips began to move. "It's never going to happen, is it?" he said. "I'm never going to get it."

Bolan didn't have time to wonder what he meant. As the last words left his mouth, Spencer raised a Colt Commander over the window ledge.

"Drop it!" Bolan ordered.

But Spencer ignored him. Instead, with a scream of rage, he aimed the weapon at the Executioner.

Bolan, Reinhardt and Vogt all fired at once.

The Executioner aimed low, shooting through the door with the hand cannon, hoping to hit the man without killing him. He knew Reinhardt would do the same—the former blacksuit knew they needed Spencer alive, needed answers. But Vogt had trained only as a police officer. He had learned to shoot to stop—but had been told the best way to do that was to fire for the chest. So he did.

Luckily he missed.

Bolan saw Vogt's round rip across the shoulder of Spencer's blue jacket while his own .44 Magnum and Reinhardt's .223 slugs perforated gray-edged holes in the door of the silver Lexus. The

Colt Commander fell to the pavement. Even before it hit, Bolan was around the front of the Civic and ripping open the door.

Spencer just sat there, stunned. Jerking him out of the car brought a small scream from his lips. Bolan held him upright but shoved him against the back window to survey his wounds. The .44 Magnum had taken him in the upper thigh, creating a gaping hole the size of a silver dollar. Shards of the femur bone extended from his slacks, but the bullet had missed the arteries. Reinhardt's rifle round, however, had hit higher and the soft-nosed .223 had ripped through the man's lower abdomen.

Spencer was going to live. But not for very long.

"Get him into the back of the Civic," the Executioner ordered. "Gypsy, take the wheel." The back door of the Honda was still open from Vogt's exit, and he and the Executioner dragged Spencer inside. Bolan pushed the man to the far side of the car and got in next to him while Reinhardt and Vogt took the front seat. They left the intersection a few seconds later, before the open mouths of the men and women behind the wheels of the other cars at the stoplight even had time to close.

The Executioner drew a Spyderco Chinook knife from his pocket and thumbed open the blade. Slicing through the sleeve of Spencer's coat, he cut a rough patch and jammed it into the man's belly wound. The pressure brought another scream from the killer's throat. The other sleeve served to slow the bleeding from his leg. The shoulder wound had skimmed across the skin and wasn't life threatening.

The makeshift bandages weren't going to save Spencer's life, and they didn't stop the blood. But they slowed it.

"Tell me who's behind all this, Spencer," the Executioner ordered.

The eyes of the man next to him were glazing over. "I'm...dying," he whispered.

"That's right," Bolan said. "So do one good thing here at the end of your life—something you can tell your Maker about when you meet Him. Tell us who's behind all these murders and what their agenda is."

Spencer's voice was weaker when he spoke again. "Kill..." he whispered hoarsely. "Kill...ia..."

"You're not in any position to kill *anybody*," Vogt told him. Tell us who's doing all this!"

"Kill...ia..."

Bolan grabbed the man's lapels. "Spencer, or whatever your name really is, you were right. You're going to die. But I can prolong the time you've got left and make it a living hell for you if you don't tell us what we need to know." He stared into the other man's watery eyes. "You left a bomb in the police department, didn't you?"

Spencer nodded.

"There are other bombs, aren't there?"

Again, a nod.

"Where? How do I find out where they are?"

"Post...board...."

"Post board?" Bolan said. "On the Internet? That's how you communicate? Through a post board?"

Spencer nodded weakly. "My code word is...*blueuniform*...."

"Blueuniform?" Bolan said. "One word?"

Spencer nodded again, twice this time. The second time, he didn't seem to have the strength to lift his head again and his chin stayed on his chest.

"What's the address to the post board?" the Executioner asked.

Spencer rattled off something unintelligible, but it sounded like numbers. Bolan still had him by the lapels and shook him. "Say it again," he demanded. "Slower."

The deputy shook his head back and forth. He opened his mouth again but seemed to have lost the power of speech.

"Talk!" Bolan said. "Talk to me, Spencer!"

Spencer rattled off some numbers. He looked as if he wanted to say more but choked instead. He took a breath, then gasped, "lap...top...."

"I looked in the Lexus," Reinhardt said from the front seat. "No laptop. All he had there was this." The former blacksuit held up the empty briefcase.

Bolan looked out of the Civic and saw they were nearing the interstate again. "Get us back to the Blazer," he told Reinhardt. "He must have left it there."

Turning back to Spencer, he said, "You didn't finish the Web address," he said. "What's the rest?"

Spencer tried to speak again, but all he could manage was another coughing, choking sound. Bolan looked down to see that the blood had soaked through the sleeve he'd pressed into the man's abdomen and was running freely to soak the floor of the car.

Then, taking a deep breath, Spencer said, "All I ever...wanted..." he choked out. "Blue...uniform...."

"Try again," Bolan said. "What's the rest of the post board Web site address."

The dying man in the back of the car shook his head. "Laptop...in...case," he said. And they were the last words he ever said as his face fell the rest of the way forward onto his chest, and his open eyes stared sightlessly at the front seat of the Honda Civic.

parking space had opened up right next to the Dakota, and
Bolan directed Reinhardt to park the Civic next to it. "Leave the
engine running," he said, then turned to face Vogt. "Take this car
back to the police department," he said. "Show them your badge,
and tell them the guy who was just there planted a bomb. Tell them
to do a search of the premises."

Vogt nodded as he and the others leaped out of the Civic. The
Houston detective slid behind the wheel as Bolan and Reinhardt
transferred the contents of the car—including Spencer's body—
to the Dakota, then pulled through the lot to where the dead man
had left his Blazer. The laptop he had mentioned was on the rear
seat. They took it and two other bags inside the vehicle.

"We need a place to look through this stuff and hook up to the
internet," Bolan said as they jumped back in the pickup.

Reinhardt threw the transmission into Drive. "I hear room 34
at the Motel 6 is open," he said. He pulled out of the parking lot,
and they raced back along the road paralleling the interstate. Bolan
searched Spencer's pockets for a motel key but hadn't found one
by the time the Dakota pulled back into the motel.

Bolan's kick caught the door just below the knob and sent it swinging back into the room. He hurried inside, carrying the laptop case to the desk and unzipping it. A moment later the computer was hooked up to the phone. As he waited for it to warm up, he heard Reinhardt shuffling through papers that had also been in the computer case. "There are notes, maps, all kinds of crap in here," the retired blacksuit said. "But I can only find one number jotted down, and it doesn't start with the same ones he gave us."

Bolan turned in his seat and found Reinhardt extending the page to him. The number was written in pencil, in the margin on a sheet of scratch paper that also had directions to the Sherman PD. "Let's try it anyway," the Executioner said. Turning back to the screen, he placed the page on the desk next to the keyboard and typed in the numbers. The computer whirled and ticked, then a "Sorry, not found" page appeared.

"In my briefcase," Bolan said. "Hand me the cell phone."

A second later the Executioner had it in his hand and was tapping away at the numbers.

"Calling Bear?" Reinhardt asked.

The Executioner nodded. A moment later Price answered, then switched him immediately into the Stony Man computer room. Bolan ran down the situation as quickly as he could. "My guess is he's left a bomb at the police department," he told the man. "And he said there are others being planted. We won't know where unless we can get on to that post board, Bear."

"Give me the numbers he gave you," Kurtzman said. "I'm going to put you on speakerphone. I want to get Akira and Carmen in on this, too. It may take some doing."

Bolan ran the numbers off as soon as he heard the speakerphone click on.

"Akira," Kurtzman's voice said on the other end of the line, "start running a probability program on what the next numbers might be. Carmen, take these numbers and see if there's some code involved."

"How long is this going to take?" Bolan asked.

"I don't know," Kurtzman said. "How long do we have?"

"I don't know," the Executioner returned. "I'm going to hang up now and call the Sherman PD. I want to see what Vogt found here. Maybe I'll have some kind of time frame on the bomb times when I call you back. Or maybe you'll have one for me." He hung up, then dialed 911. A moment later, a voice said, "Sherman PD. Is this an emergency?"

"It is," the Executioner said. "You had a Houston officer come in just a few minutes ago. Is he still there?"

The voice on the other end suddenly grew suspicious. "What is this in reference to, Mr.—"

"Belasko, Detective Mike Belasko, also Houston. Look, I'm the one who sent Vogt down there a few minutes ago. Have they found anything?"

"The bomb squad just...wait a minute...here comes your man now."

A moment later Vogt was on the line. "They found it in a small briefcase under one of the captains' desks," he said. "C-4. Enough to blow both stories off this place. Spencer came in pretending to be a Dallas cop. Some phony investigation. When he was through, he used the men's room and he must have planted it then. No one went with him, and the captain's office is right next door."

"Anything else you found out?" Bolan asked.

"No. Where are you?"

"Back at Spencer's room at the motel. Come on over. But don't bring the locals. They'll just be in the way." Bolan hung up and dialed Stony Man Farm again.

This time, Kurtzman answered direct. "Akira's running probabilities, but that could take hours," he said. "Carmen's trying simple codes first, on the assumption that these aren't master cryptologists you're dealing with."

"Anything yet?"

"No, not..." His voice trailed off for a moment, then he said, "Wait a second."

The next voice Bolan heard over the speakerphone was that of Carmen Delahunt. "Striker?" she said.

"Yeah. Go ahead, Carmen."

"I think maybe the numbers just stand for letters, *A* equals one, *B* is two, and so on. When you reach double digits like ten for *J*, they stick a dash in. If that's the case, what you gave me spells FEDPO. That mean anything?"

"Not to me. But we know there's more to the address anyway."

Tokaido's voice suddenly broke in. "Striker?"

"Yeah, Akira?"

"When Carmen hit on this idea, it narrowed my search. One of the probables is twelve, which would stand for *L,* and would make it FEDPOL." The Japanese computer whiz cleared his throat. "Could this be acronym for federal police?"

"Try it, Bear," Bolan said. "I'll do the same on this end." Quickly Bolan cleared the screen and typed www.654-16-15-12.com into the address box and hit Go.

Kurtzman's machines were faster, and before he saw it himself he heard the Stony Man computer genius say, "I think we've got a hit."

A few seconds later, a white page appeared on Bolan's screen. In the middle, a box read, Enter Code. "He said the code was *blue-uniform,* Bear," the Executioner said as he also typed in the word. A moment later, the post board appeared. Quickly Bolan scrolled down the list of subjects. There were sixteen titles, and each pertained to one of the 147 assassinations of police officers within the past few months. When Bolan clicked on the titles, he found instructions on how and where the murders were to be carried out, and sometimes a few questions back from Spencer.

Except that Spencer's name actually appeared to be Clayton Rudd. His home address, telephone number and even the fact that he worked at the Chambers County Sheriff's Department under his new identity were all there. But there was no clue as to who was giving out the assignments or answering the subsequent questions. "You reading this, Bear?" Bolan asked.

"Skimming it. Looks like he's your man, anyway."

"Only *one* of them," Bolan said. "He's killed sixteen. That leaves 131 others. My guess is there are more post boards. Does this page have any links you can find?"

"No," Kurtzman said. "But let me run a meter program over it real quick." Less than two seconds had gone by when the computer man came back. "I'm showing that there's more to this site. Quite a bit more, actually. I'm guessing you're right—each of the as-

assins has his own personal board and code. You don't have any more of the codes, do you?"

Bolan racked his brain, trying to remember all of the things the dying man had said. Many of them had been unintelligible, but he did remember Spencer saying he'd kill him. "Kill ya," if he remembered right, were the man's exact words. He had taken it as nothing more than an impotent threat. But could it have been another code word? Spencer had given him *blueuniform* right around the same time.

"It's a long shot but try *kill ya* and *kill you* and *I'll kill you,*" Bolan said. "And anything else like that you can think of."

Over the phone, Bolan heard the keyboard keys tapping. A moment later, Kurtzman said, "Nope. Nothing. Any other ideas?"

"Negative, Bear. But can't you hack in somehow?"

A knock came to the door and Reinhardt let in Vogt.

"Sure I can. But it'll take a while."

"Hang on a minute, Bear." Bolan looked up at the Houston detective. "They diffused the bomb?"

Vogt nodded.

"When was it set to go off?"

"Nine o'clock tomorrow morning. Guess he wanted to get the biggest shift possible."

Pressing the phone back to his mouth, Bolan said, "The bomb here in Sherman was set to blow at 0900 tomorrow. But if there are others, and I'm betting there are, they could be anytime."

"All I can do is get started, Striker."

"I know, Bear. But have one of your crew see what they can find out about this Clayton Rudd character who was going by A. K. Spencer, too. My guess is he changed his name in order to pass a background check for the deputy sheriff's job. And to pull off a phony ID, which would stand up to close professional scrutiny like that, he had to have some help from somebody with juice. Maybe there's a lead in there, somewhere."

"Will do," Kurtzman said. "I'll get Carmen and Akira both on it."

"Call me back as soon as you've got something," Bolan said and hung up. He set the phone on the desk next to the computer.

The hard part was about to begin. Waiting. He sat back against the hard wooden back of the chair and crossed his arms in front of his chest. They had to find out where the other bombs were planted, and they had to find them before they went off. Otherwise, the cops killed so far would be a mere drop in the bucket compared to the police officers who would be dead the next day.

Vogt still looked pale from the poisoning as he took a seat on the bed and picked up the remote control. A moment later, the news was on. The top story was a hurricane heading into the East Coast, but the cop killings were a close second. New York Senator Owen Killian's face flashed quickly on screen during which time he condemned whoever was behind the assassinations and told the public that the twenty-first century would call for far stronger federal law enforcement than even before. The senator was recommending a Senate committee look into the possibility of consolidating all federal law enforcement into one agency.

A strange tingling feeling began in the Executioner's abdomen. He couldn't quite place the source. A moment later Killian was gone and a meteorologist was standing before a map of northern Texas, stick in hand, and predicting rain over the next few days in the Texoma area. Suddenly bits and pieces of information came together in Bolan's mind.

FEDPOL. Federal Police.

Kill ya? What did that mean? The answer played at the soldier's consciousness, like a word on the tip of the tongue.

Clayton Rudd. The man had to have had someone with the stroke to create the fraudulent A. K. Spencer identity well enough to fool professional background investigators. Not as good as Kurtzman, granted, but someone good just the same.

Kill ya? Like the dawn breaking over the horizon, it suddenly became clear.

Bolan sat forward, his mind racing now. When Rudd-Spencer had said "Kill ya" he had not been threatening the Executioner at all. He'd been trying to answer Bolan's question—who was behind all this? He'd been trying to say a name, and like so much of what he'd tried to say while he died he simply couldn't get it all out. Kill ya. *Killian*. Senator Owen Killian, a man who not only had a special interest in federal police but also had the power and influence to insert as many fake identities into the computer records of the United States as he wanted.

Bolan grabbed the phone so fast that both Vogt and Reinhardt jumped. A moment later, he had Kurtzman back on the line. "You got anything yet?" he asked.

"Striker, it's only been five min—"

"Take this track, Bear. I think the man behind all this is Owen Killian."

There was a pause on the other end of the line. "The senator?"

"Look, Bear, he's been slowly but surely pushing for stronger federal law enforcement, and he's just announced now that he's recommending that they look into the possibility of one consolidated federal police agency. Humor me. Try a few things with him in mind."

"Okay. Hang on." The beeps, buzzes and whines of a large computer came back over the line as Bolan waited. A minute went by, then two. The soldier was about to suggest he call back again when Kurtzman said, "You know, Striker, I wouldn't trade that gray matter between your ears for all the gigabytes in the world."

"You're in?"

"Oh, I'm in all right. And there may not be links from Rudd's page to the others, but there are links from this one to a dozen more, including Rudd. I'm on Killian's main page, big guy. And you won't believe what I've found."

"Give me the address and code," Bolan said.

"I doubt you can pull it up on that little laptop," Kurtzman said. "That's one of the safety features he built into the program. There nothing on the twelve other boards to identify him but there sure is here, in his own little private cyber-workshop."

"Then give me the rundown."

"Short and sweet? Killian wants to be the next President. He also wants his own private army to cater to his whims, and he's going to call it the National Police Administration."

"Have you gone to the other links yet?"

"No. Give me a second." A second was all it took. "First one here is in Baltimore. Some guy who got fired from the Maryland state police is doing his dirty work for him there. There's a bomb planted at one of the Baltimore substations."

"When?"

"Tomorrow morning. Ten o'clock."

"Which would be the same as 0900 here in Sherman, " Bolan said.

"Right. You want to hear the others?" Kurtzman asked.

"No need, Bear, and there isn't time. Is Hal there?"

"He flew in a few minutes ago. I had Barb call him when this all started going down."

Brognola's voice came on the line. "And there isn't time to hit a dozen cities, Striker. Not even for you."

"I know that, Hal. You'll have to notify the local authorities and let them handle the bombs themselves. Besides, Kurtzman and I are going to take a little different approach."

He paused, then said, "You still there, Bear?"

"Yeah, Striker?"

"You said Spencer's post board had his home address and other information about him on it. How about the other eleven on Killian's hit team?"

"It's all here," he said. "But it's not going to do you any good on one of them. He already got himself killed during all this." The computer man chuckled.

Bolan frowned, wondering what the joke was. "Who was it?"

"Outlaw biker named Sam Underwood in the L.A. area. Went by Wolfman. According to what I skimmed so far, he was the only non-wanna-be-cop on Killian's payroll. Killian wasn't too happy with him. He was using the program to kill cops hounding the Redondo Beach Rebels, and also took out his ex-brother-in-law on Killian's dime." Kurtzman laughed softly again. "Seems some Houston cop named Belasko came to town and shot him."

So Officer Thurman's poisoning had been connected, after all. The personal aspect of Underwood's own agenda had just slanted the facts to make it look otherwise. Speaking back into the phone, he said, "That still leaves ten cop killers on the loose, Bear. Copy all the pertinent information about them and get it condensed for me, will you?"

"No problem, Striker."

"And Hal?"

"Yeah, big guy?"

"Get Jack on the phone. Tell him to get that bird of his warmed up out there in Reinhardt's cow pasture."

"You going after the rest of the killers?" Grimaldi asked.

"Oh yeah," Bolan said. "But it doesn't make much sense to fly all over the continent looking for them. Not when there's an easier way." He paused. "Bear, I'll explain what I have in mind when I get there."

"You're coming in, then?"

"I am. Get ready to do a little Web site posting of our own."

THE HOUSE WAS CENTRALLY located on a farm in southern Kansas just north of the Oklahoma line. A good ten miles from the nearest town of Caldwell, it had been abandoned for the past six months. The death of an owner with no heirs had meant the property went to the state. And Stony Man Farm, using a cover company called SMF Real Estate, had bought it for a song.

Bolan stood in the living room. The chairs, tables and other furniture had been covered with sheets and a thin layer of dust covered the white linen. The musty smell of a house too long shut-up hung in the air.

He waited.

As he walked around the living room, the Executioner reflected back on the mission he had just finished. All of the bombs had been found and defused by the bomb squads in the various cities across the United States. The story hadn't leaked to the press yet. Not even one more cop had been injured, let alone killed, by the assassins in the employment of Senator Owen Killian. The old title *The Man Who Would Be King* crossed the Executioner's mind as the cell phone in his pocket rang.

Bolan pulled out the phone and heard Kurtzman say, "The first two are on their way. Able Team just saw the guy from Boston drive though Caldwell. Phoenix Force reports another one—Salt Lake City—still a little farther north. And Grimaldi's got them all on screen up in the sky. You ready?"

"I'm all set up," the Executioner said. He hung up and began going around the room, pulling the sheets off the furniture. His mind fell on Jack Crenna. The tough old welder had pulled through the surgery that repaired his chest and lung, and might well live another twenty years. Bolan had talked to him on the phone and, with his usual sense of humor, Crenna had scolded the Executioner for calling the ambulance. "I was on my way to see Elsie, and damned if you didn't invalidate my ticket," the old man had said.

When he had uncovered all the furniture, Bolan carried the sheets into the back bedroom and dropped them on the floor. He closed the door behind him when he came back out.

Daniel Dixon, a man who had tried to get on the Cincinnati police force twice and been turned down for a string of armed robberies when he had been nineteen, was the first to knock at the door. The man had received a suspended sentence, but the felony conviction stayed on his record. The Executioner watched him park the rental car and wondered at a man who would be willing to commit a series of murders just because he didn't get a job he wanted. When the knock came, he opened the door to see a short squatty man with a sneer permanently etched into his face.

"Come in, Mr. Dixon," the Executioner said. "My name is Blanski, and I represent the senator. Please take a seat in the living room."

"What am I doing here?" Dixon demanded. "I got the instructions on the post board to come here and the travel expense money arrived. But nobody's said anything more to me about what this is all about."

"Please," Bolan said. "Wait just a little longer, Mr. Dixon." He smiled at the snarling man, then added, "Or should I say, Mr. Director?"

The title took the grimace off Dixon's face. At least for a moment. He took a seat in an armchair in the living room.

Bolan stayed in the foyer of the old farmhouse where he could watch the living room and the door at the same time. The man from Salt Lake City, Levi Benson, was the next to come in. He asked similar questions and got similar answers.

One by one, the cars and men continued to arrive at the old farmhouse. Bolan greeted the men and sent them on into the living room, asking each of them politely not to speak to the others until the senator arrived. He knew this request would go ignored, and it would only be a matter of time before the men learned that each of them had been promised the directorship of the future National Police Administration.

The Executioner wondered if any of them knew that a man like Killian wouldn't have hired them any more than any other police agency would, let alone put them in charge of his private army.

Gradually the whispers became louder. And eventually a voice rose to fever pitch. "Bullshit!" roared someone from the living room. "He said *you* were going to be the director?"

Only one of the ten hadn't yet arrived, and Bolan saw him pulling off the county road onto the gravel drive to the house even then. He stuck his head into the living room and said, "Gentlemen, please. I asked you not to discuss this. There has been a small amount of confusion, but this will all be worked out as soon as the senator arrives. And you have my personal promise that all of you will get everything coming to you." That quieted them. At least for the moment.

The knock came as he finished speaking, and Bolan let the final man into the house. Chet Woodring. Woodring had killed eleven cops, two of them women who were mothers of a total of six children. His excuse: he had been kept out of police work when he failed to pass the polygraph questions concerning drug use.

When the men had all assembled in the large living room, Bolan walked back in.

"Where the hell is Killian?" demanded Mark Longley from Colorado Springs. Longley had been an agent with the Colorado Bureau of Investigation but had been fired for shaking down prostitutes. "And who the hell are you?"

Bolan walked across the living room toward an old china cabinet. The dishes, silverware and other items that had once been inside had been sold at auction months before. But the cabinet wasn't empty. "As I said, I represent the senator," he said as he stopped in front of the ornately carved antique. "Now, tell me something please, gentlemen? Do you all have guns?"

Several laughs came from around the room where the men stood or sat. "Of course we do," said Peter Hibbert from Omaha, and Bolan remembered that Hibbert, too, had once worn blue. He'd also run a pretty fair "murder for hire" racket on the side, but there had never been enough evidence to convict him. He'd been allowed to resign from the Omaha force and had been a natural for Killian to recruit.

"Please put them on the table," Bolan said as he opened the cabinet door and reached inside. "Because you're all under arrest." His words had the stunning effect he had known they would, and by the time the men had recovered he had pulled out the Calico 950 with the 100-round drum magazine on the top.

Many of the men reached for pistols hidden beneath their clothing, and Tom Jantz—from Toledo—opened the briefcase he had carried into the house. He put the Uzi into play, aiming at Bolan, but the Executioner's rounds found their mark first.

All around the room, men began firing at Bolan.

The Executioner cut figure eights of fire back and forth, dodging the return rounds as he continued ridding the world of some of the most despicable miscreants it had ever produced. They were men who had sold their souls for a promised directorship of the National Police Administration; men who shamed the badges to which they had aspired, and which a few had even briefly worn. But even those who had served as officers and been fired for their evil deeds had not been cops. They had been only criminals masquerading as cops.

Forty-five seconds after it had begun it was over. The Calico bolt locked back on an empty chamber and the Executioner transferred it to his left hand, drawing the big Desert Eagle with his right. He circled the room, the .44 Magnum aimed downward, checking to see if any of the cop killers had survived. It was wasted effort.

The phone rang in his pocket, and he dropped the Calico to the carpet and took the instrument out with his left hand.

"Are you all right?" Brognola asked. After listening to what had happened, the big Fed told Bolan about Killian.

An hour ago the senator had been indicted by a federal grand jury. According to Brognola, the man's popularity had even risen a few points as his staff and two major publicity firms were working to convince America that he was the victim of a vast conspiracy by the opposing political party. There was always a chance that he'd beat the rap, and once tried he could never be held accountable on the same charges again. Not even if new evidence came to light. The rule of double jeopardy would come into play.

"Is it over?" Brognola asked.

"No," the Executioner said. "Not quite."

Epilogue

Senator Owen Killian couldn't keep the smile off his face as the Baxter Executive Protection men escorted him down the steps of the federal courthouse. Even though the flashbulbs hurt his eyes, he smiled into the cameras, using that old "honest eye contact" which, he knew, had once again saved his ass. And not only had it kept him from being bound over for trial by the grand jury, it had convinced not only the jury but a large majority of the American public that the charges brought against him had been the work of his opponents.

Killian was on everyone's lips. He had officially said nothing yet about his candidacy for President. Yet polls had been already been taken, and they showed him an eleven point favorite if the election was held immediately.

"Senator! What do you have to say!" shouted a newsman who had just shoved a microphone into his face.

Killian stared into the video camera just behind the man and gave it his most sincere smile. "That once again, the American criminal justice system works," he said. "It's the best system on

Earth, and it knows an innocent victim of a political conspiracy from a criminal."

"Senator!" screamed another reporter with another microphone. "What will be done about this alleged plot to make it look like you orchestrated the police killings to raise your own popularity?"

Killian turned slightly to the side to face the new camera. "Already a Senate investigative committee is looking into it," he said. "And we'll get to the bottom of it, I assure you. When we do, those responsible will pay the price for what they've done." He kept the smile on his face but the smile inside him was even larger. Already, he had planted some clues that would lead those investigators toward his strongest opponents. They'd take a fall themselves before this was all over.

Killian and his bodyguards took another step down the stairs but more reporters crowded in, blocking their path.

"What about the National Police Administration you've recommended?" a man in an old-fashioned fedora asked. "Is it still on the table?"

"It most certainly is," Killian said, smiling at the man. "Among everything else that all this has proved is the need for a much stronger federal role in local law enforcement. We're living in a new century. We're fighting criminals who have access to the latest technology and weaponry. If this country is to survive, it can only do so with a strong police presence. I want *everyone* to know the National Police Administration is watching them." Quickly correcting himself, he said, "Every criminal must be aware that every move he makes will be found out."

"Senator!" screamed a woman from the *New York Times.* "Your popularity has skyrocketed. What about the rumors that you've thrown your hat into the ring for the presidential campaign?"

Killian had been waiting for just this time, just this atmosphere, and just this question. Smiling boyishly into the camera, he said, "I suppose now is as good a time as any to make the announcement." He took a deep breath and his face grew solemn as he summoned up the expression of dignity he knew the public expected out of a President. "Yes. My hat is in the ring. I am announcing my candidacy."

More flashbulbs popped and more questions were shouted, but Killian knew when to leave a crowd wanting more. With the help of his bodyguards, he worked his way on down the steps to the sidewalk. He was surprised when a tall man wearing a dark suit stepped up and flashed Secret Service credentials in front of him. "Congratulations on your announcement, Senator," the man said. "I was sent out in case you made it. As you know, the Secret Service provides protection for all presidential candidates."

Killian smiled at the man. For now, he thought. Soon your organization, the FBI, and all the rest will simply be part of my own personal national police. "Yes, thank you Special Agent...?"

"Blanski," the big man said. "Special Agent Mike Blanski."

Killian turned to his bodyguards. "Gentlemen," he said, "it appears I will no longer be needing your services. Please inform Chief Baxter that I'd like to arrange to give you each two months' severance pay."

The two men who had been escorting the senator shook his hand. "That's very generous of you," one of them said. "And best of luck in the campaign."

Killian turned as the big man in the dark suit took his elbow. "Shall we go, Senator? We need to meet and put together the rest of your protection team. Right now, I'm on my own and it makes me a little nervous."

The fact that the Secret Service had sent only one man annoyed the senator. But this was no time to show such irritation—not with all the cameras and reporters around. So he smiled and let the big man open the back door of a limousine for him. He gave the crowd a last wave and was about to get in when a man suddenly jumped from the throng.

Richard Lane. The Libertarian.

"You may have fooled some of these people, Killian," the senator from Idaho screamed. "But you haven't fooled me and you haven't fooled *everyone!* You're a traitor, Killian! And somehow, some way, some day, you'll get what you deserve!"

A trio of District of Columbia police officers jumped in between Lane and Killian as Killian got into the limo and the big man closed the door. Then the man in the dark suit got behind the wheel, pressed a button on the door and Killian heard the doors lock around him.

Now that no one was watching, the senator felt free to express his dissatisfaction at the Secret Service sending only one man instead of a proper team to protect him. Leaning forward over the seat, he said, "What the hell do you people think you're doing? One agent? They send me one man?"

The big man pulled away from the curb without answering.

"Answer me, you idiot!" Killian demanded, pounding the seat between them with his fist. "Why did they send me only one man?"

The big man behind the wheel turned sideways to look at him as he drove off. "Because it's only going to take one man to do what has to be done, Senator," he said. "But don't worry, we're about to meet up with a whole army of my fellow Feds."

Killian looked at the driver's face and a chill went through his body. Before they could pick up speed, he reached for the door handle. But the door was locked. And when he tried to unlock it, the switch wouldn't move. The same thing happened when he tried the window.

The senator turned back to the front seat where the big man was now silently facing the windshield again as he drove through the streets of the capital. But Killian could see the driver's face in the rearview mirror, and the smile he had worn earlier was gone. The face in the mirror now wasn't angry. The fact was, it held no expression at all. It was the face of a man just going about his business, doing his job. The driver stopped at a stoplight, waited for it to turn green, then pulled through the intersection. He turned right, in front of a large shopping mall.

"Where the hell do you think you're going?" Killian screamed at him. "Shopping for socks? To get a cheese pretzel?" He paused when the man didn't answer, then ordered, "Take me home!"

A hard smile curled the driver's lips. "You wanted more men," he said in a low voice. "This is where we meet up with them."

They drove through the mall parking lot and then circled to the side of the mall itself. As they rounded the corner toward the delivery docks, Killian expected to see trucks. Instead, he saw a half dozen black-and-white police cars and an equal number of unmarked units.

"What the hell is going on?" Killian demanded.

The driver pulled to a halt and threw the car into Park.

Two dozen men in suits converged on the limo. Killian saw the agent lean forward toward the dash and heard a click. A second series of clicks told him the doors were now unlocked.

"These are the other men from the protection team? Secret Service agents?" Killian asked, somewhat bewildered at meeting them there.

"Not exactly," Bolan said. "Most of them are U.S. deputy marshals."

The door next to the senator was ripped open and hands reached in, grabbing him by the shoulders and dragging him out. "What—" Killian started to say. But more hands slammed him against the side of the limo, knocking the rest of the sentence out of his mouth along with his breath. More men twisted his arms painfully behind his back.

"What are you doing!" Killian demanded as soon as his air returned. He felt the cold handcuffs close around his wrists and heard the steel teeth crunch into place.

Bolan had exited the vehicle and now reached out, spinning him back around. "You're under arrest," he said.

"What do you mean, under arrest?" Killian shrieked. "I've been tried before the grand jury! I wasn't indicted! Isn't this double jeopardy?"

"It's not double jeopardy," Bolan said. "It wouldn't be under the law. Besides, these are different charges." A hard smile set at the corners of his mouth. To Killian, the man looked like a wolf about to pounce on a lamb. No, he corrected himself. More like a sheep dog about to destroy a wolf.

"A lot has happened around the world since you began all this, Killian," Bolan went on. "There are new statutes on terrorism. And everything you've done fits the definition of conducting an ongoing terrorist operation."

"You mean a trial?" Killian asked. His voice sounded less-animated now. More composed.

Bolan leaned in a little closer to him. "That's right. You'll be tried on the terrorist charges. Not to mention treason."

The usual cockiness returned to the senator's voice as he said, "I beat the charges before. I'll beat them again." Then the widening smile he saw on Bolan's face suddenly sucked the confidence out of him again.

"You'd better hope not."

TAKE 'EM FREE

2 action-packed novels plus a mystery bonus

NO RISK
NO OBLIGATION TO BUY

W

DEATH LANDS.®

Skydark Spawn

Available in
March 2003
at your favorite retail outlet.

In the relatively untouched area of what was once Niagara Falls, Ryan and his fellow wayfarers find the pastoral farmland under the despotic control of a twisted baron and his slave-breeding farm. Ryan, Mildred and Krysty are captured by the baron's sec men and pawned into the cruel frenzy of their leader's grotesque desires. JB, Jak and Doc enlist the aid of outlanders to organize a counterstrike—but rescue may come too late for them all.